The

Game

Nancy Jardine

Rubidium Time Travel Series

Book 1

Artwork: Neil Saddler

Editor: Jeff Gardiner

The Taexali Game

Find Nancy Jardine online:

www.nancyjardineauthor.com

ISBN:1511938730
ISBN-13:9781511938730

Dedication

I dedicate this book to my former pupils at Kintore School, Aberdeenshire, Scotland, some of whom were the inspiration for me to write fiction, and in particular this time travel novel. At the end of a term's study of Celtic Roman Britain, during the school session of 2004 - 2005, my primary seven pupils (aged 11-12 years) were tasked with writing a short adventure story where a local Celtic tribe was invaded by legionary soldiers of the Ancient Roman Empire. The resulting stories being excellent, I jokingly claimed I'd write a full length tale some day. This novel has gone through many draft versions over the years since it was started, but I always knew I'd publish it some day. I also dedicate it to those who are reading it —I hope you enjoy this historical era of Roman Britain as much as I love writing about it.

Acknowledgement

I give a hearty round of thanks to my editor, Jeff Gardiner, who gave such great advice during the edits to the manuscript. His suggestions were spot on and he was the best ever cheerleader as we readied the story for publication.

I'd also like to give huge thanks to my cover designer, Neil Saddler. From a few starter ideas, he has produced the fabulous cover on the novel which encompasses the location, my intrepid trio and the Roman usurpers.

Author's note:

Historical records for the invasion of northern Scotland in AD 210, by the Roman Emperor Severus, are very scarce—those available mostly written in Latin or Greek by writers of the era, or later. The Celts left us no real evidence in writing, so a lot of the information I've used in my fictional story has been gleaned from archaeological evidence and interpretation. My use of contemporary place names in Aberdeenshire, Scotland—and especially around the village of Kintore—has been deliberate, to give my readers a sense of the geographical setting, though the events portrayed in the story come purely from my imagination.

Chapter One

Aran Bruce was pounding the fancy brass lion against the wood when the door yanked open, half-hauling him inside the house. If he hadn't been astride his bike, he'd have been sprawled knees first on the hallway floor. Regaining his balance, he glared at Brian while massaging his shoulder, pretending it didn't hurt.

"Change of plan." Brian blocked the doorway.

"What's wrong? We arranged this ages ago." The mulish look on Brian's face didn't cheer him.

"I'm doing something for Callum."

"Yay. Callum's stuff's fantastic." Whooping as he wheelied free from the bike frame, he ignored the way it scratched against the wall before coming to a clunking halt at the window sill. His mood gone sunny again, he shoved his way inside. "Fresh air's free anytime."

"You won't want anything to do with this one," Brian sneered, closing the door behind them. "Fianna's got to do it, too."

Aran went for a commiserating smirk, though wasn't a good enough actor to pull it off. Brian's twin sister Fianna was an irritating fly but he would easily put up with her because Callum Fraser's stuff was awesome fun. The man worked with advanced interaction techniques which were so amazing they were insane.

"Don't worry, mate." Aran was sure it would be fine.

At five feet ten, he towered over Brian by a head.

Nudging him out of the way, he bounded along to the workroom and launched himself inside. Shrugging out of his backpack, he dumped it inside the door. Against one wall, a bench held three transparent display screens of different sizes, but very little else. There was no messy tangle of wiring, keyboard and the bits and pieces which clogged his workstation. Of course, Callum Fraser's bench was different from almost every other computer station on the planet since the remote keyboards and touch pads were hidden from sight. Even the computer itself was invisible to the uninitiated.

Slipping into a chair, he faced the largest screen. "Callum off having a fly cup?"

"Nah. No tea break that I know of." Brian's head shook as he settled into another chair alongside. "He was in Los Angeles. The nerds were showing off their latest, though he should be back at the lab in England by now."

Aran winked. A very screwed-up wink. "The 'hush-hush it's a big secret' place?"

"Do you think you know everybody's secrets?"

He ignored the tick-off and guffawed till Brian began to grin, knowing his mate wasn't capable of holding a grudge for any length of time. "So what needs testing?"

"Don't know yet. I've to call him." Brian growled when he glanced at the time on the screen in front of him, lightly cuffing his ear as he reached forward. "You've made me late."

His chair whizzed along the wooden floor when Brian edged him out of the way. It was the weirdest thing ever to watch his friend's hands delve straight through the largest display screen to type away at something he selected from the options available, which floated around in multi-dimensional heaven. He hadn't been allowed to use the largest screen computer technology yet, but had gamed with one of the flanking screens which was nearly the same—at least that's what he'd been told. That fantastic experience, which had been so realistic, had left him wanting more, a lot more of Callum's latest innovations.

The natural light of the room blinked off when automatic shutters ghosted across the expanse of windows on the wall behind him. The speed of their operation used to amaze him, but it now happened so often he was blasé about it. He wheeled closer to the middle screen that Brian was working on; much easier to see now with no sunbeams causing distortions.

"Callum's been working for ages on this new development. Nobody's to know anything about it."

Brian's disembodied hands typed furiously at a keyboard behind a photograph of the Fraser's back garden in Kintore, Aberdeenshire, when a series of bloops emitted, yet the front image seemed very complete. It was incredible. He couldn't stop staring. The multi-dimensional technique was way beyond 3D.

"I shouldn't even be telling you this much." Brian turned to face him.

Aran was sheepishly disappointed but knew Callum's work was shrouded in confidentiality. "Okay. I'll see you around, then."

Brian made no answer and returned to tapping like mad so he slunk out of the chair and headed for the door.

"Hey! I'm joking." Brian's shout halted his exit.

"Callum wants you to test it, too."

"Really? That's brilliant." Aran's face relaxed as he turned back.

Callum Fraser appeared on screen wasting no time with pleasantries. "Hi, guys. Aran—glad you're here. Brian—where's your sister?"

"Sorry. I was going for her when Aran came to the door."

Brian fidgeted, the freckles on his face merging in an embarrassed, red glow. Callum's comment wasn't exactly a chastisement but Brian was sensitive to what he thought was criticism.

"Does your mum know you're at our house, Aran?"

Callum's inquiry sounded casual as he looked directly at him but Aran could tell there was more behind it. "Yeah. I've got permission. Brian and I are going on a long bike ride today. Mum packed a picnic."

"That's what you thought Aran, but I don't believe you'll need your picnic right now if you want to try something for me." Callum's chuckle was deafening.

He guessed his eagerness was way too easy to spot, and that was no surprise since he felt the anticipation zapping free from his eyeballs.

"Go and fetch Fianna, and while you're off to get her I'll send your mum a message and tell her you're happy about the plan. She's already agreed that you can stay with us for a few days."

"Yay. Will this be more than one demo?" One of his fists repeatedly slapped on his open palm.

"Who knows? This is vastly different from our earlier interactive games." Callum's smile was enigmatic; that cheeky kind, like the *Mona Lisa* painting. "When Fianna's here we'll start. Go and get her."

He sprinted after Brian to the garden where Fianna and Jennie were planting vegetables. Jennie was Callum's wife but she wasn't the twins' mum. Ages ago, he'd learned that it was only after their mother had died of cancer, when they were almost eight, that Brian and Fianna had been told they had a living father. Their mother never mentioned him while they were growing up, so they assumed a dad was never going to be part of their lives. Since the woman had never told Callum about the twins being born, it came as a huge surprise when the authorities informed Callum that he had children who needed someone to look after them.

It was cool that Callum had taken them straight into his home. He'd insisted he'd not earned the title of father, since he'd not seen them growing from babies into toddlers, so the twins were encouraged to call him Callum.

Aran reckoned it was because of their unusual beginnings that Callum allowed the twins to have a go at so many of his brilliant new trials. An incredible amount of trust had built up between them in a shorter time than seemed usual for a newly-together father and children.

"Hurry up!" Brian urged from the doorway.

Fianna peeled off her muddy boots at the back door, thrust her grubby arms and hands under the tap in the utility room sink, and flapped them dry as they scurried back to the workroom. Plonking himself down on a chair, Aran waited as Fianna wiped off the last of the water droplets on her manky jeans and then stuffed her long red hair into a scrunchie.

"How're you doing, Fianna?" Callum asked when she raised her head to the screen. "Been a grubby little urchin, again?"

"Maybe I have, Callum." She thumped down onto a chair, a determined look forming.

Fianna hated it when Callum teased her and, like Brian, her freckles seemed to blush as well.

Callum's cheery grin slid away and was replaced by a sober expression, which instantly captured all attention. "Right. Are you ready for something really different?"

"Can we get started?" Brian's whine accompanied all three heads as they nodded wildly.

Callum assessed each of them in turn. "This development is totally innovative. You have to accept that it's not a game, as you know them, but more of an interactive story where you're a crucial part of the plot and at times you will drive the action. The people in the story need your help to get them out of a very sticky situation. Picking up clues, and working out what's needed to aid them, will be what's necessary for the story to have a good ending rather than a disastrous one. We've set it up so that you will help to create the rest of the plot, as and when it happens. I'm going to let you have a go because…"

Aran's response slipped into the silence. "We're smart-arses and we're desperate to try it?"

A small grin appeared on Callum's face but the seriousness was still there. "It's because I trust the three of you to do the correct things. Aran—go to the bottom drawer of the unit under the window. Fetch over the three metal bands."

He zoomed back with three heavy bands too excited to think through Callum's words because they were a bit odd. Games always had their unique procedures; they just had to learn the rules but Callum had said it was more like an interactive story, so maybe there wasn't a set of rules to abide by. He didn't care either way; it was always great to try something new.

"Each one is named. Pass them out carefully. They're more delicate than they look," Callum warned.

Three chunky bands lay glinting on his lap. One was gold, another was silver and the third a deep bronze, the surfaces all decorated with different patterns. They looked kind of ancient as he read the engraving on the inside edge of each of them. He passed the first one to Fianna—the bronze—and then found Brian's. Beaming like mad he realised he'd scored the glistening gold one.

Callum drew their attention. "Those micro-computer armbands need to be kept on all the time. Slide them over your left wrist and push them as high as they will go. They need to fit snugly against your skin."

"How does it fit so well?" Brian mumbled as he glided it in place.

Callum's eyes crinkled. "Confession time. I measured your arm when you were sleeping, to get a good fit. Same with Fianna. I had to guess Aran's. Is it too tight for you?"

"No." He slid it up and down a little to be sure. He stretched his arm so that Callum could see where it fit. "It's fine when it's here."

"That's good. Keep it safely in place. Now each in turn, I want you to put both arms through the screen, making sure you go through all the way to your shoulders. Count to two and then slowly remove your arms again. You go first Aran, followed by Fianna, and then Brian."

As Aran scooted directly in front of the screen, he felt the blood pop inside his temples; that first experience of something new such an exhilarating sensation. Reaching the tips of his fingers through the screen the anticipation mounted, even though he could feel nothing different. It was like stretching through any old air and yet he knew it wasn't. Having done as requested, he moved aside to let Fianna in next.

After Brian was finished, Callum nodded at them. "Fantastic. Now slip your thumb along the top edge of the armband till you find the tiny dot of metal and press it firmly."

"Wow. That's neato." Aran whistled at the flap which opened. A display pad was revealed along the length of the inside. There were eight tiny icons on the part that lay flat down against his arm, all of different colours.

Callum gave them instructions. "The technology has gone through a series of test runs, but my team are using you lot as guinea pigs—so be prepared for something never tried before."

"Eeek. Eeek." Brian's noises echoed around the room.

Callum called their laughter to order. "Hey! Listen well, all of you. Press the yellow sunglasses and focus on it for at least two seconds."

One…one hundred. Two…one hundred.

Callum yelled. "Got them. Your armbands have transferred your retinal details, and your finger prints have been taken when you depressed the icon."

"You make that sound so real." He grinned at Callum's image.

"Do you doubt my skill, Aran?"

He knew when to grovel. No way did he want to offend Callum. "Absolutely never."

"Now press the purple icon, the one that looks like a curled DNA string."

A strange tingling wound its way around his arm where the metal of the armband contacted his skin.

"That's a really weird feeling," Fianna squealed. "What's happening?"

"Your computer is now linked directly to your DNA structure. It'll make adjustments as you go through the adventure."

"The computer will message us through our skin?" Fianna's green eyes looked huge when she beamed at him.

The vibrations settled to a warm glow all around his arm. The other two looked like they felt the same thing. "That's cool."

"What about the other icons, Callum?" Brian's finger tips hovered.

Aran guessed his mate itched to test them out.

"Patience, Brian. The black question mark is for help if you're really banjaxed, but only use it as a last resort." Callum's grin widened even more as he continued. "The jeans ensure you have appropriate clothing; the red lips icon is a translator which only needs to be pressed once for a new language. The white 'X' on red is your stop button, but that's only to be pressed when you agree to end the experience. You must all be of the same mind about that. Messages will display on the other flap. Don't worry; you'll get further instructions later when we discuss your purpose in more detail, but right this minute I need you all to press the one that looks like a green traffic light."

"Green for go?"

The grin on Fianna's face was a younger version of Callum's as her finger hovered, his own finger pressing as instructed.

A horrendous whooshing pained his ears from deep behind his eardrums, the pressure so fierce Aran thought he was about to pop into a zillion smithereens. Stinging pins jabbed him all over, piercing every pore in one massive zap. When his stomach hit the roof and he forward-flipped over and over and over, he felt his grin flubber, the wobbles at his cheeks in contrast to the fearsome tight blast at his scalp.

No way could he keep his eyes open.

Chapter Two

Aran's front flipping stopped as abruptly as it started. His eyes flicked open when he teetered to a halt outside an impressive pale-stoned building with lots of shining glass which twinkled in the sunshine. Electronic doors slithered open in front of him.

"Wow. What the heck happened?"

His voice came out a bit funny, the way it sometimes does after a particularly scary fairground ride, hoarse and jittery—and like his stomach still felt. Or like those silly eejits he'd seen on TV whose voices had gone all funny after bursting helium balloons with their teeth. He shuffled his feet to get a better balance. "Where are we?"

Callum's disembodied voice instructed, "This is the National Physics Research Facility. Go inside and see our latest version of a Rubidium Time Slip."

"A what time slip?" Fianna's voice asked the air around him before she herself settled in alongside, Brian bumping him on his other side.

"That was a cool way to get into your story, Callum." Brian disentangled himself from his elbow and straightened up.

"The story's not started yet, Brian. I need you all to learn a few things first. There's someone at the door to meet you, so I'll see you soon." Callum's voice faded.

A dishevelled guy beckoned them. He looked about eighteen but Aran knew the man had to be much older if he worked at the facility.

"Hurry up, you lot. I'm Ronald. Callum sent me up

to get you." He urged them across the main foyer of the building, a huge cathedral-ceilinged space that was sparklingly clean yet empty, apart from a dour looking security guard who sat positioned at a desk near the main door. Ronald's squeaking feet led them towards a bank of elevators. "This way. We can't afford to waste a single second."

The guy's abrupt stop made them all smash into him. A hearty chuckle escaped, the man creasing up. Aran wanted to join in though hadn't a clue what was supposed to be funny.

Ronald gurgled. "You don't understand yet, but you will. Come on."

He followed, leaving a gap in case there was another collision, thoroughly confused by the fact that there had been a real one already. The guy was pretty solid to crash into—which was a bit weird in an interactive story.

"I'll answer your question now, Fianna. The Rubidium Fountain is the most accurate atomic clock that's used worldwide." Ronald halted at a lift where his eye and handprints were taken on the simple keypad at the side of the doors.

The pad throbbed, a nasal voice floating around. "Thank you, Ronald, you may enter."

Aran knew it was silly to be crushingly disappointed as he glanced around the huge foyer. "So, this Rubidium thingy isn't new technology?" A whisper of warm draught whiffed around him as the lift doors closed.

"Subterranean Level 3, please," Ronald instructed, and then turned to him. "Old or new technology, Aran? The answer is both. What you're going to experience is our most advanced innovation."

A big smile began to spread, tingles of anticipation overtaking Aran's nasty little disenchanted ones.

Ronald's eyes seemed amused by some secret he wasn't divulging. "It's super advanced technology based on well-used techniques. Some of the research at this facility is so secret you can't enter the main laboratories, however, we are authorised to investigate from our demonstration rooms."

The lift doors sighed open and they all trooped out. Ronald stopped at a viewing panel about half way along a gleaming corridor. Inside the room people busily worked through screens similar to Callum's back at his house in Kintore.

"Is that a Rubidium Fountain?" Brian indicated a huge screen on the opposite wall, the area around it completely enclosed in glass and chrome, like a humongous and fancy shower stall.

"Not quite. That one's called the Rubidium Time Slip." Ronald's finger to his lips invited confidentiality. "It is rubidium driven, but it's much more advanced than the ones currently used for co-ordinating universal time around the globe."

The same computer voice droned again after Ronald had peered at the keypad outside the door. "Enter now, Ronald."

Aran tripped in after him, the twins at his heels.

"Why does it let us in without scanning?" Fianna asked.

"Good question. Think about it." Ronald's smile was a tease.

"Our armbands?" Fianna sounded smug as though knowing the answer was a doddle.

"Exactly." Ronald nodded to all of them. "We've everything we need from the bands to give you the best experience ever, including knowing who you are and where you are at any given time."

Aran looked at the other two. This trial was nothing like the games experiences he'd had before. "Like a tracking device?"

Ronald guffawed. "Oh, much better that that."

"Where's Callum?" Brian's question was tentative, maybe even a bit suspicious.

"A doubting Thomas, are you?" Ronald's chuckle quivered around them. "Open your armbands."

He popped the little knob. Callum's carrot-topped image smiled at him before speaking. "I told you this trial would be very different. Aran, you're nominally in charge since you're the oldest, but you all have to look out for each other."

Brian fidgeted alongside him.

"Yes, Brian. That's a dig for you to look after Fianna—even though I know it's usually the other way round."

"I'm thirteen now, Callum, not three," Fianna protested.

Callum laughed at his daughter's reaction, her freckles so scrunched up. "Oh, I do know that, Fianna, or I'd not be letting you try this for me. Pep talk over."

Callum's image disappeared before Aran could ask where he was. His stomach did another sudden wobbly when the armband snapped shut by itself with the tiniest of pings.

"That is so cool." Brian was clearly impressed, his eyes still staring at his own closed armband.

Ronald led them to the glass enclosure. A screensaver inside displayed a field of light golden corn waving in a light wind on a sunny day, the sky a dense mid-blue and unmarred except for the occasional fluffy white cirrus trace. Near the bottom was the time and date as would be seen on any computer except that the time extended beyond the digital hours and seconds to micro-fractions of a second which flickered too quickly to keep up with. "That will indicate the extra leap second for the Rubidium Time Slip when it's inserted." Ronald pointed to the whirring bit as the doors slid open. He ushered them inside.

Aran didn't know what the guy was talking about but was intrigued when Ronald remained outside the cabinet, the door panel gliding tight again. Turning round to the display screen, he read the question which now hovered above the date.

"Which number?" Fianna mouthed the words. "Is that question for us?"

"Definitely." Callum's voice rang loud and clear around the enclosure, his image appearing superimposed on the corn field background. "Type in two one zero."

"Why that one?" Brian asked.

Callum looked desperate to get them started as he waved towards a keypad. "I chose it because Aran was going on about it recently, before your school broke up for the holidays. Type in two one zero, press the green icon and zap—you'll start your adventure."

Brian was still doubtful. "How does that work?"

"Your armbands make use of the time leap second." A hearty laugh went along with Callum's information.

Aran wanted more information as well, though a time leap sounded intriguing—even if the words made little sense. "There's no other equipment needed?" he asked, making eye contact with Callum.

"Nope. The Rubidium Time Slip works as a courtesy of the leap second, which currently happens when time around the globe is universally co-ordinated. We've added a little dabbling here and there of some cellular material. Go on. We've made the transfer as simple as we can."

"Okay." He only partially understood the leap second process, having read about it somewhere, but if Callum was happy with the technology, then he was confident too.

Callum continued. "There are some people out there in the story who need you three to help them. They're living in dangerous times but just a tiny nudge from you will set them on a safer path, from expertise that you can share with them. You'll each have to do your own bit to make their situation become a more secure one, by working out what's necessary as you go along."

Fianna snorted. "You're sure we can help them? My memory recall isn't nearly as nano-second quick as Aran's is."

Callum looked serious. "You all have a whole barrage of great skills at your fingertips which will be really useful to these people."

"Like what?" Aran elbowed Brian when he guffawed in his ear.

"You're a fantastic musician, Brian." Callum beamed at his son.

Brian looked sceptical. "You're sending me off to play them magical tunes that will make their life safer? Tell me another one, Callum."

"Brian. Believe me. You can impress them

immensely and, in turn, they can teach you a thing or two as well. Your other leisure pursuits will be useful as well."

"Call two one zero! I'm your resident computer nerd." Brian's voice was a nasal drone.

Callum's hearty laugh rang around the enclosure. "These people live in an era which was long before computers were invented, but you've loads of skills as well as musical and computer ones, Brian. When an opportunity presents itself, I'm completely confident that you can help them. You'll also, very likely, find that this experience will change how you view the world."

"Are you being deliberately vague, Callum?"

"I sure am, or there wouldn't be anything for you all to work out in this interactive mystery."

Not to be outdone, or outshone by her twin, Fianna shoved Brian aside before she faced Callum. "If he's going to be such a great help, what skills am I supposed to flaunt?"

Fianna was miffed. She wasn't musical at all and Aran usually kept out of her way when she was bothered. He distanced himself from her—a few centimetres—but enough to be out of reach.

"Use your instincts, Fianna. You're much better at getting a job done than your brother, and you know it. You've got brilliant practical skills and you're nicer to people than you think. You're likely to be the one who senses that people are in jeopardy before your brother, or Aran realise it. Watch and warn. Maybe sometimes get a job done yourself, because it will be the most successful way. Think of those as your main objectives."

She scoffed before turning away from Callum's

image.

"Fianna. You're the most nosey young female I've ever had the pleasure to know and believe it or not, you'll have to be snooping a lot to help these people. You'll ferret out information better than the other two. Never fear about doing your bit in this quest."

"It's a quest?" Aran perked up. He liked a good mystery hunt. "What do we need to look for?"

"Information. Visual evidence of the time, but you also have to find the answers that will help these people stay alive, Aran."

He sensed Brian's change of mood as his mate moved closer to the screen.

"Alive? As in not dead?"

"Exactly, Brian. Many of these people will die if they don't get the correct help from you three." Callum nodded encouragingly.

"That sounds far too serious and way too exciting!" He wanted to get going immediately. "You've not said what I need to contribute, Callum."

"You have an infinite capacity for storing trivial details, Aran, and for once it'll be the perfect answer for helping these people. The solutions they need are in your head. You need to concentrate on remembering things you've learned, facts that will help them at the right time to make life, and not death, decisions. You're going to be the front man of the trio but you'll need the twins' help to back you up."

He nodded. "I guess we can do that."

Callum pointed to their armbands. "If I need to contact you, your armband will vibrate. The display will give instructions."

"You missed telling us about one of the icons,

Callum." He champed at the bit, but wanted all the symbols to be explained properly.

Brian chanted what he remembered. "Question mark for help; Sunglasses for retinal info; DNA string the main link; Lips for translation; Jeans for good gear; Green for go; White cross on red for stop. How did I do, Callum?"

"Spot on, Brian," Callum praised, "though never use the help button for silly questions."

"Okay," Fianna answered. "We've got that, haven't we boys? Let's get going."

Aran groaned. Fianna in bossy mode meant trouble. He glared at her. Though not happy about it, she buttoned her lip.

"Hey!" Callum clucked. "Be nice to each other, please. Activate the jeans icon now, since you're about to start."

After pressing, Aran looked at his clothes. "Nothing's different, Callum. Isn't it working properly?"

Callum's deep chuckles reverberated around the enclosure. "Trust me, Aran. It's working. The clothing function will kick in automatically, once the adventure is set in motion. We had a few naked disasters with that one during testing..." Callum stopped at Fianna's echoing guffaws and then straightened his face before he continued. "So we know you can't wait till later to activate that icon. Now, about the other functions. Remember to use the stop button only when you've all agreed that you want the experience to finish and press it at exactly the same time. If you can't all agree, then don't stop the story." Callum's expression sobered. "Are you sure you all want to try this?"

"Yes!"

"How long do we have to wait for the leap second to kick in?" He hoped it wouldn't be too long as he counted things off on his icon pad.

"That's the absolute beauty of it. There's no wait at all. We've perfected the use of the time slip facility. Fianna, type in two one zero and get going."

Fianna's fingers hovered excitedly before she reached through the screen and depressed the keypad.

Brian reminded them again about the last icon that hadn't been explained. "You still haven't told us about the analogue clock, Callum."

"That's the time leap function," Callum replied. "Only use that one in dire emergencies because it will reactivate the leap second facility, and will end the whole encounter."

"I don't get the difference between the stop button and the clock button." Brian sounded annoyed that he couldn't work it out.

"The stop icon ends the adventure but you all have to press that at exactly the same time to make the transfer smooth." Callum's wide grin showed his slightly over-lapping canine teeth, a trait both twins had inherited. Then his grin faded. "However, the clock is different. It can be activated by an individual but we've not quite perfected it yet; it's still too abrupt."

"So, you're saying…the clock icon is more of an ejector seat?" Aran asked.

"Exactly. Only use the clock facility if you feel one of you is in mortal danger, and will not survive."

"Us, as well as these mysterious people? In mortal danger…as in real death?" Brian's face was a picture, his expression an 'as if'.

"Most of your challenges will be tense and exciting—though many will be dangerous. Some of the people you meet will be pleasant and helpful yet others may be quite the opposite. You need to find out as much as you can about the people you encounter and tell us this information when you return. You'll also need to work out who you can trust and who needs your help the most. It's only if you're sure that one of you truly faces death that the clock icon should be used."

Exhilaration flared while he absorbed Callum's words, though actual as opposed to virtual death sounded way too final.

Callum tut-tutted. "Aran, you might love adventures, but remember if one of you presses the clock icon you'll all be catapulted home."

"Got it!"

"You still want to join this adventure story?" Callum asked.

Their 'Yes' rang around the cabinet till Brian changed tack. "Wait. You're still too vague, Callum. I need more info about the rules of this thing."

Callum nodded. "Okay. Here's a task list. Work out where you are, who the people are, and when, because it won't be your own time. After that, you'll need to suss out what the greatest threat is to all of the people you meet, and then what you need to do to help them cope with it. You have information that can help even those who seem to be the nasty ones. Helping them might seem extremely dangerous, but it's also part of your task list. You must decide who most needs your knowledge and assistance and give your advice sensibly because it will have far reaching consequences if you don't get it correct. All of this will take time to work through and it's likely that you'll even need to have sleep-overs on some of the decisions."

"Wow! Is that all we need to do?" Fianna was now the one delaying them.

Callum sighed affectionately. "Okay, then. Here's the biggie. Your ultimate task is to help solve a mystery regarding a particular name. There's a local hill in Kintore which has a current official name on the Ordinance Survey Map but it's sometimes called *'The Gallows Top'* and at others, it's thought to be related to the Gaelic word for *'hatchet, or axe'*. Historians aren't sure why it got these nicknames. We want you to find out."

"That's everything?" Brian was like a terrier worrying a raggedy bone.

Callum was on a roll. "Well, if you need even more on this quest, bring us back some physical evidence related to the story."

Fianna nudged into her twin. "Stuff your whinging questions and let's get going. I'm fed up with you already. Maybe Callum should let Aran and I go together and leave you behind."

Aran didn't like the sound of that. An adventure with only him and Fianna didn't appeal. He was so glad when Callum merely chuckled and asked them to listen again.

"Getting you all here to the Physics Lab was a bit shaky because you didn't all press at the same time, so what you need to do is activate the Green for Go icon at exactly the same moment, when I give the signal word of 'Now'." Callum's smile encouraged. "Set your finger over it and be ready for the command… NOW!"

Chapter Three

A different whooshing sensation made its way through Aran's armband, tingling all the way round his arm, billowing over his whole body. It set him to tumbling, yet again, though this time in backwards flips. It didn't seem like it happened as many times as before, though maybe he was becoming used to the weightless tipping over when he slowed to a halt.

The sounds of a softly plucked harp rippled around, a mysterious harmonious hum. Dense woodland blossomed in front of him, building up from the tiniest image, becoming clearer and clearer till it was all around him.

"Ugh. Something hit me. Get it off me now!"

He heard Brian squeal beside him as his mate flapped and slapped at his face, jumping around like a lunatic. Grey-green velvety leaves from a silver birch sapling feathered over his cheeks when he moved forward. The plucking of the harp fainted away and was replaced by birds chirruping above him. The noises were accompanied by a soft soughing of the wind as it ruffled through the branches. Woodland noises. Realistic noises and woodland smells. He sniffed hard, and then wished he hadn't.

"That's absolutely mingin'!" Fianna gasped. She shielded her nose with the fingertips of one hand when her feet squelched in the muck she'd churned up after plopping into place beside him. With her other palm, she scrubbed leaves and tiny mites from her forehead.

The stench of rotting foliage on the forest floor,

and something much more obnoxious, bombarded him. Whatever he'd stepped on hadn't been left by one little animal. They were in a forest but it wasn't too dark since the shrubbery close by was mainly of saplings and scrubby ferns.

"What on earth's happened to us?" Fianna squeaked. "Look at you two."

Instead of ragged jeans and thin T-shirt, Brian wore a faded red tunic with baggy mucky-yellow trousers underneath. Aran looked down. He was even more gaudily dressed.

"Cool clothes, Aran, I love the checks." Fianna giggled at his elegance.

A dull brown tunic covered his chest and breeches of brown and green checks clad his legs. Draped around his shoulders a long cloak hung to just below his knees. Brian's cloak was roughly woven dark-grey wool that tied round his neck with a woollen cord, but his was different. It was newer looking wool of a dark mossy green colour. It was a finer weave with a large, ornate gold brooch fastening it in place at his right shoulder.

"Very fancy." Brian laughed as he pointed to the brooch.

Fianna's dress was a simply joined pale lilac rectangle of material with openings for her head and arms to slip through, reaching half way down her calves, drawn in at the waist by a twisted rope, the knotted ends dangling down from the middle.

"Look, you two. I've got a real knife." She whooped as she pulled it free of a stiff leather sheath that was threaded through her belt but in her enthusiasm, it got caught on her cloak. "Eugh! How come my cloak's the yucky one?" She stopped complaining pretty quickly though, when she realised the blade had ripped a fine slice in the coarse wool. "Friggin' heck! It's really sharp. Watch you don't lose a finger." Using her knife she pointed to Brian's before sheathing it.

Fianna's cloak was much longer. It almost reached the ground, was made of a cow-pat-brown weave and looked like a coarse potato sack.

He and Brian had sheathed knives, and all three of them had a leather bag which dangled from a cord angled across their chests, but the most magnificent thing of all was the metal band around each of their throats. He peered down. Around his neck was a heavy circlet of dark gold formed like a twisted rope. Brian wore a dull thin silver band, but Fianna's was a tubular bronze choker.

She whistled before she slid her fingers across her neck ring. "Get a look at these. Have you two noticed they match our armbands?"

He hadn't, but she was right.

"Hey, Aran. You look really cool. Fierce and much more grown up. I'm not sure about the dried whitish clabber, but your hair spikes on the top are brilliant, and the rest hanging wildly down past your shoulders is…" Fianna's face was a picture, seeming short of the exact words she was looking for, tact not something she was noted for. "It's tangled like a bird's nest but your tattoo's brilliant."

"I've got a tattoo?" He quizzed both of the twins, looking at all the bare parts of his body that he could see. "Where?"

"It's on your forehead." Fianna reached up to rub it with her finger, to see if it would wear away. He wasn't keen on her getting so close to his nose as she peered at it. "It could be an animal of some sort, like a fat sheep or maybe a pig?"

"Have I got one?" Brian's question was hopeful.

"Nope." He scrutinised Brian's forehead thoroughly, rubbing off a fair amount of mud with his fingers. "Nothing but dirt."

Fianna touched the coarse material of her clothing, and then felt the finer material of his tunic. "Okay, smarty pants, so when and where do you think we might be?"

"I guess we'll find out soon enough." His wide I'm-really-enjoying-this sort of grin slipped free. A sudden flutter of birds caught his attention as they swooped over on the far side of the clearing, startled by the strident squeal of an animal in the distance—either in pain, or not particularly happy with something. "Have you noticed these on the ground?" At his feet were two spears: one shaft quite crudely made.

When Fianna picked it up a splinter pierced her skin. "Ow!" She yelped again and threw it down in disgust. "That shaft is way too jagged." She sucked a fine bead of blood from her finger and stepped clear of the weapon.

Aran lifted the other spear. Drawing his arm back, he pretended a throw. It fit him quite well, a bit like the javelin he'd been practising with at athletics, but with a super-sharp looking tip. "I like it. It's got pretty good balance."

He peered at Brian's feet when his mate cautiously lifted the spear Fianna had tossed down. Like his own feet, they were encased in leather shoes like bags roughly fitted by pulled laces of leather. The spear looked quite heavy as Brian mimicked his movements, but since Brian had never been much good at throwing a ball, never mind a sharp spear, it was gingerly laid down again, keeping well clear of his toes.

"Where do you think we fit on the historical time line?" Fianna asked.

"Remember our history project on Celts and Romans?" Tentatively testing the point of his spear head he continued, "The clothes and neck rings? These seem like Celtic torques to me. The checked breeches and tattoos were worn by Celts, as well."

"Yeah," Brian nodded his agreement before shoving his messy long hair away from his face. "Our group made loads of neat stuff."

"The Celts lived two thousand years ago, didn't they?" Fianna was checking out his torque as she answered, her finger poking at one of the knobbly rounded ends of his gold band.

Batting her hands away from his neck, Aran was in his element, horrible history being his forte. He loved everything historical, but especially the gory nitty gritty. "The Celtic period lasted for ages. Clothes and torques like these could have been worn anywhere between 500 BC and approximately AD 600. If this story is set in Celtic times that would be so cool!" He lowered his spear, and set it on the ground, tip pointing to the sky.

Although he was nearly a year older than the twins, they'd been in the same primary school class at their small Aberdeenshire country school, and had done the same history topics.

When Fianna fingered her own neck ring, the string of her dangling pouch twanged against her thumb. Slinging it over her head, she rummaged inside the soft leather before she pulled out something quite hard. She sniffed at it, and then fingered its texture. "It's like an oatcake."

She held it out to him. He sniffed it. Then felt the bumpy texture. She also had two pieces of wood. One was a short stick with a smoothed end and the other a small flat square with a central depression—also quite worn out but burn-blackened at the centre. Her only remaining object was a smoky-smelling brown lump.

"See what you two have got," she ordered, stuffing her things back into her pouch before sliding it across her chest again.

Pulling out a brown misshapen object, he sniffed it and then put it to his lips. "Hey, it's like beef jerky! Mmm. Not bad at all." He sucked hard on it to extract the smoky meaty taste.

"What the baloney am I to do with these?" Brian sounded disgusted to find a little collection of very smooth rounded pebbles and a neat little leather sling in his bag, though dangling it upside down proved it contained nothing else.

He wasn't sure if Brian would be any good at using a sling, either. After rummaging inside his own bag, he pulled out a bone comb, the teeth irregular and widely spaced. He held it out.

"Looks like deer horn." Brian fingered the surface of the comb then popped it back into the bag, grinning like mad. "But looking at your rat's nest of hair, I guess you don't use it much."

A matted lump of course, greyish hair, and part of the skeletal head of an animal with a long jaw-line and fiercely sharp canine teeth were also in his pouch. A dog or maybe a wolf? Brian fingered the jaw gently to feel the spiky line of teeth then snatched it to mimic an attack on his chin. A weird squealing nearby added spooky effects to his melodramatic acting.

"Listen to that. Great background sounds here."

"Stop messing around." Cuffing Brian's shoulder, he reached for the grisly bone. "Give it back."

"Had a good set of gnashers, didn't it? Fancy that snarling you to pieces?" Brian cackled.

Aran grabbed it and stuffed it in his bag.

"I love this story already, everything feels so real. Oh, hey! My armband's buzzing." Brian sounded really excited.

His was vibrating, too.

"It's started." Fianna's shriek rang around.

Reaching for the opening knob on his armband, he depressed it. *'Good start on your task list but you must find sanctuary now!'* There was almost no time to read before the lid pinged shut.

A twinkling excitement lit up Fianna's eyes. "Deadly serious already. What should we do?"

Having stuffed all his pieces into his pouch, he slung it back around his neck. "We find cover."

Brian whooped, and wheeled around to scan the copse of trees. "Our adventure has started."

Three pairs of glittering eyes assessed the dell, most of the trees nearby too slender to be any good to them. The forest floor around them was full of little hummocks and dips, covered with mosses, ferns, and lots of low densely-laden bushes, but nothing big enough that looked safe to hide behind.

"Can you two hear that?" Head cocked to the side, he listened intently.

The flapping of wings and the scuttling of small animals cried their distress, the creatures scattering in all directions. Some of the tinier birds swooped right past his spot, an undulating flutter of darting swifts. Somewhere, off to the left, was a noisy pounding as though many feet tramped through the forest.

"Yup." Fianna clenched up a spear and held it tight in her grip above her shoulder, her eyes gleaming. "Are you ready to fight them?"

"Move, Fianna." Brian urged her. "They're getting closer."

Aran wasn't sure now that it was a comfortable thudding. "I don't like the sound of whatever is coming. The message didn't say get ready to fight, it said find sanctuary, and that's safe cover. Pick the best tree to climb." His spear point swung around.

Horrifying squeals and heavy grunting jolted them into action. He didn't have a clue what came towards them, but now he didn't want to face it head on. From the sounds of twigs snapping and popping it wasn't only one large animal coming their way.

"That tree back there's good for all of us." Fianna gestured wildly to an old and gnarled oak about thirty metres behind them.

His longer legs covered the distance much faster than the twins. He was up the first few footholds before Brian even reached it. The oak had plenty of foot and hand holds, but the difficulty was to keep hold of the spear, and he could see that a few times Fianna came close to dropping hers, hampered as she was with her long dress and cloak.

"This bit will be safe enough," he gasped as he stopped at a point where sturdy branches grew close together on the trunk. The tree was in full leaf which meant he could see the other two, but not everything that was directly below. Panting with the effort of the mad dash, he didn't dare make any other noises as gut-wrenching squeals and an angry human voice reached the foot of the tree.

Who fumed down below?

Adjusting himself slightly, he peered down through the sun-dappled foliage. He could see a girl, maybe a bit older than he was, but he had no idea what she was yelling because her speech was a strange foreign language. He could hear the rage and desperation in her tone, but her words made absolutely no sense.

"Wow! I almost lost it." Fianna grinned, grasping the shaft of her spear. Nudging Brian with her elbow, she thrust the weapon at him needing her fingers to open her armband.

"It's the lips. Isn't it?" he checked.

Nodding, Fianna pressed the red lips icon. He did the same.

"Take your spear back." Brian urged, not wanting to miss out on any of the action.

Soon they were all beaming widely because they could understand the girl below—each and every angry word.

"You will never get me without a fight!" The girl wheezed, her breath wrenching out of her lungs as she wavered to the left to avoid the ugly beast that charged her yet again. The boar got close enough for one razor-sharp tusk to slash the arm she held across her ribs. "Aaiee!" she cried as it almost gutted her.

A dislodging tremor vibrated right up the trunk when the heavy body of the boar thudded against the rough bark of the old oak tree, after it skidded past the girl. Its irate squealing was even more intense when the creature found its tusks embedded in the gnarled surface.

The spear the girl weakly brandished aloft wouldn't be nearly enough to kill the hefty animal. She was too close to it, and her strength seemed gone. Aran could easily see that. The only escape for her would be to climb up the tree, but to do that she would have to lead the horrid animal away from it first, because the ugly boar was amazingly agile, and wouldn't be pinned to the bark for very long.

"Yes. Follow me first. Though your kind are the emblem of my tribe, you are a loathsome creature," the girl crowed at its snorting face.

Her angry yells rang across the glade while she struggled on a few more steps. The beast worked one tusk free, its grunts an unimaginable volume, so loud it hurt his ears up above.

Gasping for breath the girl continued to taunt it. "I will lead you a merry dance before your sharp tusks get me a second time."

Fianna's eyes were huge. "Gruesome. That thing really slashed her arm. Look at the dripping blood."

"Ssh. You idiot," Aran chided as the drama unfolded below, his own heart hammering because the beast looked convincingly fearsome. Pawing the ground it rocked its bulk, back and forth, the folds of leathery grey skin wobbling grotesquely as it worked its second tusk free.

"What do you wait for?" The girl nagged again, her squealing matching the wild boar, but he could tell she was exhausted. Glaring at the ugly mass of animal, her voice rang out over the clearing. "What takes you so long? By all the gods, I am ready for you. Come and get me." She held her spear stiffly out in front of her body, ignoring its trembles.

"Stand fast, Princess of Balbath. I am here to help

you." The voice that answered her came from the other side of the copse.

"Princess?" Fianna squawked, her eyes a-glow.

"Be quiet and listen." Aran glared for all he was worth, annoyed that Fianna had distracted him.

"Duhlain? I am so glad you have come." The girl answered though didn't take her gaze from the pawing and snarling beast, her body bent over her injured arm which leaked a ton of blood.

"When I divert it be ready with your spear, Seonagh, since mine alone will not kill it." The boy's voice got louder, his pounding feet scattering leaf litter and shredding twigs as he sped towards their tree.

"Aha!" Brian's grinned commentary was theatrical because he could now see the young boy across the glade. "The warrior boy, Duhlain, comes to the rescue. He's puny and thin for a hero, but looks mighty steadfast."

Fianna's mirror-image green gaze glittered expectantly at her twin then winced as the boar bellowed its fury just before it disentangled itself. "Oh, oh. Hold on. It just might get even bloodier."

"I am ready, but my foot remains weak, Duhlain." The girl called out as she retreated very slowly from the beast that now scanned back and forth between the two humans, "And my strength fails me."

"Where is Tyrnan?" The boy's question came as he manoeuvred even closer.

"I sent him to tell my father that I was returning to the settlement," she yelled over the boar's grunting. "I cannot keep pace. My scouting skills are worthless today."

Aran avidly listened to the exchange, processing

the information. Seonagh—girl. Duhlain—boy. Tyrnan—another boy but not around? Boar—definitely below and not best pleased.

The beast grunted and bleated, turning itself around in circles, its black beady eyes sparkling. Its deadly tusks rose skywards, the ears pricking up to attention, its head turning agitatedly towards the boy, and back to the girl. The beast didn't know which way to turn since there was, now, more than one quarry.

Brian tracked Duhlain as the boy deliberately paced about in front of the boar, and continued his running commentary to the others up the tree. "The warrior boy is thin as a wisp, but he's swift."

Aran's chuckles were easily drowned out by a dull rhythmic thumping on the ground a short distance away as Duhlain demanded the attention of the wild animal, drumming both his feet and his spear on the forest floor. Like the twins, Aran had got into the best position to see the action.

"Over here beast. Come and get me!" Duhlain roared as he grappled in the leather bag which hung low in front of his chest. A rapid whirling of stones flew from a sling to sting the beast's flesh, setting it squealing around. The incensed boar circled wildly as the boy pelted it with more stones from the little hoard in his pouch, some of them biting deep into the wobbling thick flesh, making small wounds, the blood trickling red trails down the folds of hairy grey pelt.

"Wow. I'm impressed. That's some really neat moves, warrior boy. You'll have to teach me how to use my sling," Brian praised, sharing some wide grins and thumbs up signs with his sister.

The pounding of the animal's trotters joined its unearthly shrieking as it faced Duhlain full on and lumbered towards him.

The warrior boy yelled back. "Come on, beast! This is for you." A glinting spear thundered through the air from his hand and caught the boar full in front, but it wasn't nearly powerful enough to fell it.

Seonagh galvanised into action and sent her own spear into its back, though she was too close to get any real muscle into it. The creature whirled back towards her, its agonised howls even more horrifying than before. The two spears buried in its flesh jiggled and vibrated, trickles of blood seeping through the thick hairy pelt.

"Oh, oh. It's getting nastier." Fianna grinned like a mad gamer. "I like this story."

Aran found a better vantage point, seeing both Seonagh, and the furious beast. He wasn't feeling nearly as excited about the events as Fianna was. She was thinking it an exciting, if bloody, game—he wasn't convinced of that at all. It was all too real. The creature was going to be upon Seonagh any second. She had absolutely nowhere to run to, and had no energy to escape it. He could almost taste the fear down below as the girl staggered aside, the boar still able to change tack to lumber towards her.

She had to be one of the people that Callum said might die.

He didn't want the story to end so quickly but had to prevent her death. Clenching the spear tighter, he squinted down through the foliage.

"By Taranis!" He called up the god of the Celts, remembering the name just in time. "Don't let me miss and hit the girl."

Chapter Four

"That was bleedin' close."

Brian gawped at the sight down below, his words brimful of admiration.

Aran's jubilant grin disappeared fast. It was disgusting. The spear had forced a pathway through the trembling leaves and had made an almighty squishy mess of the beast's head on impact. Like a balloon bursting, dark red gob and grey-white blobs had fired up and around. He'd heard the bone snapping, and had witnessed the blood and brains gush.

What kind of interactive game story were they involved in? It was alarmingly realistic and the stench of blood wafting upwards was authentic as well. Brought up on a farm he was no stranger to the metallic tang.

The boar had rocked from trotter to trotter. It had then keeled over in one massive thwump at Seonagh's feet, trapping her legs and had pinned her down. From above, he watched her manic breathing, her lungs straining, her gaze wild with panic or anger—he wasn't sure which. He knew his throw had been so close she must have felt the rush of the spear as it hurtled past her shoulder, before thrusting into the animal beside her. The singing of the spear's passage had probably shocked her as much as the proximity of the creature.

Duhlain sped over to her. "Seonagh, the gods heard you. The mighty Taranis above sent his spear down to save you."

Seonagh lay shuddering, the boar's tusks poking ineffectively into her stomach. The scraggy pelt scratched her shins when Duhlain struggled to disentangle her from the deadweight carcass, the weeping boar blood and messy flesh splashing their clothes and legs. Eventually free, Seonagh and Duhlain knelt side by side, their lungs still heaving. Then they raised their chins upwards, holding their trembling hands high in supplication.

"Taranis, god of the skies, I thank you. You sent down your thunderbolt spear to aid me in my time of need." Seonagh's intonation was seconded by Duhlain.

From above, Aran heard Seonagh's prayers but didn't dare move as the drama unfolded.

"What's going on?" Fianna inched herself along the limb to get a better view. The snap of a small branch cracking off under her thigh broke the near silence below, a rustling noise following as the wood jounced its way down through the heavy foliage. Losing her hold on the branch, one hand still gripping at the flailing spear, her cry echoed around. "Help me, Brian, I'm slipping."

Fianna's legs were horridly reddened as she slithered downwards. Her arms grasped to catch anything that would stop her headlong descent, the spear wedging itself amongst the small twigs and leaves, still in her tight grip.

Aran grabbed at her cloak and dress to prevent her uncontrollable dive, hissing madly. "Be quiet. They'll hear you."

Righting herself when he yanked at her clothing, Fianna moaned in his face. "It's way too late. They've already seen me."

"Okay, so, we're rumbled." Aran shrugged before pulling aside a branch for the three of them to look down through the canopy of leaves. Two pairs of astonished eyes gaped up at them.

Brian found a foothold to descend. "What are you waiting for? Let's do that interacting thing."

When Aran and the twins scrambled down the tree, and landed on the ground, Seonagh and Duhlain jumped up and scuttled back a few paces, avoiding the carcass of the boar. They whipped out sharp knives from their leather belt-pouches and held them out at the ready, their stance defensive.

"Hi. That was really close wasn't it?" Aran greeted them, taking a step forward; amazed he was thinking in English, though he knew it was a foreign language that came out of his mouth. The neatness of it made him grin till he noticed that the sharp blade in Duhlain's hand wildly gestured for him to halt. The warning made him feel less sure of his welcome. He stayed put, though he attempted the friendly approach again.

"I'm glad that devil didn't get you." He looked at Seonagh but pointed to the boar. "Jeeze. That was a vicious beast."

Seonagh raised her eyes, her pupils like cartoon concentric spinning plates. He wondered, for a moment, if his babblings didn't make any sense to her since she looked so bewildered. Duhlain nudged closer to her.

Fianna, last to touch down having been hampered by the spear, went right up to Seonagh and in her typical fashion rushed straight in. "Are you actually a princess?"

Aran's groan was quite distinct because Fianna

could be rude without always meaning to be. She was admiring the finely wrought silver rope around Seonagh's neck, but he knew from the disdainful look that she was scathing about the plain brown dress, which was similar in design to the one Fianna was wearing. Seonagh's simple hairstyle of two long brown braids hanging down her back also got a good deal of disbelief from Fianna. There was nothing fancy to Seonagh's hairstyle, not a hint of any special clips or jewellery holding it in place. It was exactly the same way Fianna's long hair was plaited.

Fianna pointed her spear tip towards Duhlain. "He called you princess, didn't he?"

"This is Seonagh, daughter of Tuadh, the chief of the Taexali of Balbath; therefore she is honoured with the title of princess." Duhlain stammered the words. His face was a sickly pasty grey-white, the knife in his hand a trembling glint, yet he still repelled any advance, defending even though he was much smaller than all of them. "Who are you?"

"I'm Fianna."

A shocked gasp came from Duhlain.

Fianna ignored the noise and continued. "That's my twin brother, Brian, over there."

Aran squirmed at Fianna's disgusted expression since it was the one she usually put on when people noticed the twins looked almost identical apart from the lengths of their hair. He knew for sure that Brian didn't want to look like her either. "And this is our friend, Aran." Fianna put on a cheesy smile, just for him.

"I know of Fianna," Duhlain muttered, a dismayed look now puzzling him as he and Seonagh inched even closer together. "But I do not remember those other god names."

"Gods?" Aran gulped. Gods were a pretty big thing to the Celts who tended to be extremely superstitious. He processed the conversation, frantically trying to recall where he'd read the word Taexali.

"Did the mighty Taranis not send you to help me?"

He cringed at the wary look on Seonagh's face.

"Taranis?" The twins' simultaneous question wasn't unexpected. He was used to them often asking or answering at exactly the same time, but Duhlain and Seonagh looked horrified by the in-tandem response.

"If not Taranis, you must then be Cernnunos, shape-shifter, and god of the forest. My thanks, Cernnunos, and that of all my tribe goes to you for saving the life of the daughter of our chief." The young boy's expression was a mask of dismay. Throwing himself flat on the ground Duhlain wobbled another invocation.

Aran was stunned when Seonagh flung herself prostrate onto the forest floor, as well. He looked down at the boy's shaking torso, and at the hand which could barely hold the knife. He would normally have laughed out loud at being called a god if he hadn't realised how earnest the younger boy was, but Duhlain wasn't joking, he clearly believed in Cernnunos. Not only believed but was so terrified with all the shenanigans that he almost hyperventilated.

Feeling very uncomfortable, he urged Duhlain to his feet, pulling him up by the bare elbows since the boy wore no cloak covering his arms. Bracketing the boy's skinny, shuddering frame he forced Duhlain to look up at him since the lad only reached his mid-chest. "I'm not Taranis and I'm not Cernunnos! And the gods didn't send us."

Convinced now that they had catapulted back to Celtic times, he remembered a little about the god Cernunnos, recalled that the forest god wasn't always kind to humans who disturbed the peace of his forest. He'd read tales about Cernunnos having a fondness for eating naive children who ventured into his domain. A scary god was Cernunnos—he had seen some bloodcurdling images that had been carved of him.

Duhlain continued to tremble.

His repetition was firm. "The gods didn't send us."

The young lad wasn't convinced but the shudders gradually receded. Aran took a deep breath before trying again, modulating his tone to a soothing one, encouraging Duhlain to believe him. "We were up in the tree, and it was obvious that Seonagh needed some help, so I used my spear."

He felt Duhlain's breathing even out, and then waited till some colour seeped back to the lad's face. He let his hands drop from Duhlain's rigid shoulders before he stepped back a pace, now sure the boy wasn't going to collapse in a heap. Truth to tell, he was still a bit thrown by this reality thing himself, because it felt as though he actually had been clutching Duhlain. The lad might be mostly skin and bone… but he was as real as touching Brian or Fianna.

How wonderfully weird. Despite the tense situation, a quiver of excitement crept across his cheeks.

Seonagh rose to stand right next to Duhlain, though neither of them seemed at all convinced about his explanation.

Aran watched as Duhlain pointed at him. "You are a warrior of the Taexali?" The boy raked his fingers through his matted brown hair, and pushed it carelessly back from his scalp. "I do not understand this. You are real people?" Duhlain's gaze didn't waver for an instant.

"Of course we are!" Fianna giggled before looking at Brian and then across to him. "Erm…aren't we?"

Aran knew what Fianna was thinking. What exactly were they? Were they projected images that could somehow touch their surroundings? On the other hand, were they really in the forest? He still wasn't too sure, but it wasn't the moment to look uncertain. "We're as real as you are." He thumped his chest to reinforce his statement.

Duhlain startled him when he leapt in front of Seonagh again, wielding his knife at them all, forcing them back, his fear turned to antagonism now that he'd recovered. "How did you get here? There were no strangers on our territory."

"You carry the mark of our tribe." Seonagh pointed her knife at his forehead. "And you all wear treasures around your necks and arms—but we do not know you. Who are you?" She slid her own knife forward.

"We're from a different branch of the Taexali tribe," Brian said, picking up the conversation. "We're from quite far away. You just wouldn't believe how far away. But we've come to visit you."

Aran was happy for his friend to take the initiative with the storyline.

The huge smile Brian summoned was supposed to be friendly, though Aran wasn't so sure it worked when it didn't get any positive reaction. In fact, Seonagh's aggression increased. She took a menacing step towards them. Brian sidled in closer to him because, although Seonagh wasn't as tall as he was, she was bigger than Brian and he was fairly sure Seonagh wielded her knife a lot better than his best mate would.

Brian improvised again. "We weren't sure how to reach your home."

"You have come to Balbath to speak with my father, Tuadh?" Seonagh prodded closer to Brian, her voice and knife working as one.

"Yes." Aran decided it was time to join in. "That's where we're going, but since you're here now we'll just follow you."

Thwhomp!

The spear that embedded itself in the ground between himself and Seonagh stunned him, the vibration of the shaft twanging and humming well after the impact. He jumped back from the girl as though scalded.

"Seonagh. Is there trouble?"

The deep boom of the questioner made Aran whirl around, so silently had the warrior come upon them. The very sound was scary enough to Aran, but that wasn't a patch on the look of the man who could just be made out in the speckled sunshine. A giant of a warrior loped across the glade towards them. He wasn't so old, but he was awesomely ferocious looking. Fianna nudged Aran's elbow.

"He's totally cool." Her low tone was somewhere between awe and wonder.

The warrior's long dirty-blonde hair hung well down below his shoulders, rippling in untidy waves. Two thin braids framed his severe looking face. Above his brow, the hair was short and spiked out stiffly from his scalp. Aran looked at the man's hair closely. Fianna had described his own hair as being whitened by some sort of gunge. He wanted to feel the top of his head to compare it with the warrior standing before him, but he didn't think such sharp movements were a great idea.

A small dark blue mark decorated the warrior's brow. It looked like an animal, maybe even a boar, though he wasn't sure. He was too far away to see the detail, but there was no way he would willingly go closer to confirm his thoughts.

A bushy moustache on the warrior's upper lip drooped down the sides of his grim looking mouth; the ends of the whiskers reaching the underside of his otherwise shaved chin. One cheek had a brutal looking scar that sloped from the edge of his eye to just short of his ear, the skin still reddened and puckered, not long healed. One huge fist gripped a slender blade, the deadly-sharp edge glinting in the mottled rays flickering through the trees.

Aran regretted the quick peep he'd dared at the man's face since the warrior's menacing black eyes glowered at them all when he stepped purposely between them and the princess, before his gaze focused on the dead animal and the blood around their feet.

"Are you hurt, Seonagh?" The warrior scanned the blood smeared on her.

"Not so much, Tyrnan. This is mainly boar's blood." Seonagh pointed to her clothes and legs.

"The creature pursued me, but Duhlain and this other young warrior helped kill it. They saved my life because it was sure to disembowel me."

"And your arm?" Tyrnan growled again not yet satisfied with her wellbeing.

Seonagh looked down at her arm where a steady stream of blood ran down to her fingertips and dripped off, less than there had been earlier but still a reasonable flow. "This is where the boar scraped me. A flesh wound only and nothing to fuss over." She swiped the blood off with her dress and then examined the cut.

Aran noted the deep slash, about six or seven centimetres long, that had scored through quite a few layers of skin. Blood oozed from the whole area, the edges of the cut ragged and an angry red. He glanced at Brian who wasn't usually too good when it came to blood and bits, but his mate had buttoned up his feelings fairly well, his teeth biting into his bottom lip, his gaze averted. He was fairly sure if it had been Brian who was injured he'd have easily bested the boar's squeals.

Peeling off a thin cord from her belt Seonagh mutely handed it over to Tyrnan, her wounded arm outstretched. Her face was pale, but she remained completely silent, her expression blank, showing no sign of any pain. Tyrnan trickled a few droplets of liquid over the cut, from a skin he carried on his belt. A cleansing of sorts. Grunting and muttering, the man's movements were assured and purposeful as he repeated the treatment, wiping blood away with a piece of cloth that Seonagh took from her waist pouch. The warrior still looked absolutely scary, his mouth remaining a grim straight line, his eyes a black wrath.

Friendly doctor's bedside manner? Brian clearly didn't think so; a horrified gasp whiffing past his lips when Tyrnan squeezed the edges of the wound tightly together. It must have been excruciating, but Seonagh didn't utter a sound. Aran was very impressed with the princess's self-control. Brian, on the other hand, now looked like he might pass out.

Tyrnan suddenly barked at Fianna, his anger a petrifying bellow. "Why do you stand there gawping?"

Fianna was riveted to the ground staring vacantly at the warrior. If Tyrnan hadn't been holding Seonagh's arm he was convinced Fianna would have received a good sound blow from the back of the man's hand, before he blasted on at her. "Fetch the healing mosses!"

Fianna was spared from more of Tyrnan's thunder when Duhlain thrust a pad of moss and lichens into the man's hand, a bundle that the boy had swiftly pulled up from somewhere close by. In a few quick twists of the cord, the mosses were packed on and Tyrnan had the wound dressed tight and secure.

Aran was seriously impressed... and amused. He'd recently done some first-aid training at his Scout troop. Antiseptic wipes? Butterfly strips? Clean gauze? Sticking plasters or bandage? Nope! Not a one. He couldn't suppress a small grin from escaping, but he made sure the terrorizing guard didn't catch sight of it.

It was only after he'd finished with the princess that Tyrnan turned to him and addressed him formally, though the words were grudging.

"My thanks go to you. I should have been at Seonagh's side to keep her from harm." Guilt across the man's features warred with a good dose of anger and a lot of suspicion.

Seonagh groaned. "You cannot be in two places. The fault of your being away was mine, but it matters not because I still live."

The warrior had yet to be convinced as he manoeuvred himself directly between Seonagh and Fianna's spear.

Tyrnan noted Aran's tattoo, thrusting the tip of his knife towards it. "Warrior of the Taexali? You will explain how this killing of the boar happened."

Aran shuffled his feet under Tyrnan's intense glower, but Seonagh responded before he could speak.

"Duhlain and I were too close to the beast to put enough power into our throws." Her features softened a hint, the bright blue of her eyes glistening with the memory. "The stranger's spear slashed down upon it from the heights of the tree, like a thrust from Taranis."

"From the tree?" Tyrnan rumbled before prowling closer. "Why were you in the tree? And where were you two?" The man whipped around to confront Brian and Fianna, towering way above them. The warrior peered at them, one after the other, as though he couldn't fathom how near-identical the twins were.

Fianna exhaled loudly, almost a whistle beside Aran's shoulder when Tyrnan yanked his spear out of the ground using his left hand. Without casting his gaze upon it, Aran felt the warrior expertly twirling the earth off on the bottom of his fancy green cloak. The piercingly sharp point was then waved around to reinforce the man's inquiries, the other slender blade never out of his right-hand grip during the process.

Both weapons were perilous. Fianna nudged him for his attention and then winked.

She was definitely impressed by the Celtic warrior. The grunt Aran wanted to make had to be stifled.

"What were you doing?" Tyrnan was becoming repetitive.

Fianna looked excited. He wasn't sure how he was feeling. If he gave the truth, would his explanation be believed? He attempted a small smile as the warrior's scepticism continued. "We were lost. We went up the tree to get a better view."

Tyrnan assessed in tense silence, his reptilian eyes half-hooded, while he slowly circled their little huddle.

When the warrior walked behind Fianna, the blade of Tyrnan's deadly, sharp knife nudged her spear tip – in towards Aran's cloak. He felt a nip at his shoulder before she yanked it away, but he didn't dare utter a word, or make a move. He had no doubt now that Tyrnan interacted with them in a totally animate way.

Completely cool but he'd rather the spear prod hadn't been so accurate. A suspicious stinging of his flesh made him sure something wasn't imagined.

Callum had said this experience would be completely different from anything ever before. His pulse bubbled, excitement clashing with caution, because these blades could rip people to shreds… real blood… real tragedy. He dared a glance at the dead animal a few paces away. That bloody mess he'd made of the boar's head was real gore and the next bloody mashing up might be his own face. His stomach lurched since that wasn't actually a pretty thought. When he thought about it, the smell of animal blood couldn't be a fabricated one either. His nose curled up.

The boar was a skanky beast!

Nausea bubbled up his gullet.

His mind worked at warp speed. The danger they currently faced could have mortal consequences though Seonagh would probably not be a target again. Yet they'd barely started; had worked out almost nothing, so far. That must mean this sort of threat couldn't possibly be dangerous enough for them to end the programme, but what on earth would be calamitous enough? A twisted excitement flooded again and brought his thoughts to order. He made himself concentrate on the present danger; the threat from the warrior's piercing knife.

The guard completed his circling noting their clothing and the fine torques they wore around their necks. Ogling the large brooch pin Aran sported at the shoulder of his cloak, Tyrnan used the knife tip to peel the metal away from the material. Aran's breath hitched though he stood his ground. Tyrnan's focus was intent, and puzzled. His eyebrows rose, his upper lip hair so close it almost brushed Aran's chin. "This belongs to you?"

His head bobbed. He was tall for his age but Tyrnan topped him by more than a whole head and all of Tyrnan's muscles bulged. Not like a weight lifter, just a man who was extremely fit and naturally strong. He squared his shoulders, not actually feeling at all confident, though instinct told him that he needed to face up to Seonagh's guard.

Tyrnan scanned the forest around them before his interrogating gaze pinned him to an imaginary pole.

"Where are your elders?"

Chapter Five

Elders?

Aran strained his body away from the warrior whose stare menaced its way across the gap between them. His eyes flicked across to Brian, his mind whirring through how to describe Callum, and his team.

"You were not on your journey alone?" Seonagh challenged before swinging a question towards Brian, appearing to find him an easier mark to intimidate. "Where are your guardians?"

Brian's halting speech came out in fits and starts, words tripping off the cuff. "We had guardians when we left our home but we ended up separated from them."

"These surely are the most troubled of times." Tyrnan nodded solemnly as he paced in front of Brian, appearing vaguely sympathetic.

It was a ruse Aran wasn't in the least swayed by since he was sure there wasn't a compassionate bone in Tyrnan's body.

"Where were you headed for when you were waylaid?"

"To Balbath," Aran interrupted quickly, allowing the guard to think what he wanted to.

"You bring a message for Tuadh?"

Tyrnan's question snapped when he whipped around, his face thrusting right up close, which meant the warrior's knife was also incredibly near Aran's throat. After his small nod the man pounced again, grabbed his cloak at the neck and fisted it tight, the knife in his hand no impediment because he'd flipped the blade to the side.

"You will deliver your message to me."

"No!" Aran struggled against the grip at his throat, a clench that increased till it was an agony to breathe. "No," he croaked again, determined not to show fear. Yet, he knew it wasn't his own expertise, or strength, when a quick flick of his arm dislodged the warrior's grasp. He was free. For some unknown reason the warrior had allowed it to happen. "I can only give my knowledge to Tuadh in person."

What the heck the message was he couldn't work out, his thoughts frantic as the warrior padded around him. What could be believable?

Seonagh was as fierce as Tyrnan, her knife also too ready. "Tuadh is my father. Your communication can be delivered to me."

Aran had just dug a large hole for himself. Now he slid further into it, because what had seemed at first like a little white lie now assumed larger proportions. Yet, the truth wasn't an option either. What could he say? There is no message. We're just here to create an interactive story with you. We haven't a clue why we're here. He didn't think Tyrnan would appreciate any of those. Eventually, he settled on a delaying tactic.

"Tuadh will appreciate what I have to say to him."

"How strong was the enemy force that attacked? Separating you and your guardians?"

Seonagh asked him so abruptly, he floundered.

"Our guardians sent us on ahead so I can't give you an answer to that question."

"Cannot?" Tyrnan wasn't budging an inch.

The warrior's fist was back at his throat, an even

tighter grip on his cloak. Tyrnan's spear tip goaded his shoulder this time, pressing hard enough to leave a good solid bruise.

"Or will not?" Tyrnan's breath fanned his chin when the guard literally hauled him off his feet and onto his tiptoes.

He refused to flinch as he dangled, his lips clamping together when he drew his head back as far as he could from the warrior's hot breath. Tyrnan was pretty scary, but he now reckoned that if the warrior was going to kill him he'd have done it already. Getting better at giving non-answers he replied, "I can't."

Expressions of doubt passed between Seonagh and Tyrnan, the man reluctantly relaxing his grip.

Aran slumped down almost knocking Brian over, so close had his friend plastered himself to his side.

A heartbeat later, the warrior sheathed his slim knife before his muscular arms folded across his wide chest, his spear tight in his grip. The guard's expression was dark and angry as a winter storm, words dragging through his clenched lips. "Your explanation had better be good or you will regret toying with me."

One side of the warrior's mouth curved up in a parody of a smile that put dread into Aran's heart, because it wasn't in the least reassuring. Tyrnan didn't look as though he'd believed one single thing he had said before the man turned slightly away from him.

Tssh–ick!

The sudden high pitched scrape sent shivers down his back. His wasn't the only pair of alarmed eyes now riveted on the warrior's glistening long-bladed knife as Tyrnan drew it from the longer sheath at his waist.

The edge was flourished in front of him; a gleam back in Tyrnan's gaze when the man noted Brian's fearful reaction to his longer weapon. It made the warrior's short knife seem like a simple little butter spreader. The deadly element of the story ratcheted up a notch.

"Oh, bleedin' heck..."

Aran felt Brian's knees buckling beside him. A sudden large lump in his throat prevented him from breathing properly when his mate's weight tugged at his cloak.

"Here, Duhlain! It will take us some time if we are to take home the kill." Tyrnan's boom commanded, the weapon brandished close enough to ruffle the edge of Aran's tunic.

The kill? Him, and the twins? A glacial avalanche chilled to his toenails, his indrawn whirlpool of breath almost sucking him into the vortex. The weirdest thought flicked across his tortured brain—Where's the damn portaloo when you need one? Darting a glance at Fianna, he realised that Brian was the only twin feeling a little bit nervous.

Fianna was hiding a worshipful smirk.

She couldn't possibly, truly, fancy this Celtic warrior? Could she?

The way she was casually draped around her spear was as though it was something she did every single day. Rather Tyrnan than me, he thought. There was no way he wanted to be the object of Fianna's drooling attention.

When Tyrnan stepped away from them, and bent to lay down both his spear and the long blade, Brian's relieved sigh whiffed out.

The warrior drew off the long length of rope that coiled diagonally across his chest and tossed the loops to the ground before turning to the boar. Stamping his foot hard on the beast's carcass he yanked out the three spears, dark red blood and other grisly bits surging from the gaping wounds. The loud suck of the blades coming out of the flesh was revolting, and the pong emanating from the gap was even worse. Fianna sniffed alongside him.

Tyrnan straightened up with the three weapons, and then held them out shaft forward to Seonagh. "Claim your own first."

Aran was relieved when Seonagh claimed her own then passed one to Duhlain because he hadn't a clue which one he'd thrown. A good warrior should know his own weapon? He was pretty sure of that.

Tyrnan held the third spear pointing skywards while he regarded him, his gaze hooded. "You use your spear well, young warrior, given that it was embedded deep into the skull of the boar." Then with a grudging nod of acknowledgement, man to man, he thrust the spear at him. "Ensure you know who your real enemies are, young warrior of the Taexali, when you next use it."

He reached for it but received Tyrnan's uncouth guffaw right in his face. Any hint of mirth immediately vanished as the warrior retracted the spear with a grim announcement. "Not just yet, Taexali youth, if that is what you are. You will get no spear till I know exactly why you have infiltrated the territory of Balbath."

When he refused to respond Tyrnan remained immobile, his arm muscles flexed around the weapon. After a tension laden pause, his reactions were so swift Fianna almost keeled over alongside him. The warrior seized her spear before she knew what he was about and, using both hands, fired one spear after the other, well away from the little group. Aran was stunned by the expertise and speed. Tyrnan's nod to Duhlain was understood as the boy obediently cantered off to retrieve them—the salutary lesson over. Whipping out his slender blade Tyrnan then gestured to their knives.

"Relinquish them." No compromise, nor delay.

Wow! The lightening-fast guard meant business. He was now totally impressed. From the looks of it so was Fianna, but Brian still looked scared stiff. For some reason Tyrnan unnerved his friend.

He slipped out his blade and laid it down, the twins following suit. These Taexali tribespeople didn't trust them at all and he itched to know why. He had some inkling that the Taexali tribe lived in northern Scotland but couldn't remember anything else about them.

Maybe he should have lied to Tyrnan? Maybe he should have pretended to be the god Cernunnos that Duhlain was so terrified of? Unfortunately, he didn't think that warrior Tyrnan would be afraid of Cernunnos. Aran suspected Tyrnan would be afraid of absolutely nothing.

Seonagh swooped up their weapons and popped them into her own knife sheath. Jabbing her own blade-point in their direction, she silently manoeuvred them a little bit away from the dead boar, her measured gestures nearly as intimidating as Tyrnan.

"Are we prisoners?" Fianna's whispered question at his ear was a good one but her excitement was at odds with the enquiry.

Was this the next stage of their adventure?

That would make the story more exciting. His

heart tripped. Right now, the prospect of an escape was a thrilling challenge, but their chances of making it happen looked pretty well nil. The thought of being used for Tyrnan's javelin practice didn't appeal.

Tyrnan used his long blade to make strategic slits around the carcass. Being the son of a farmer, Aran acknowledged that the warrior had opened the blood vessels to let the blood drain more quickly. Then the rope was expertly twined around the trotters, tying them together. Duhlain went rooting about for a strong pole-like branch, grubbing around in the fern strewn undergrowth till he found one stout and straight enough for his purpose. Satisfied with one, the young boy hacked off some unnecessary twigs with his sharp knife, and then threaded the pole between the strung up legs of the beast. The boar may have been short of stature, but it looked heavy, a dead weight, with blood still dripping.

Aran goggled at the proceedings.

"Move." Seonagh urged him and the twins when she lurched forward.

"Nay!" Tyrnan's command halted them. "You go first, Seonagh. Our uninvited visitors will follow."

Seonagh set off without delay. Tyrnan sheathed his long blade before he picked up Aran and Fianna's spears.

"Seonagh!" His deafening command made her head swivel back. Two spears winged their way to thud in the ground just ahead of the girl. "Take these."

Seonagh deftly pulled them out of the ground still on the move, no lessening of her lurching speed.

"And you three? Make sure you remain a few paces behind Seonagh."

Tyrnan warned them on with his own spear.

Aran's gaze lingered long enough to see the warrior hefting up the animal carcass with Duhlain, each of them bearing an end of the pole over a shoulder, the bulky animal hanging between. Duhlain stumbled, not having the same height or strength as the warrior. The pole slipped from the young lad's shoulder and tumbled the beast to the ground.

"I am sorry, Tyrnan." The boy was ashamed.

Aran knew his strength and height would be a much better match for carrying the carcass, but when he moved back to take it from Duhlain one disapproving growl from the man told him his friendly gesture wasn't appreciated.

"Nay. The boy will do well next time. He must learn a man's tasks. Move."

Yet again the spear ruled.

"So, what have we found out about this story?" Brian whispered as they loped after Seonagh who set a spanking pace, despite her injuries.

"We're definitely back in Celtic times and the warriors here are really cool." Fianna darted yet another glance backwards.

"You best ditch the adoration, Fianna; I'm pretty sure it's not mutual." Aran ignored the returning slit-eye she sent him. "What I'm sure of now is that the Taexali tribes lived to the north of Dundee, and well into Aberdeenshire."

"Taexali Tyrnan. Cool. I love the sound of that. Probably Celts of north east Scotland, but we've no idea yet of when. How do we work that one out?" Fianna's mood changed to inquisitive.

"Watching alone probably won't do it. I guess, we need to listen for clues." He had no other answer to give.

"Should we keep going with them to Balbath?" Brian was hesitant, his constant checks backwards almost making him trip.

"Tyrnan's knives and spear are a bit too sharp for comfort to do anything else. He's demonstrated how he'll not hesitate to use them if we try to run off. For some reason he doesn't trust us. We need to follow till the action heats up and we can find out why."

Brian gasped. "You don't think we've had enough action yet? Seonagh's been gored by a raging boar. You just killed it with a spear and splotched its brains all over the forest floor and your neck is red raw where you've been sliced by a rapier sharp knife."

Aran fingered the skin above his torque, surprised to find it wet. At some point Tyrnan's blade must have nicked him after all.

"That's a trickle!" Fianna added. "We've all had real knives brandished in our faces, and in case you've forgotten it, brother, we're prisoners." Her outburst broke Brian's tension, and the three of them grinned at each other.

"That about sums it up so far. And, you'd both better be thinking up what my message to Tuadh might be," Aran warned the twins. "Seeing as I haven't a clue, yet."

Thwomp!

The twanging spear bedded itself in the ground only a hairsbreadth from Brian who jumped like a scuttled rabbit and sprinted the next paces.

"Enough of your talk. Respect our forest god."

Tyrnan's method certainly shut them up. They walked. And walked on for quite a while.

After the guard had goaded them through a belt of

trees, the land flattened out just below Aran in a natural plateau. The breath lodged in his throat as he gaped at the scene. The rush of sheer exhilaration made his steps falter.

High turf banking a little below him created a huge barrier. A wooden palisade towered behind it, separated by a dark shadow that he guessed to be a deep ditch. By an opening in the banking, a walkway zigzagged up to wide wooden gates which presently stood open. The tops of many houses were just visible over the wooden stockade, smoke seeping through the conical roofs. There were too many buildings to be easily counted since it was impossible to see far into the enclosure, but there were a lot of little spirals of smoke making their way straight up into the air, it being a very calm day.

In the distance, and well behind the settlement, rose a solitary hill with a grey frill around its peak. It snagged Aran's attention for a moment, something about the shape not quite right, yet familiar.

Exchanging a swift glance with Brian absolute glee coursed through him.

Seonagh rushed on ahead, seeming eager to get inside the walls.

It was a real live Celtic hillfort. Not one in a book, and they were to drive the plot of the story.

Expectation settled to a nice little hum. Trading fleeting looks with the twins, he guessed the next bit was likely to present more challenges. He grinned. They smirked back. This wasn't anything like the reacting-to-quick-death games that Callum had let them play before. These were real people; real sounds and smells, and some of the stenches were pretty similar to the fertiliser slurry on his dad's farm.

At the beginning of the walkway, two men sat scraping and sharpening a randomly dumped heap of spears. They greeted Tyrnan with a nod, getting to their feet as Seonagh reached them. One of them laughed heartily, a beaming smile breaking across his features. "A short scout today, we see, though not unsuccessful. We can feast well on that."

Aran was thankful to see the man pointed to the boar and not him since he had been shouldering the carcass for most of the journey, Duhlain clearly not up to the task, though the young lad had given it his best shot. Scrutinising them all in turn, the guard looked to Tyrnan for an explanation. The other one circled them all, taking stock back and front.

Tyrnan's chuckle wasn't friendly at all. "This Taexali youngster claims he has a message for Tuadh. I came across him and the other two in the Forest of Bendauch, though how they managed to get into our territory has still to be explained. They became separated from their companions, who may already be dead…" Tyrnan's eyebrows rose almost to his hairline as the warrior shared some hidden message with the guards. "Or worse."

Aran wondered how much worse you could get than being dead, but wisely kept his mouth shut as Tyrnan explained about the boar and the part he had played in helping Seonagh.

The guard accepted the explanation, his companion taking to his heels into the settlement without uttering a word.

"Though, if they are not dead," Tyrnan went on, "their guardians will probably make their own way here, so be on the lookout for Taexali strangers approaching."

Seonagh led the way round the pathway to the main gates, bypassing more young men who were dotted about, doing chores here and there, sharpening even more already frighteningly sharp tools and weapons. Busy, certainly, yet Aran realised they were on guard, too. Brian shared his suspicions, their glances connecting. Fianna, on the other hand, was ogling them all as though they were models on a catwalk.

Her attitude was disgusting—he hadn't realised she'd become a silly hormonal female!

He wondered why so many young guys were posted around. Were the people of the settlement expecting some imminent attack? No wonder Tyrnan was suspicious of their presence.

Otherwise, the settlement was a hive of activity. Children were dotted here and there outside the strange round houses; some played games, though others transported things—wood, pots, jugs and flat platters. Hens and dogs scuttled and ferreted around everyone's feet, but other animals were secured in large pens alongside some of the roundhouses.

"Are those scrawny things goats?" Fianna whispered alongside him.

Some of the animals were pigs—not like the boar killed in the forest—but a much smaller, pinker species. Not the same as on his dad's farm, but definitely pigs. The animals Fianna pointed to were quite different.

"No, they're sheep." His reply was low making sure Tyrnan didn't home in on their conversation as they trudged along. "You can see something like them on some of the Scottish islands. My dad's farming magazines have features on them. Wild sheep like those are called Soay.

A sudden loud hammering drew his attention, coming from a place towards the back of the settlement. The sharp ring of metal on metal tinged beat after beat. An acrid pall of smelly blackened smoke rising up into the air made Aran fairly sure the noises and burning haze came from a smithy. Closer by, food aromas tempted his nostrils: delicious meaty smells, though these mingled with the pong of damp wool and burning wood. Unfortunately, there was another odour he identified that wasn't at all pleasant. Not as sweetly pungent as the chemical-aided slurry on his father's farm—it was different and much more cloying.

Their little group came to a standstill as Seonagh pointed towards the source of the stench. "Our midden area lies beyond that screening."

He almost laughed at the look on Fianna's face. The compost heap took on a new dimension.

"Not yet, thank you." Brian's mutters sounded embarrassed, even a hint disgusted at the thought he'd maybe need to use the facilities soon.

Fianna just giggled.

His needs were more immediate and he wasn't being a cautious numpty about it. He nodded to Tyrnan. In tandem, they laid down the carcass of the boar.

"I'll just check it out. I'll be back in a moment, you two." He loped off behind the screening.

Back in record time, he grinned at the twins, leaned towards them and winked before he whispered, "Beats slurry spraying with my Dad any time."

Seonagh turned to Duhlain. "Your deed today will

not go unrewarded, Duhlain. I will make sure that my father hears about it. My thanks go to you again."

"I am honoured." Duhlain was embarrassed by the attention he received, barely able to contain his prideful smirk.

"Tyrnan? Take the animal to Agnas. She can prepare a beast as fast as a blink. It will be on the spit without delay."

Tyrnan didn't immediately answer Seonagh. Aran felt the inquisition return when the warrior's scariest glare settled on him before his hand waved them off. "Do nothing rash. Remember well that you are the strangers here."

Following Seonagh prevented the need to reply, even if Aran had wanted to. There were so many guards watching their progress that any attempt to flee would have been really stupid.

Close to the largest of the buildings, Seonagh paused. "This is the dwelling of Tuadh."

Built round a bigger circular base than all the others, Tuadh's house was constructed to the same design. Its sturdy walls of firm, regularly placed short posts were filled in with solid material like straw-mixed clay. The upright posts were about Aran's height, though the conical roof of the building towered up to about four times the height of the walls. The massive stout posts that made the framework of the thatched roof met high up in the centre, and at their low end the posts rested securely on top of the walls, extending out a little.

A young guard was seated at a jutting porch built out from the roundhouse but on seeing Seonagh, he leapt to his feet. His question was incredulous. "This is the warrior who must speak to our chief?"

Scepticism positively oozed from the man as he scanned them for weapons.

"Is my father within?"

"Aye, he awaits your return."

The entrance passage was short in distance, built to the same height as the walls.

"Follow me." Seonagh disappeared but the guard remained, corralling them in with his spear.

Brian made to follow her into the tunnel, though changed his mind when he realised it was gloomy. "After you, Aran. You're more special than me, and that mark on your ugly mug proves it."

Aran felt the push as Brian sent him in.

"I'll just come last." Brian made it like he'd just done him a favour.

When he glanced back, Fianna was smirking.

Was she checking out that young guard as well? Must be the different environment, he thought, since he hadn't been aware of her being so interested in young men at home. Then again, how would he know? He tended to keep out of her way most of the time when he visited the Frasers.

The short passageway was made of woven stout twigs and branches, stuffed in between with mosses and dried grass. The smell was immediately heavy, yet not unpleasant, a kind of candle-like fragrance and a marked contrast from the smells outside. It was very dim, and grew even gloomier with each of the four long steps that it took to pass through the short passageway, since the light from outside was blocked by their bodies. In front of Aran, Seonagh pulled aside a curtain of woven wool that protected the interior from draughts.

He coughed loudly when heavy smoke hit his

nostrils and made his eyes stream. It billowed around the interior and was accompanied by many other strange smells and noises. Side-stepping to the right on entry to the room, his head banged against something dangling by the doorway. It whipped back to tap him a second time. Terrified he'd knock it down, he felt around in the dimness to stop it spinning. A cold smoothness settled under his fingers. Little by little, it came into focus. Right in front of his face.

He gawped at it his hands jerking back. "Oh, shi…ugar!

Chapter Six

"Yorick?"

Aran recoiled, the cough returning to choke him. A grisly skull dangled from a leather thong threaded straight through its crown. It was smooth in places; gruesome tufted tresses still growing from its sides.

"Yuck!"

He squirmed away. Surely it couldn't be long dead, if it still had hair on? His vision had adjusted to accommodate the smoke but he wished it hadn't. A short string of skulls dangled on each side of the doorway. A pulse pounded at his temples. They weren't plastic—plastic hadn't been invented. The skulls hung in their grimness, the eye sockets balefully staring as though blaming him for their being there. He felt his eyes fill up. He convinced himself it was on account of the smoke—not for any other wimpy reason and squared his shoulders to prove it to himself again.

Trophies.

He almost hyperventilated when the word flagged up in his brain. A trophy was a little silver cup you won for winning a race or being the best in the football team—but Celtic tribes? They beheaded their enemies, and then left the skulls outside on poles for the birds to peck away at the flesh and clean the bones bare. The skulls were kept as a mark of respect for the brave fate the original owner had come to, the cranium believed to be still full of that person's wisdom.

Aran wanted to keep his brain feed intact.

Reading about skulls in a book? Looking at

illustrations? Easy peasy. Seeing and touching was another thing entirely. Standing right next to them in the gloom of this strange-smelling roundhouse made the hairs on his neck stand up like a cat bristling before a spitting fight. He shuddered at the thought it might be his fate, disgusted to think somebody could twirl his skull around.

Ugh!

Tearing his gaze away from them, he felt their malevolent eye sockets now on his back. Had they been brave warriors who hadn't been afraid to die? Alternatively, were they poor souls who had been scared out of their wits at the moment of death, just as he felt right that minute?

"Those usurpers have the gall to descend on us, again?" The warrior who spoke was beyond angry.

"Why do they revisit?"

The rising clamour inside the room in response to the questions broke Aran's preoccupation with the skulls. It seemed as though everyone present wanted to get in on the action.

Were the people bawling about him and the twins?

Breathing erratically, he stared towards the centre of the large room where the light of a recently lit fire illuminated the dimness: a fire which spat and sparked, most likely caused by the use of still sappy, damp wood. The smoke, unfortunately, didn't billow up to escape through a chimney, or a hole in the roof: there wasn't an escape route at the highest point of the roof timbers. Instead, the pungent smoke floated around the inside of the roundhouse, hugging the low walls and clouding the whole area with a ghostly-whitish pall above the heads of the men who sat at the far end of the hearthside: all of them fierce-faced in the flickering firelight.

Drawn by the arrival of him and the twins, two of the men peeled away from the others. They zipped down the room towards him, one on each side of the fire as they sped past curtained off areas that lay against the walls.

Friggin' heck! Escape sounded like a fabulous strategy.

Steeling himself to look behind, there were a couple of small reed torches barely flickering above the entrance door. Their metal sconces jutted out from the wall near the dangling drops of skulls now almost obscured by Brian and Fianna who, like him, struggled with the smoke. The young guard had entered behind them and now stood sentry at the doorway, his spear still in one of his crossed arms—though the smoke didn't seem to bother him at all.

Aran blocked out the creamy-white craniums and took note of the glistening array of weapons stacked around. A bright and shining shield hung to one side of the door, a large metal rack holding many spears below it. More shields were scattered at the bottom of the wall. On the other side of the entryway, there was a collection of metal cutting and scraping tools spiking up from a low metal holder that resembled a lattice bucket.

A small armoury he could choose from, but he reckoned that was way too rash a thought. Being pummelled by the looming warriors just didn't appeal.

"...at least a whole legion!" The words echoed inside the large room.

Men at the rear quarrelled, their voices rising over a general bubble of noise, something angering them to shouting pitch. It was impossible not to tune in though Aran couldn't hear full sentences. Attack. Death. Desecration.

Again.

He hadn't mistaken the word legion. That had to mean the Ancient Roman Army—he was sure of it. Anticipation flared the resulting fluttering in his tummy now from excitement. It sounded as though the story would involve Romans as well.

He bit back a grin.

Nodding to her helpers, Seonagh tugged his elbow and forced him past the wattled-walled cubicles which hugged the walls to his head height, almost all the way around the room. The twins were likewise escorted in behind him till Seonagh stopped at one of the arguing men. Only some of them sat down on low stools, the others ranged themselves alongside sitting cross-legged on the many rugs that lay piled around the fireside. The man Seonagh brought them to sat at the end of the long fire area bordered with large flat stones. It was a prime position facing the entrance door.

"Father?" Seonagh's soft word was ignored. By all of the men.

So, this was the chief of Balbath. Aran was impressed.

The warrior's broad torso was daunting, his body bent forwards, his feet balanced evenly on the beaten earth and bracken covered floor. The biceps of his bared arms were like knotted tree branches as he flexed a small switch of hazel wood, back and forth, bending it to almost breaking point, while he played with it across his thighs. His powerful body was topped by a thick waving mane of reddish-brown hair that hung well below his shoulders.

"They are still only rumours, Tuadh." A man beside him spat the words, yet it also seemed as if he attempted to calm the rest of the men down. "Nobody among us can confirm."

"I will have proof," Tuadh shrieked. The switch flicked on the floor sending up a cloud of dusty earth and bracken fibres. "Reports that are unverified, and petty jabbering, are useless to me."

The switch in his hand whipped furiously in the air narrowly missing the wool-clad legs of his neighbour. Aran noticed the other warrior didn't even flinch. How the man ignored it, he couldn't fathom, because he found it impossible to avoid following the constant flicks.

"Father?"

Seonagh waited again after her second interruption. Though still softly intoned, there was more of a steely determination to her words. She appeared unaffected by the anger that roiled around the small group of warriors and didn't seem particularly bothered by Tuadh's furious body language and livid tones. Incredibly, Aran noticed that she didn't cower from the thin piece of wood which could so easily be used as a punishment to the unwary.

"What?" Tuadh's voice rose to an even higher pitch. When he turned around, the chief's eyes were more frightening than his switch. Piercing blue, they looked so enraged it took a few blinks to register who stood alongside him. His voice was so deep it barked from his toe nails. "What do you trouble me with, girl? Cannot you see this is not a good time?"

"This uninvited visitor has a message for you." Seonagh was patient, untroubled by her father's antagonism, Aran making no resistance to her dragging him forward. "He is the young warrior who came to my aid today and killed the boar."

The men in the little group fell silent when Tuadh leapt up to his feet. Aran almost rocked over from the slaps that came across his shoulders in greeting, the chief's palms landing so hard he stumbled back. Like a set of skittles, he knocked back into Fianna who toppled Brian to the ground. Seonagh clucked her way along and plucked Brian upright again as though it was a regular occurrence.

"A deed well done, lad!" Tuadh boomed, his tone only slightly less angry. Aran felt the riveting gaze locking on to him as he righted himself. "You have proved yourself worthy today—with that at least. For the rest, we will just have to see."

One huge bear forearm tightened across his shoulder, almost scrunching his bones to a pulp. That funny fluttery nervous feeling happened again in his stomach as he latched onto the words 'at least'. What could Tuadh mean by that, and what was the rest?

Tuadh was an extremely powerful warrior. The switch of hazel lay down at his feet just ready to jump up and flail him. As Aran stared down at it, he was convinced it was twitching of its own accord. Vile-tasting bile rose up and almost made him puke. Being intimidated wasn't actually the greatest feeling.

"Sit beside me here, branded warrior, and we will talk for a moment before the council assembles."

He was powerless when the chief plonked him down on the vacated stool next to the one Tuadh had been sitting on. The warrior who had been seated on Tuadh's right now stood just behind his back. The most distrustful look yet passed across the man's features—and that was saying something—since everyone at Balbath was suspicious.

Aran let his gaze drop to the floor, unable to confront them. He needed to summon some willpower again to assess what was likely to happen to him. The fire was warming up but it wasn't the fresh blaze that scalded his innards.

"Now is the time for truth young warrior."

The steely edge to the chief's words kept Aran's nerves frayed as much as the man's shoulder purposely butting against him when Tuadh twisted round to peer at the twins, though he made no attempt to invite them to join him around the hearthside. The two warriors closely flanked them, so dismissal of the twins by Tuadh was swift. Turning back to him it was the pin at his neck which claimed the chief's attention.

A strong forefinger wiggled it away from the material of his cloak. "This is a crucial message you bring me. Are you aware of its import?"

He gulped and nodded his head, just a little bit, while frantically thinking about what the fancy brooch might mean. Mercifully, he didn't have to reply because the chief was impatient.

"You have something else to add to this message on the Pin of Funach?" Tuadh's fist clutched at the brooch so hard it was like Tyrnan strangling him all over again, the golden torque he wore forced upwards into his gullet. As a measure of silent intimidation it worked. It really worked. He could barely shake his head, could barely breathe.

"Your father?" Tuadh's furious features were so close their noses almost collided. "Who is he? Tell me true."

Aran flinched from the chief's intensity. The rattling of his teeth didn't make it easy to answer. Swallowing awkwardly as some smoke billowed towards him from the fire, his mind raced ahead. His father's name? His brain was paralysed. All he could do was croak.

"Darren."

Tuadh looked impressed. "Durran, of the Durris is your father? The warriors of your settlement skirmish well enough."

Skirmish? The chief sounded like an old enemy of Durran of the Durris, but Tuadh was on a roll though and wasn't remaining quiet. It gave Aran time to think, and breathe.

"Durran was not with you in the forest?" Tuadh fired questions at breakneck speed, giving him no time to reply which was just as well since he didn't know what to answer. A shake of his head was all Tuadh needed to barrage on. "Who are your companions?"

The fist at his neck relaxed slightly when the chief looked behind. Aran adjusted the torque before he answered, squinting around himself. It had been throttling him, just as Tuadh had intended. "Brian and his twin sister, Fianna."

Tuadh looked Brian up and down, taking in his carrot-red hair gleaming in the firelight. "Come forward, boy! Kneel."

Brian knelt as requested, his knees not looking too steady. The chief's large fist reached forward to grasp Brian's neck ring. "You also wear a fine torque of the ancient Taexali. And your father? Would I know him?"

"Callum." Brian's answer squeaked. Aran guessed

he didn't much like Tuadh's breath fanning his face either, the strong teeth menacing.

"I know of no Callum at the settlement of Durris." Tuadh addressed the man seated on his left. "Do you know of one who is named Callum?"

"There is a son of the old chief, Ternan, named Callum and he is said to have the old man's very likeness."

The warrior leaned towards Brian to look closely. "Ternan was called the red fox often enough, and that's a very good name for you too."

"Er... I'm sometimes called little red fox." Brian bit his lip.

Aran knew Jennie sometimes called him that.

Brian's shaky finger pointed to Fianna so the man could see her too. "And so is my twin sister, Fianna."

The man alongside the chief guffawed, slapping his thigh hard. "There should be no doubt then, Tuadh. No doubt at all, since Ternan also had a tamhas of his own likeness."

Tuadh dismissed Brian with a flick of his wrist, sending him sprawling across the floor. His focus returned to Aran as one of the brawny warriors plucked Brian aside and wedged him back towards the closest curtained enclosure.

The chief rounded on him, that horrible fist squeezing again at his throat. "You must have some other message for the council?"

Being shaken like a rag doll was an interesting experience but it was definitely not the most comfortable thing to happen to anyone. Being well grown for his age, Aran had never envisaged anyone being taller and strong enough to make him dangle so excruciatingly that the blood at his toes screeched in agony as well as at his neck. He was mightily relieved when a sudden hullabaloo at the doorway made an answer unnecessary, all eyes drawn to the stream of men who entered the roundhouse.

One among them was noticeably different from the rest. He was an extremely tall man, though it wasn't just his height that made him stand out. In one hand, he held a large wooden staff that was even taller than he was with a knobbly top. At the entrance, he stacked his spear in the nearby rack, his companions piling up their large collection of weapons likewise. In addition to the staff, the tall man bore a stringed instrument, like a small harp, slung across his back over the top of his cloak.

Tuadh dropped Aran like a pebble into a pond and strode off to greet the new visitors, Seonagh trailing after her father.

Taking advantage of the interruption, Aran picked himself up before scurrying well away from the fireside and went closer to the twins, soothing his poor neck and knees as he went. The men guarding the twins were standing a little away, talking to another man who had left the fireside.

"We should try to say very little. That way we might learn more. Agreed?" he croaked since a hoarse whisper was all he could manage.

Brian nodded his bottom lip out, happy with the idea.

Aran had a hunch Tuadh's questioning of his friend had been as terrifying as he'd just found the chief.

"Fianna?" True to form, Fianna was too busy being nosy to even hear his question properly. "Fianna! Are you listening to me?"

Brian pulled at her arm to get her attention.

"What?" Fianna was torn between answering and watching the developments over at the doorway. "Yes." She barely looked in his direction. "Whatever it is, I agree."

Aran was annoyed with her, but was sure she knew what he'd said. "You say almost nothing so that you don't give the game away. Remember that when you want to open that nosy mouth of yours."

"Okay, keep your hair on." Her words spat, irritated he'd interrupted her viewing. "Maybe we should all watch what's going on now and find out about the Romans as well as the Celts. I heard the word 'legion', though maybe you two missed it?"

Aran sighed. Bossy boots Fianna in full fettle was probably right.

The new arrivals walked towards them trailing behind Tuadh. The chief's face was grim when he halted quite close to him. That deep distrustful anger engendered more waves of alarm.

Flippin' heck! It suddenly occurred to him. Did the chief think they were Roman spies?

The new visitor reminded him of a predatory raptor swooping on its unwary prey when the old man stopped in front of him and held his gaze for long silent moments. Without uttering a single word, the stranger pounced to lift his brooch. A peculiar hint of a smile hovered around the man's lips.

"The Pin of Funach. How comes the lad by the message?" The stranger quizzed Tuadh.

Aran felt Tuadh's fingers nip his shoulder. "Answer the question."

"It tells its own story." He was unwilling to say anything that was untrue.

Patience was clearly not Tuadh's strong point, the chief thrusting him aside before addressing the visitor. "The lad's only message seems to be to wear the warning sign."

"Perhaps, or it may tell a story we do not wish to hear." The visitor's declaration was cryptic. "I see hidden depths in this young warrior. Information he does not disclose, but plundering him for it will come later."

No longer interested in him, Tuadh swept Aran away with one impatient slap of his palm that sent him flying. "You will remain over there!" The chief's demand wasn't just for Aran to obey; the young guards alongside moved into place.

Pulling at Brian's sleeve, he back-paced a few steps, Fianna hovering nearby. Rubbing sore body parts was getting to be a common occurrence. He wasn't sure which now hurt the most as he massaged his shoulder.

"Listen carefully. We need to find out what makes them tick."

A nod from the twins was all he needed.

The chief sat back down in the middle position where observation of all movement in the roundhouse was easier. Arranging themselves closely around Tuadh, most of the new arrivals sat on the stools and low herb-stuffed skins. Behind the stool Aran had recently perched on, the man with the clarsach lingered next to Tuadh, towering high as he carefully removed the instrument and set it down on the hard-packed dirt floor. A bulging pouch and the staff were also laid aside before the visitor took his place at the fireside.

The men had a hurried low conference, their gaze

raking in Aran's direction a number of times. The atmosphere in the long room was electric, the tension almost unbearable as everyone else quietly muttered while awaiting events to unfold. The general noise level rose as the minutes passed till not only were the group by the chief bickering again, all the other huddles were having their own agitated conversations.

"Romans… attack again… thousands."

Aran's focus darted from one group to another, waves of exhilaration almost swamping him.

Eventually, Tuadh bellowed at Seonagh who had remained close. "Summon the rest of the elders and order the women to see to our guests' needs."

Instead of squeezing past, Seonagh shoved Fianna into one of the curtained off compartments that lay to Tuadh's rear, and then thrust him and Brian in after. Tying open the woven cloth door with a thong, she gave orders. "Remain inside unless Tuadh asks for you."

The young guards were close enough to make Seonagh's words seem unnecessary.

Having issued her instructions, the girl dashed away. The talking at the fireside became fractured again, back to groups having low conversations amongst themselves.

In no time at all, Seonagh returned and the newest visitors were ushered into other curtained stalls around the huge room, a fleet of young girls carrying in wooden bowls of steaming water for their use. Aran realised they must have had them prepared already, given that they were brought in so quickly. Indeed everything seemed to be rushed now and yet it was all happening as smoothly as a well-oiled machine.

Their guards remained stationed outside their enclosure, so he huddled with the twins. A quick scan around the cubicle took no time at all. There was a raised platform of packed earth hard against the roundhouse wall, topped with layers of bracken and ferns and above that a blanket of simply sewn-together skins. A piece of woollen cloth was folded at the end. The only other thing he could see was a large iron hook on one of the partition walls which were wattled like the entry way into the roundhouse.

A sleeping compartment and nothing else.

"You reckon the door curtain is for privacy?" Brian looked doubtful since the weave of the cloth was quite open, a bit like Fianna's potato-sacking cloak, but he asked anyway.

"More like to keep out the smoke from the fire," Fianna giggled, "And to keep down disturbances like your noisy snoring."

Aran didn't think keeping down the noise was possible since the sleeping area was open to the rafters. Dismissing the surroundings, he concentrated on the fireside activity.

The atmosphere inside the roundhouse became so tense he could almost taste it. More and more bodies spilled into the room hollering and bickering as they squeezed into the circle around the fireside which was now two rows deep. He'd read that the higher ranks of men and women placed themselves closest to the fire around the chief. He couldn't see much difference between the assembled people, except maybe a glint of gold or silver here or there, but he guessed that they knew their place in the tribal hierarchy. Very few of the tribespeople could be called really old, though many had a worn look that indicated hard lives.

One youngish woman Tuadh referred to as his hearth-wife, Orla, wore a very fine dress of red and dark yellow checks. The thin golden torque around her throat glittered in the firelight as she took up a standing position behind the chief.

A rough head count of somewhere between eighty and a hundred tribespeople made Aran softly whistle.

The recent visitors emerged from behind the curtained partitions to re-join the throng, water still dripping off some chins. The tall man had changed into a long tunic of pale grey material, bordered in black with a gold pattern into the weave of the hem and neck.

Aran's heart thundered.

A druid?

Chapter Seven

A bardic druid?

Aran's excitement soared. He'd read that bardic druids told stories of the Celts in song and verse as well as being priests of the faith. That they were skilled secret agents was an even more thrilling thing to remember.

Tuadh surged onto his feet, his fist rising high into the air, the noise dwindling to nothing. Furious, yet heartily rousing, his voice boomed over the seated people.

"People of Balbath, of the ancient Taexali, and now allies of the Caledon Federation of tribes—the Roman army again marches across our lands, even though the legions of Emperor Severus trod our soil flat last Lughnasadh. You know how destitute we have been of grain crops over the snows and days of darkness because they carried off the best of our harvest before they burned the remainder, and left us scrabbling for winter fodder for our animals. How many of you had to glean food from our revered forests in the depths of winter, risking the wrath of our god Cernunnos, because the woods and streams were our only source of food?"

A tide of mumbles rumbled around the room.

"Aye! They left us lean and hungry. Now the news is that Emperor Severus flies in our face yet again. The Roman legions stride south towards us, again killing everything in their path that shows a hint of resistance."

Appalled gasps halted Tuadh.

An old female elder's frail question broke into the

disgust. "Are our constant attacks not sufficient to rout them from our lands?"

"Did their ships not take them away from the northern shores of our Vacomagi neighbours?" asked a warrior alongside her.

"Why do they return? What have we left that they can steal from us?" This wail came from another of the elders.

Tuadh's shout was meant to calm the disorder… and it did. "We do still have our successes when they infiltrate our woods and hills, but that only happens when we lure in small numbers of them. One Celtic tribe cannot fell a legion of Romans when each soldier wields his powerful gladius and uses his shield like a snail cowering into its shell."

One of the warriors opposite Tuadh jumped up, his sheer fury evident in his clenched fists held fast to his thighs. "After they left us in dire straits last Lughnasadh it was said they would not return to Beinn Na Ciche and our Garioch area since they had already laid waste to our soil. We were told that they would sail back to Rome using their fleet of vessels which we have noted many times, plying back and forth off our Taexali shores. Why has this not happened?"

"Listen well to our druid brother who has the latest tidings from north and south. He can explain all to us." Tuadh's hand rested briefly on the tall man's shoulder before he sat down again.

The druid's gaze wandered over the whole company, authority settling around him like a cloak as the man waited for his own little group of followers to settle.

Aran didn't believe it was a coincidence that two

of the druid's men now flanked him and the twins at their doorway–and it wasn't a reassuring guarding. The two men had earlier dumped their spears and shields but they still wore enough metal at their waists to mean business, even if they never said a word. Aran was aware that Brian sidled closer but was more conscious that Fianna was losing her cool. Being cornered wasn't something she tolerated easily, her expression one of barely restrained temper. He guessed she wasn't as drool-struck about the two older warriors as she had been by Tyrnan.

The druid's voice rang to the rafters. "For those who do not know me, I am Mapon. Severus dislikes that we of the Caledon Federation still attack his men at every opportunity out in the open. However, due to the bravery of our fallen brothers and those maimed ones who still survive, Severus and his son have turned their legions about and are now marching south again. They slash everything in their path that shows any resistance—land, man and beast. "

"Did they not journey on to the lands of the Broch people?"

Aran's attention sharpened. A broch was a round tower built of stone but he hadn't read anything about the Romans having captured the People of the Brochs. His excitement spiked as he caught Fianna's raised eyebrows, indicating she knew nothing about them and was wondering if he did. He gave the tiniest head shake. He knew almost nothing at all about the Broch people except that the ruins of brochs tended to be north of Inverness.

Mapon was very solemn. "My druid brothers tell me that the Romans did not venture far beyond the Lugi territory.

Aran smirked in Fianna's direction. The Lugi tribe lived around Inverness, so that fit with what he knew of the Roman occupation of the far north.

"Does that mean the Lugi have made new treaties with Rome?" Tuadh was incensed.

Mapon bit down on as much anger as the chief. "From what I am told, all the tribes north of the Caledons have recently made some kind of an arrangement with Emperor Severus."

The room erupted.

Fianna cupped her hand around his ear to whisper. "Have their lands been left untouched?"

He nodded, leaning towards her. "The Romans went north of Inverness but don't seem to have had any resistance from those tribes."

Many questions similar to Fianna's flew around the room, the druid giving quick answers which matched what Aran had just mentioned.

Mapon continued, "Now that he is sure the far north will do his bidding Severus returns to the Garioch area to teach the Caledons and the Taexali another lesson. Caracalla is even more brutal than his father. He leaves land unusable for many seasons. This makes Rome happy. They believe that if they continue to destroy our fertile Taexali land they will eventually destroy the will of our people."

Aran itched to talk to Brian who had just nudged his elbow. He had a good idea of what the date was.

Mapon's next words were sombre. "Thousands of troops march towards Beinn Na Ciche and the Garioch area, even though Severus will not reach here till after the advance forces led by Caracalla."

A huge clamour broke out as the assembled council scorned a military leader who was carried like a baby. The mood of the crowd shifted. Mockery reigned.

Aran felt the tug at his cloak.

"Do you know anything about this?" Brian sought confirmation.

He nodded.

"Nay, People of Balbath." Mapon quietened the crowd. "You know that Severus is no baby and no wounded warrior either."

Fianna jostled him while the throng mumbled and fidgeted till Mapon regained their full concentration. "It's AD 210 isn't it? That's why Callum had me type in that number."

He dipped his head having come to the same conclusion. Though why that particular date, he still hadn't worked out.

Mapon carried on. "You have already seen that Severus is old and crippled, yet that is not what causes him to linger behind his frontline troops led by Caracalla. The Emperor gains a full report before he begins his own travel for the day. His campaign is planned in meticulous detail. Severus misses nothing throughout the lands the Romans have named Britannia. But we must not forget that the emperor also tests the strength of his merciless son."

Mapon continued to outline the strategies Severus made every single day, his emphasis building up the tension in the room.

Aran huddled into Brian whispering into his ear. "Severus was a military general for most of his life, and he campaigned all over the Roman Empire."

Mapon held the gathering spellbound. "Severus' ultimate purpose is to return to Rome and declare he has every last piece of our Celtic lands in his palm.

We, of the Taexali; the Caledon peoples of the north; and a few of our southern Miathi brothers, are the last disruption on the western barrier of Severus' Empire, the last resistance for him to totally subdue."

Bold interruptions broke Mapon's flow but only for a moment since Tuadh signalled the sentry at the door to wield his flickering torch high in the air. Silence reigned again.

Fianna giggled, her eyes now twinkling. "Hey! We need that for our school assemblies."

Aran's answer was cut short when one of Mapon's guards yanked Fianna out of the cubicle and thrust her to the side, keeping her hidden by his bulk. She was protesting but was making almost no noise. The guard was either gagging her or she was wise enough to keep silent. Aran hoped it was the latter. It took a few seconds for him to realise that Brian had been similarly dragged away from him.

That put paid to any more sharing of information.

Mapon sounded solemn. "Our enemy moves swiftly enough, given the baggage carts they pull with oxen and mules. Unlike you, who have been almost starving, the Romans still have plentiful supplies. When not reaped or bargained from our fellow Celts, their supplies are replenished from the sea. After the first spring thaws, Severus built a special fort near the end of the stone wall that crosses Brigante lands and it is now from this place that he sends those provisions northwards to our Taexali sands."

"Do their vessels deliver new soldiers on Taexali shores?" The cry came from a warrior further down the room.

"Aye, they disgorge auxiliary soldiers at many of our beaches." Mapon held up two fingers. "Two days ago, ships of their Classis landed between the mouths of the Rivers Don and Dee. All land to the south of the Dee is under total Roman control. The Taexali there have ceased to skirmish."

Tuadh was back to bellowing. "I do not understand these orders. If Severus and Caracalla are still to the north of us in the lands of the Vacomagi, how do their troops control everything south of here?"

Mapon cooled the chief's temper. "You forget that Severus has two sons. The younger son, Geta, has not been tramping the northern earth with his father and brother. Since last Lughnasadh, Geta was left to maintain Roman control of all land to the south of the great stone wall and he has done that very successfully. The Brigantes south of that wall no longer challenge Rome."

"But that is on far off territory." Yet another angry warrior challenged what Mapon was telling them.

"Aye. The territory may seem a long way away from here but the Roman Army can march quickly from the great stone wall on their newly strengthened roads. They could reach Balbath in this many nights." Mapon held up his two hands, all fingers and thumbs stretched out. "What is more important is that, if the winds are fair, their vessels can travel that distance in a much shorter time."

"I have heard that the Roman fortress at Raedykes has again been reused and repaired. Is this a truth?" The angry shout from the crowd interrupted Mapon's flow.

Raedykes? Aran suppressed another exhilarated grin. He knew exactly where that was—just south of Aberdeen.

Mapon raised his hand for silence. “It is true and I will answer your question. Severus is still to the north of your Garioch area, accompanied by Caracalla. However, Geta follows his father’s orders and makes some new ones of his own. Sufficient troops have been gathered by Geta to control all land to the south of the River Dee.

“Where does Rome get all of these Roman soldiers?”

Aran thought that a very good question. He knew that many of the auxiliary soldiers were acquired from Celtic tribes which had been conquered by the Roman Empire and some of those currently in Scotland might even be from southern Britain.

Tuadh jumped up and scanned around like a madman, all eyes following the chief’s outstretched finger. When it settled on him, Aran swallowed hard before Mapon’s guards dragged him out towards the chief.

“Is the stripling’s settlement at Durris already taken?” Tuadh asked.

Mapon’s nod was firm. “Aye. Durris has fallen. Roman forces flood the flatlands around their old Roman base at Raedykes. The warriors of Durris fought bravely, yet were too few to defeat the Roman troops.”

“Durran sent his son to us with the Pin of Funach to escape the carnage?”

Mapon nodded. “Perhaps, or it may be that it was to send a general warning. On the other hand, the young warrior coming with the pin may signify some other thing.”

Tuadh’s eyes sought out Aran’s again. “Were you there when the Romans attacked?”

Aran's reply was careful. The guards held him tight and he didn't feel like a repeat of Tyrnan's arm locks. "I haven't set sight on any Roman troops."

"Does the boy tell it true?" The call of the old woman at the far end was strident.

A gaggle of denials mixed with questions disturbed the air, the crowd stirring into action.

Tuadh held his hand high. "Who is alive to tell the fate of the Durris settlement?"

"Some kinsfolk escaped to the hills, though they were vastly outnumbered by the slain." This answer came from one of Mapon's guard.

"How can we defend ourselves against such a fighting force?" The old woman was despondent.

Mapon took a deep breath and stood as tall as his aged body could muster. "No single settlement can continue to repel this evil. Unity is strength. We must mass together to face Rome. Some twenty thousand men of Severus' legionary and auxiliary troops advance towards you.

Chapter Eight

"So many?" Tuadh sounded gutted.

"I have scattered my druid companions far and wide, into the hills of the Caledons. They go to the far west to warn of this new development, those closer to us here already know." Mapon now sounded cheerless, his earlier energy dissipated.

"What must we do?"

"I wish I could tell you what you want to hear, Tuadh. I have few suggestions and none of them are good. You can continue to defy smaller groups of the Roman Empire's soldiers and die under the gladius. You can flee to the hills of the west and make a new life there as hunters, rather than as farmers. Or you can make more peace treaties with them."

"Only cowards flee!" someone cried.

The next outburst came from an elder of the tribe seated close to Tuadh who first spat his disgust into the fire. "Treaties are worthless. The Roman word is not to be trusted."

The room erupted in a fury of disruption, the anger able to be snatched from mouths.

From what Aran had read, the word of the Celts couldn't be trusted either since they continued to attack Roman patrols after signing treaties saying they wouldn't do it any more. He looked round at Brian and Fianna to tell them what he knew.

They weren't there!

A hurried scan of the room gave no sign of them. Where were the twins? The cold slither down his backbone just got worse. He was supposed to be looking after them.

He strained at the tethers still holding his arms.

Over the clamour, the most hideous noise blasted the very timbers of the roundhouse and made them creak with its force. The weirdness of it bombarded his ears; its horrid wailing like the squealing of an animal in pain, not unlike the wail he'd heard from the wild boar in the forest earlier in the afternoon. Every voice immediately ceased its babbling. All focus was back on Mapon, the long metal tube topped with a pig-like animal head to his lips.

A carnyx.

Aran had seen photos of the Celtic battle horns but hearing the sound up close was truly awesome.

Mapon passed the instrument down into Tuadh's hand. "We have resisted the Romans imposing their gods on us and though they have forbidden my druid teachings, I still continue. We of northern Britannia have not yet become a subjected people of the Roman Empire. But, if we do not find a way to deal with Caracalla, I see only death or slavery as our fate."

Slaves.

The very mention caused another furore.

"Be still!" Tuadh's command silenced the crowd.

Mapon's arms extended high to encompass the whole room. "I call for all tribes of the Garioch area to stand united against our common enemy. From dawn tomorrow, Blairdaff assembles the local tribes below the hillfort on The Mither Tap, highest peak of Beinn Na Ciche. Delnabo, the high chief of the nearest Caledon hill tribes musters there, too. Will you join them? You must decide, but you must decide now. The Romans march at a fast pace."

"Will we fight like Celts, or will we become their

minions like some of the tribes to the south of the green wall, those who have already made worthless negotiations with the Roman scum and have become just like them?" The question came from a very angry warrior.

Aran guessed that not all of those present wanted to be peaceable about meeting the Roman enemy.

"The Romans infiltrate in many ways, my friends. You must decide where your loyalties lie." After he spoke, Mapon's unfriendly gaze whipped around to settle on Aran.

The tiniest nod from the druid had him dragged to Tuadh's side once more, his arms twisted behind his back. Facing him, near the entryway he could see the twins being dragged into position. Brian now looked as angry as his sister, both of them writhing against their keepers.

"They may even have sent these striplings to spy for them."

All eyes swivelled from Aran to the twins and back again, the mood of the crowd murderous.

"But they wear treasures of the Taexali."

"Aye, they do." This came from Tuadh. "And we all know that it is not often that a young undecorated warrior wears a special mark of our tribe like the red foxes down there. That alone is suspicious."

Mapon shouted down the fireside. "How did you come by your torques, little red tamhas foxes?"

Down the room, Fianna struggled to free herself from Mapon's warrior. Instead of answering the question she bawled to all and sundry. "Perhaps you should ask why my father gave me this." Drawing back her cloak, she lifted her arm aloft so that all could see her arm ring, a newer bronze than her torque.

Aran glared for all he was worth. Was Fianna going to do something totally reckless like open her armband? His arms were held fast. There was no way he could press any of his buttons.

"And Callum gave me this one." Brian followed suit, not to be outdone by his twin.

The assembled crowd seemed shocked on seeing the twins wearing matching armbands and torques, Brian's silver arm ring glistening more than the ring round his neck – a very substantial piece of new silver.

The guard who held Aran dragged back the green cloak to bare his arm as well, displaying his matching golden arm ring. His pulse spiked as he wriggled to free himself but it was to no avail. Were they going to be stripped of their armband computers?

He couldn't let that happen!

Callum had told them they must take care to wear them at all times.

"Did the Durris chief give you this one?" The question was muffled as Mapon's nose almost touched Aran's arm.

Aran looked down at Mapon's bent head; the druid seemingly transfixed by the scrollwork pattern on the golden armband. He couldn't control the tremor in his arm, but it didn't matter because the guard wasn't letting him go. The fact that Callum had given him it didn't seem like the answer the druid was probably looking for.

Surprisingly strong fingers gripped around the armband and dragged him closer to the fire. Rotating his arm back and forth, holding it aloft and then letting it down, Mapon read the pattern all around the ring.

Aran had looked at the squiggles earlier. They didn't mean anything to him, yet they seemed to mean something to the druid.

"This arm ring bears a different message from the torque." Total silence had enveloped the room so the druid's explanation was heard by all. Mapon's free index finger pointed down the room and rested on the twins. "Bring the tamhas, the twin red-foxes, to me!"

A few seconds later, a reading of Fianna's ring and torque brought a tiny smile to Mapon's face though he made no attempt to tell the congregated people why. His eyebrows rose when he read Brian's, though that generated no smile before his attention turned to the company.

"People of the Balbathan Taexali, heed me well! These rings have important messages for us. This changes the status of the bearers very much indeed. These youngsters must be treated with care."

"They are not Roman spies?" The speaker sounded disappointed by the druid's declaration.

Mapon's expression changed to one of intrigue, as though winding up the crowd. "I can tell you that these striplings do conceal much mystery. However, I vow that you will learn much from them before you all reach the foothills of The Mither Tap. Tuadh?"

The chief was instantly alert and ready.

"You will see to that."

Tuadh's nod was curt.

Aran wasn't sure if the chief looked forward to it, or not, since Tuadh appeared puzzled. Mapon continued to scan all of the assembled people around the room.

"Henceforth, you will treat these wearers of both new and ancient treasures fairly, as honoured guests of the Taexali. Now, we must move on to other matters."

Aran remained tense as the druid continued to inform the crowd about other news. He and the twins weren't under quite so much suspicion but their secrets were going to be wrenched from them.

The big question was how Tuadh would see to it.

It wasn't easy to sidle back from Mapon, since everyone was focused his way, but he managed to do it very gradually over the next minutes as he worked through the possibilities for horrible extraction of information. The rack probably wasn't invented in AD 210, and maybe they didn't do the ghastly pulling off of nails he'd read about during the Middle Ages, but he was fairly sure the Celts would have their own incredibly painful ways of torturing out information.

He was relieved when he noticed the twins had followed suit on either side of him and had also backed-off from the druid. All of them out of the limelight—or more accurately the flickering firelight.

"Bennachie." He felt the hefty nudge from Fianna as she whispered in his ear. "Pay attention! He's talking about The Mither Tap."

He gave himself a mental kick for losing the thread of the conversation. He'd been so intent on disgusting agony that he hadn't been listening properly. Glancing at Fianna, he could see she was following in her focused nosey way. For once, he had to applaud that was a good thing. She'd be able to tell him what he'd missed.

Bennachie. Beinn Na Ciche. They said it a little differently but the name was still recognisable.

Alongside him, Brian flashed a small grin of understanding. "Mapon's talking of the hillfort being used."

Now Aran knew why the hill he'd seen earlier was familiar, as they'd approached Balbath. It was part of the range he knew of as Bennachie. In the twenty-first century, the dark grey fringe near the summit of The Mither Tap was the tumbled stones of an ancient hillfort which showed up as a bumpy frill near the peak. In AD 210, it was a newish fortification, standing sound and proud, giving enemies fair warning of the strength of the warrior defences in the surrounding Garioch area. Maybe The Mither Tap had been called *The Gallows Hill* because people had been hanged there? Maybe hanging enemies was something the Celts did that he'd never read about?

He wished he'd paid full attention to what Mapon had said. Second hand from Fianna was going to be embarrassing.

Mapon's voice rang out once more, hushing the throng. "I cannot remain with you for the Rites of Beltane which fall tomorrow's eve. By first light, I must move on to Tap o' Noth to be there before the Roman usurpers reach that hillfort."

Surprise greeted this bombshell. Gutted disappointment fluttered around the gathering.

"However, I will leave you my acolyte to conduct the ceremonies."

The druid's voice paused once more, savouring the total hush around the room. Aran looked keenly at Mapon's face as it was illuminated by the firelight. It softened a fraction, the old man's dark eyes glittering, and then to his astonishment a huge smile emerged. The man held both hands aloft, spreading wide arms and fingers dramatically. "But, as I am with you now, we can celebrate the ring messages these striplings carry to us, though the small bere should be watered. You must all remain vigilant."

A huge cheer went up around the room that was roundly deafening. Aran watched agog as the room thundered with the stamping of feet and of hands drumming on the earthen floor. Fianna covered her ears with her palms to block out the hullabaloo. Brian joined in with the general stomping though Aran guessed his best mate didn't understand the sudden change of mood around them any more than he did.

A different kind of excitement gripped the room that was as strong as the fearful tension of before. Mapon swooped down and then plucked his clarsach aloft. The thumping stopped at his signal. His smile remained. "People of Balbath we have this lull. The Roman army is not yet here. You are all weapon ready and your sentries are watchful. If it is your wish, I will recount the greatest tales of our ancestors."

A cacophony of noise greeted this as many people shouted out at once. Tuadh held one hand in the air. "We have food for everyone tonight. Let the fare be brought in first."

"Remain here, and wait for me." Seonagh indicated they should enter the same cubicle as before. "I must help with the food, but I will not be long."

"Can I help you?" Fianna asked.

Seonagh looked suspicious. "You are now our guest, Fianna. Guests need not help in Balbath."

"I'd like to… be honoured to."

Aran noted that Fianna was trying to match Seonagh's formal patterns of speech. After a curt acceptance, Seonagh took Fianna's elbow and sped off with her.

Hanging his cloak on the iron hook, he climbed onto the low cot and stretched out.

Brian copied his example after a quick scan outside the cubicle. "Do you think we should have let Fianna go with Seonagh?"

Aran was surprised to hear genuine concern in Brian's tone. "Five minutes ago I would have said no way, but after Mapon's declaration, it seems we've been granted some sort of reprieve from being spies."

"Yeah. But I don't trust the way that their mood changes so easily. And Mapon didn't say what messages our rings carry."

"Good point, though everyone accepted that they must be good because Mapon was satisfied." Aran wasn't too sure of the way their moods changed either, but he was more interested in the fact that Mapon seemed to have so much influence over the people of Balbath. And especially the fearsome Tuadh. That was slightly weird.

"What do you reckon we've learned?" Brian asked before settling flat down on the cot, head to toe with him.

"I think we're close on the time of one of the biggest Roman treaties of north east Scotland."

"In AD 210?"

Aran raised himself onto his elbows before answering. "Emperor Severus and his son Caracalla came to Britain in AD 208 to teach the Celtic tribes a lesson. The Governor of Britannia told Severus that loads of northern tribes were in revolt and were causing huge problems. He hinted in a letter that it would be a good thing if the Emperor showed up to scare them into submission."

"Why couldn't the guv do that himself?" Brian wriggled around to get more comfortable, sending up some dusty chaff from the bracken mattress with his feet.

Aran moved his nose away from the fine particles that danced in front of him. "He claimed he didn't have enough troops to keep order in England and come north of Hadrian's Wall to tackle the Scottish Celts as well."

"So the Emperor just upped sticks and headed off to Britain? That was kind of him."

Aran ignored Brian's sarcasm. "It was good kudos for an emperor to show they had the upper hand all over the empire so Severus took the opportunity to make himself look good. He landed in England with his two sons, his wife and his Danubian guard."

"Was that his special forces?"

Aran chuckled before he tucked his crossed arms under his head to make a pillow since there wasn't one. "Absolutely. His specially hand-picked guard from his own regiment. They were the best trained in the empire, totally loyal and were paid more than the usual soldiers."

"So gold was their motive for looking after the boss guy?"

Again Aran laughed. "Yeah, and I just remembered that Severus came to Britain with tons of gold, pretty well all that he could rustle up from as many places as possible."

"Was that to bribe the tribes?"

"Spot on, Brian. That was exactly what it was for. He used some in northern England to placate the Brigantes who lived south of Hadrian's Wall. That was so he could rebuild a lot of the forts and guard towers along the length of the wall and keep the peace there."

"These Brigantes had wrecked his forts before Severus arrived?"

"Sure thing and they'd killed a lot of the soldiers who'd been stationed on the wall in the years leading up to AD 208."

"Is that why the guv had said he didn't have enough troops?"

Aran felt the pins and needles starting in his arms. "Partly, but also because some of his four legions of soldiers had been sent to continental Europe a while before then and he was already short of manpower for keeping Britannia under control." He rubbed his forearms before relaxing them by his sides.

Brian was now the one who raised himself up on one elbow. "Did Severus come with plenty of spare troops?"

Aran drew up his knees and scratched his legs, wondering if the bracken was mingled with more than moss. "Roman writing claims he came north to quell the natives with around fifty thousand troops."

Brian whistled before thumping himself back down flat. "That must have been awesome to see them all marching north."

Aran ditched any sarcasm. "Truly awesome indeed. It must have been immensely scary to see those guys marching in formations, a cohort of around five hundred at a time – some cohorts of legionary soldiers and many more of them auxiliaries. Followed by another unit and then even more, interspersed with the mounted ala forces."

The image he'd just portrayed silenced both for a

moment. Eventually Brian asked, "Did he march those fifty thousand past Balbath last year? I heard Tuadh say they had been here already and flattened the earth."

Aran rolled on his side to see his mate better. "Not as many as that reached here. They had to do a lot of fighting and skirmishing all the way up Scotland. The tribes in Scotland were relentless in organising constant small raids which gradually whittled down the Roman numbers, though no big battles were noted down."

"How do you know all that, Aran?"

"While you and Fianna were building a dinky crannog-on-the water settlement as your joint project, I worked on the post 1970s aerial discoveries of Roman Marching Camps in north-east Scotland."

"Hey. Fianna and I won the craft competition, I'll have you remember."

"So you did, and that was a miracle since you two hardly ever agree about anything." He fielded Brian's nudge to roll him off the narrow bed and carried on talking. "Remember our class going to the Roman Marching Camp at Logie Durno?"

"Sure," Brian sounded bored already. "All we saw were mounds of earth, a pile of standing stones in a field and lots of farmland."

"Yes, you numpty, but the Roman Marching camp at Durno could have supported as many as thirty-two thousand soldiers in it."

"You're joking!" Brian sneered. "You don't mean that thirty-two thousand Roman soldiers might be gathering a few miles from here?"

"I do." The thought awed Aran just as much now as when he'd read it on an internet site.

Brian wriggled upright again and sat cross legged, his expression one of excited horror.

"Holy crap of the Celtic gods! Are we going to be fighting a gigantic, humungous battle tomorrow?"

Chapter Nine

"Get your cloaks and come with me. Hurry now!"

Seonagh was impatient.

"Reckon we're being taken prisoner again?" Brian grabbed his cloak and towed after Seonagh who was already half way down the fireside.

Aran shook his head. "Don't think so. There are no guards." What he meant was no guard in particular since the room still held plenty of brawny warriors.

Ushering them quickly past lots of roundhouses, the one they entered with Seonagh was noisy. Sitting all around the fireside were many children, chattering like bubbly jocks. Young girls served the littlest kids with bowls where they sat cross-legged on the ground.

Bent down, handing out bowls, Fianna's gaze lit up on seeing them arrive, a fake cheesy grin splitting her face. Aran knew what that meant: she had learned a thing or two.

Seonagh pointed to a space in front of a large cauldron. "Sit there." Reaching for wooden bowls she scooped out ladles of sludgy goo from the nearest huge pot. After handing them a bowl each, she filled one for herself and sat down.

Aran took a quick sniff, Fianna doing the same when she sat alongside. He accepted the round flat bread offered by a young girl.

"Thank you." Seonagh put down her bowl after popping her bread inside it and stood up again as though just remembering something. She clapped her hands then held her arms high up in the air. All the children in the room stopped their whispering. "We have guests among us tonight. Are you listening, Colman?" The little boy in question reddened before he nodded. Seonagh continued. "I am going to tell you all a story."

Aran heard a tiny grunt near him as one lad dropped his eyes to the full bowl waiting in his lap.

Seonagh giggled. "A quick story, I see how eager you are to eat. This branded warrior is named Aran. To him I owe my life."

Surprise sprang from many lips. Aran felt a red heat of embarrassment rush to his cheeks.

"Today, in the woods of Bendauch, I was challenged by a mighty boar."

A few hands crept up to cover mouths as eyes brightened in anticipation of the story unfolding. Seonagh's gaze sought out one of the boys seated at the far end of the room. "Duhlain. Come and join us."

When the lad was close by, Seonagh continued. "I would have been badly gored by the boar if Duhlain hadn't come to my aid first. He was very brave, though he and I alone could not kill the powerful beast. The fatal wounding came from this warrior, Aran, so to him I owe my thanks and my life."

He felt sheepish when Seonagh pulled him to his feet.

"The hearthside of Balbath is yours for as long as you wish to share with us. Eat your fill."

A huge cheer went up around the room with much clapping and shouting. The children obviously liked to make as much noise as their parents but Aran was glad it was over quickly, the last sounds deadened by slurping mouths.

He set to, finding he was hungrier than he

thought, using the last of his bread to wipe the bowl. "Great soup."

When Fianna was finished, she grinned and then whooped. "Weeds! I just ate fat hen weed and buttercup soup. Won't Callum be surprised?"

Brian looked at his empty bowl. "Really? But you never eat your greens."

Aran was amazed at Fianna's enthusiasm. "You knew what it was before you ate it?"

"Sure. Seonagh told me when I asked what the green slime was."

Brian gave her his bowl to add to the stacked pile in her hands. "I'm proud of you, sis. No fuss about eating your greens, even when you knew. There's hope for you yet."

Seonagh presented Aran with a large shiny plate she'd filled from a pile of already carved meat that sat at the edge of the fire. "Choose first. You have the Curadmir—the Hero's Portion—of our table. It is your right, and then it is the turn of my friend Duhlain."

It was the scraggiest bits of the animals that had been given to the children, but he didn't care since he loved the fattiest, most burnt bits of barbequed food anyway. The prime cuts obviously went to the adults.

"Are these all the children who live at Balbath?" Fianna was counting as she asked.

Seonagh laughed. "Nay! These are the children of the council elders who gather in my father's roundhouse. During council times, the children eat in here. Do you do it differently at your home?"

Aran butted in, in case Fianna would give the game away. "Sometimes we gather the children together, though there aren't so many living there."

He had two much younger brothers and a baby sister so he wasn't exactly lying about the children being together at times.

"Balbath is larger than many other settlements," Seonagh answered. "Do you often journey with your guardians to visit other settlements, Fianna?"

"No. We don't normally travel very far."

Brian snorted almost spitting out the last of his bread.

Aran hid a grin because they'd done some strange travelling that day already.

Fianna was, thankfully, keeping her cool. "Do you go visiting, Seonagh?"

Seonagh wore a resigned look. "I have rarely been anywhere else than Balbath territory." She brightened quickly when a pleasing thought popped into her head. "Though, before last Samhain my father took me to visit Foveran."

Brian's whisper was low at Aran's ear. "What's this 'so van' time?"

Turning away from Seonagh he mouthed back, "Halloween."

Brian winked and made a surreptitious thumbs-up sign.

Seonagh's eyes sparkled in the firelight, with the remembering of her journey, her voice growing more excited. "I had never been so close to the waters of the sea before then. It was strange; it frightened me a little at first as I stood before the surging ripples. I thought the sea god, Manaan, would carry me away, and take me into his foamy depths."

A woman approached Seonagh before she could explain further. "Tuadh bids the warrior, and Duhlain, to come to the gathering."

Aran jumped up, followed closely by the twins. Hurrying in behind, he almost collided when the messenger turned around at the open doorway. "Tuadh only asked for the warrior. Not the tamhas. The little red foxes should remain here."

"I will vouch for them," Seonagh said, reassuring the woman before she spoke to one of the older girls. "Mhairi, you will be in charge during my absence."

On the way back to Tuadh's house Seonagh gave instructions to the twins. "When we get inside you two stay back at the doorway."

"Can't we be with Aran," Fianna asked.

"Wait at the entryway till you are called," Seonagh again ordered. "You know that the unbranded are not allowed at councils."

"Are you usually at these gatherings?" Fianna asked Seonagh.

Aran reckoned it was a great question. Seonagh had no obvious tattoo so it was hard to tell if she was of branded status, or not. "Only when summoned: my duty is to watch over the children of the elders when they are at council."

Fianna was baffled. "I thought you'd always be there beside your father."

"Surely it cannot be so different at your settlement? Stay here," she warned on entering the chief's roundhouse, pointing to the skulls.

"Ugh."

Aran looked back to see Brian cowering away from the grisly objects, looking into the empty eye sockets and grimacing at the teeth as though they'd bite him.

Tuadh was seated as he had been before with a cluster of people around, the druid still in place beside him. Signalling for him and Duhlain to stop a little way off, Seonagh went forward and tapped her father's sleeve, gaining his attention. "You asked for Aran and Duhlain?"

Her father stood up, his arms wide stretched. The ripple of noise faded. "Duhlain. Come lad, you first. Mogran?"

A brawny warrior rose from his place, a beaming smile on his face, acknowledging his son standing beside the chief.

Tuadh announced to the whole room. "This brave son of yours did a great service to my daughter, today. He helped the mighty boar to meet its end."

"But my spear didn't kill it." Duhlain was embarrassed.

"We know that, lad. Praise is given for your part today. It is well earned."

The chief slapped Duhlain's shoulders, rocking him off his feet, and back into Aran who reaffirmed that the chief was very practised at the manoeuvre. Regaining his balance, he helped Duhlain to do the same.

"Your next attempt will likely earn your warrior's mark if you kill a large beast," Tuadh announced to all. "You learn well, Duhlain."

Mogran strode around the circle to clutch his son by the shoulders. "You have not even reached ten summers, yet. I feel great pride at your prowess, my son. Soon you will take your place alongside me in the battlefield." Nodding to the chief, the public acknowledgement over, Mogran ushered his son back to the door where Duhlain melted away through the entryway.

Tuadh turned to Aran. "Now you. You played

your spear well and we will not forget your brave deed."

Aran readied himself for the usual greeting. Though more prepared, it still cannoned him off his feet. He was taken aback when the man scooped him up and propelled him into the circle of seated men, presenting him to the whole assembly.

"This young Taexali warrior's spear felled the boar. My thanks go to you, Aran of the Durris." The chief scanned the seated tribespeople before he continued his voice again a booming threat. "But we have yet to learn why you breached my territory. We will have more knowledge from you. Sit down, lad, and give me answers!"

Aran felt like the meat in a sandwich about to be nibbled slowly as the men stared. The food in his stomach churned dangerously; terrified in case he'd be asked difficult questions. He had no time for long wondering, though, since the druid's gaze lingered on him, an uncomfortable boring.

"It is some time since I was with Durran at his settlement, though I have heard much of you."

"You have?" Aran was mystified.

"You progress well, lad. A druid learns many things. You have a fine teacher in Donald Urchain. He has spoken highly of a youth who has much knowledge, and now that I see you face to face I know it must be you, since there is great wisdom in your eyes."

Aran had a history teacher named Mr. Donald, but he didn't think that was who Mapon referred to.

Tuadh raised his eyebrows before launching in with a barrage of questions. "What did your guardians tell you to do?"

Aran scrabbled for something realistic. "Callum's instructions were to work out what to do for the best when we got here." He hoped the dull flush of his embarrassment wasn't visible in the firelight, though he'd done his best to be truthful.

This wasn't the place to divulge the list of targets Callum had set them because he wasn't doing such a great job, yet, of solving the quest.

Mapon added a question, delivered slowly and deliberately. "Are we about to be launched into a great battle?"

It was impossible to prevent the alarm from registering, Aran unable to completely conceal his knowledge. "There may still be more battles against the Roman Empire, though not such a great one as there was many, many generations ago when they first infiltrated these lands."

The druid regarded him with piercing shrewdness. "Smaller skirmishes rather than one large battle? Are you a seer that you know this?"

"I'm not a seer." The answer was brave, though inside Aran quaked. "Yet, I know I'm right."

Mapon continued to study him, his head nodding, as though working through momentous thoughts. The druid held eye contact, the perceptive glare drilling into Aran's soul, making it impossible to break free. Eventually after what seemed a very long time the druid turned to the chief.

"Keep this stripling close by you, Tuadh. He has much to tell you on the morrow about the Roman forces in your area, though not right now, not in the dark of night."

Tuadh waved him off. "Sit behind me, lad, and listen to our tales of the great battles."

Seonagh softly tapped her father on the shoulder. "What of the tamhas? Do you wish that they be seated together with Aran?"

"Have your wits fled, daughter?" her father upbraided her.

"Nay. Seonagh's question is a fair one," Mapon answered. "It is fitting that they join us for the remainder of the feast because they are as much a part of our future as the warrior Aran."

Seonagh signalled the twins.

"Thank goodness we're allowed to be with you, Aran," Fianna whispered for his ears alone, as she scooted in behind him. "I don't want to miss anything exciting."

"Your daughter should also join us." Mapon's command left Tuadh little alternative but to agree.

Mapon stood up with his clarsach and rippled his fingers across its delicate gut strings, all talk in the roundhouse ceasing. The bard in him was mesmerising when he sat back down, his tales of the gods and of mighty battles unfolding. They were story songs where sometimes his deep voice chanted like a poem as he let his clever fingers pick over the instrument and at other times, he sang. The sounds were all melodious, his audience riveted on his performance.

"Bluddy brilliant." Brian's grin was infectious, his itching fingers plucking at his tunic.

Brian was great on his fiddle and could pick out a tune on his guitar, but Aran didn't think his best friend had ever tried a harp.

Eventually Mapon stopped and stood up. Holding his hands aloft, once more his fingers outspread, Mapon's voice rang out over the throng. "People of

Balbath, it is good that you have feast times. They fortify your soul, and your body, for the fray that is as inevitable as each day dawns. Till I meet you again in safe circumstances, may our gods walk with you! This gathering is now ended."

"I didn't think it could get any noisier, yet it has," Brian bawled into Aran's ear as the whole room got to its feet cheering the druid. There was a great deal of clapping and thumping of hands on shoulders for what seemed like ages then the tumult died down to a general buzz as the room gradually emptied, the tribespeople spilling out through the entrance tunnel.

Aran counted that the only ones left in the room, apart from him and the twins, were Seonagh and a small group surrounding Tuadh and Mapon: probably those who would be sleeping in the chief's roundhouse.

The druid's gaze turned to him once more. "I charge you to stay close by Tuadh and help him well during the coming days. You have useful things to tell. I know it from deep in here." Aran was mesmerised when the man thumped his knuckles once at his forehead and then thrice at his chest. "The chief will have need of your knowledge."

Mapon turned away to find Brian reverently stroking the clarsach, his fingers following the carving of the wooden curve. "You believe you could play this?"

"Err… yes, I think I could," Brian jumped back from the beautiful instrument, terrified he'd angered its owner.

"Play," Mapon handed the clarsach into Brian's amazed hands.

Feeling the heavy weight, Brian looked like he'd

drop it. Sitting down slowly, he let his fingers ripple over the strings. Listening carefully to a few of them in turn, he picked out a very simple lullaby. The hush around Aran made him aware that mystified eyes and ears had tuned into his best friend's musical ability. The mingling of Brian's freckles meant he was mortified.

"You are a bard in the making." Mapon nodded before gently removing his harp from Brian's reluctant hands. "Perhaps you will own an instrument like this and like me you will give her a name. Meriel is my name for this cheer bringer."

For a long moment, Mapon stared at Brian as though seeing right through him. "You are an interesting one, indeed. You have reserves of strength though your pathway through life will be different from your warrior friend here. You will teach through your heart."

Brian was unable to answer. Aran was sure Mapon was paying his mate a compliment, though about what he hadn't a clue. When Mapon's stare turned to Fianna, Aran had a hard time suppressing a grin—they were all getting the treatment.

"Soon-to-be warrior maiden," Mapon said holding Fianna's gaze. "Keep your great curiosity within bounds. It will stand you in good stead, but you must observe with caution. And listen to what your gut tells you."

"Err… thank you." Her answer was hushed.

"A word outside, Tuadh," Mapon commanded before he moved towards the doorway. The few men left around the fireside followed in their wake.

"We must retire now," Seonagh told them as she laced back two nearby curtains. "These two stalls are free for your use."

Outside the stars glimmered in a clear darkness, the moon almost full when Fianna wandered off with Seonagh leading the way. Aran lingered with Brian by a dying fireside that burned near Tuadh's dwelling, squatting to warm their hands at the faint embers, the night dark holding a tiny chill.

"Do you find Mapon a bit weird?" Brian nudged his shoulder toppling him over onto the hard packed ground, the surface worn by many feet tramping back and forth. "What do you reckon he meant when he said your knowledge is going to be useful to Tuadh? And I'm going to teach with my heart?"

"No idea, mate. Maybe he means you won't be wielding a sword too much, but will get your point over by other actions." He got back onto his hunkers finding the perfect balance point, not wanting to be caught out like that again, not even by his best buddy. He'd been literally put off balance a time too often already and he wasn't enamoured by that. "I like Mapon, even though he's a bit scary. I'm more concerned that Callum sent us to share our knowledge but I haven't done any of that, yet."

Brian nodded. "Yeah, but Callum said we might need sleep-overs on some of the decisions. I didn't think he really meant proper sleep but it would appear that's what we need to do."

He got to his feet to stretch his legs. "I think you're right. Callum also said I might be staying with you over a few days, remember?"

It was too dark to see Brian's face as they sauntered away from the fire. "So he did."

"Is it this one?" Brian whispered at Fianna's door hanging a while later.

The roundhouse was almost pitch dark, apart from some glowing crimson embers on the fire, yet the gloom didn't seem to bother the ever ready guard at the entryway.

Fianna's head popped out. "Of course it's this one. I've been waiting for you for ages. Where have you two been?"

"We went for a little scout around." Brian deliberately kept his voice low in case anyone was nearby.

"Nothing to report," Aran told her. "Plenty of guards are posted around, but they didn't challenge us."

"They knew who we were." Brian looked to him for confirmation.

"Yeah. No chance of escape."

"Escape? Do you want to?" Fianna sounded disappointed. "Seonagh promised to show me the chariots tomorrow and all the other tasks needed for some big festival that's happening. By the way, she left you drinks in your cubby hole. I've had mine already. It's a warm spiced milky drink. "

Aran popped in behind the door curtain and came back with two wooden beakers. Handing one to Brian, he sniffed the other before sipping. "Spicy?"

Fianna shrugged. "Not exactly, just sort of different."

Brian burped his appreciation, having drained it in one gulp.

"I want to see the training ground as well. I fancy trying out another spear throw and maybe even use a real Celtic long sword. That's going to be so cool." He pretended to parry with his empty cup but Brian was having none of it.

"Nope. I'm not that keen to be sliced in half by one of their swords." Brian shuddered at the thought. His next question was whispered, as though afraid that someone might hear them talk. "Right now I'm knackered and want to sleep for a week but maybe we should arrange some kind of signal if this lot get really nasty with us overnight. A password for danger… or something? In case we need to pull the plug on this strange escapade."

"Good idea." He nodded. "What do you think, Fianna? You pick something since you're the one in there on your own."

Her eyes sparkled in the dim light. "Fantastic!"

"Fantastic?" Brian wasn't impressed.

"I don't mean that for a password. How about… OOH."

"Ooh?" Brian pursed his lips, thinking it through. "That's an absolutely crappy suggestion."

"O-O-H." Fianna enunciated each as a letter. "Out Of Here!"

"Okay! That's pretty neat." Aran liked it.

Fianna sounded decisive, still convincing her twin. "If any one of us is in deadly trouble we shout O-O-H. We press escape and zap away from the adventure."

Chapter Ten

"Rise now, for the sun god, Lugh, already sends us day light outside."

Aran felt someone's fingers nudge his elbow. He blinked his eyes to clear them of matter, and to get rid of the stinging from the swirly pall around him. He felt a bit woozy, yet an excitement surged through him that he couldn't quite explain.

Orla, the chief's hearth-wife, spoke again as she tied back the door-hanging with a leather thong. "Wash quickly. Seonagh's brothers await you."

A chill filled the roundhouse. The dim light from the struggling fire made it still seem as night-time, the smoke coming from the died-down fire which had been revitalised with sappy wood.

"Waken up, sleepy head!" After he struggled over to the washbowl Orla had left for them, he splashed a few droplets of cold water towards Brian, feeling a bit jittery on his pins. "We're going out with Seonagh's brothers. Maybe we'll get to do a mock battle with real swords."

"I'll only be trying to kill you." Brian peered out from under the cosy covers. "I feel rubbish. Like I've been drugged, except I don't know what being drugged is like."

Aran felt his stomach lurch.

"Could that milk have had something in it?" Brian's legs swirled around, his feet dangling to make contact with the floor as he ruffled his already messy hair.

"To make us sleep?" He didn't like the implications of that, after the event, but he was still alive to tell the tale; or maybe more accurately to create the tale.

"I fell asleep the minute I hit the sack." Brian's feet slapped the rushes before he moved over to him.

He had as well.

Brian scooped water up to his face, his mumbles just able to be heard. "If we'd been in any danger our armbands would have warned us, wouldn't they?"

He hoped that was true though he'd not even thought about it the previous night. It seemed that although Callum had said they'd be crucial to the action, some of the decisions were out of their hands. He resolved to be more careful about everything.

"Fianna!"

He thought of her at the same time Brian lurched out of the stall. Subdued noises outside told them that the roundhouse occupants were already up and prepared for the day. A huddle of men clanked their weapons as they were extricated from a depleting stack, their goodbyes quiet before each man slipped through the entryway. In contrast, Mapon noisily took his leave, thanking Balbath for his hospitality.

Before vanishing, the druid made one long look in Aran's direction but said nothing, the only acknowledgement a tipping of his staff towards him.

Fianna was already at the fireside, her question bright and cheery. "Sleep well you two? I slept the sleep of the dead."

Brian glared and then looked at the bread and water she handed him, his mood turning zany. Flapping the bread in front of his nose, he lurched around, his eyes agog. "Zombie food. Oh yeah!"

"You had any of this, yet, Fianna?" Aran hoped her answer would be good.

"It's okay. Not like our bread, it's much drier and flatter. I shared a piece with Seonagh a few minutes ago. Hurry up. They're waiting for us."

That made it sound legit if Seonagh ate it as well, but Brian continued to clown around, faking a choking fit.

"Stuff it!" His grin was hampered when a wad of dry bread stuck to his teeth. He gulped down the wooden beaker of water and made for the entryway after Fianna.

Brian nudged him. "Today's guards?"

Seonagh's older brothers, Liam and Thain, nodded to them when they stepped outside.

They all met up with Tuadh at the armoury. Rooting about like one of the domestic pigs snuffling in the pen nearby, the chief was elbow deep in a huge muddled heap of bits and pieces of broken armour and horse fittings. Seeing them all enter, he straightened up and beckoned Aran to the pile.

"Take the others away!" he ordered Seonagh who stood at his side. "I want to speak to this warrior alone since Mapon believes he has much he can tell me. His faith in this young man is great. I pray that my faith will become so too, since we are in need of help from the gods." Seeing Seonagh and the twins still hovering he shouted again, his impatience getting the better of him. "Go. You are of no use to me just now."

"Father. Mapon said that the red-haired tamhas are also part of our future."

Tuadh sighed, quite noisily. "True enough, girl. Wait yonder." He pointed to the opposite side of the pile.

The room was also crammed with spears and other

weapons: some broken but many looked searingly sharp. Leather-covered oval wooden shields were dotted around the area, a few very battered looking, yet others seemed reasonably new. There were two wicker battle chariots to one side. They'd seen better days, and needed a good bit of repairing to make them useful again.

"Well, lad!" Tuadh boomed at Aran. "Will we need many warriors and all of these weapons when we next challenge the Romans? Will their forces outnumber our own? Can you tell me that?"

Pointing to the motley collection of broken bits, his answer was tactful. "I believe you will need these repaired if you decide to fight the Romans."

"You are right about that. We need every warrior in the north bearing as many arms as possible." The chief strode around tossing worn weapons into different heaps. "Repair every possible piece here, without delay!" he ordered the man who patiently trailed around after him.

Taking him by the arm Tuadh strode outside to the fresh air, the others trailing in behind. "And these battles? Where will they be sited?"

Aran gulped. Very, very slowly he answered sure that his reply wouldn't be welcome. "I don't believe there will be any more large battle sites against the Romans. Places of smaller skirmishing I can't be sure of either, but I can tell you about two places where the Romans will make overnight camps, where they'll gather together and regroup their strength."

"Gather their forces together? I have heard they march as one body. As they did before. What can you mean?"

"They do march together as a unit, though they

also establish contact lines with their fleet."

"Aye. I have heard tell of that." Tuadh strode around the settlement expecting Aran to follow him. "Will they make a short encampment as they did many long seasons ago?"

Aran risked a reply. "Caracalla follows the usual Roman pattern. Shelters made of strong leather will be carried by his pack animals or in the baggage wagons—each shelter good for eight men to sleep under."

"Aye. I know of this from last Lughnasadh. That way they can shelter anywhere they choose."

"That's true. Except they always make camp near a source of fresh water and wood for burning fires: for heat and for cooking." He tried hard to give useful information. "They need large amounts of water because they have many men in their cohorts…" He coughed loudly, nearly biting his tongue out in his haste to cover up Roman terminology in case the word cohort wasn't familiar. "I mean in their huge groups of fighting men."

Tuadh pounded a pathway past the smithy. "Mapon tells me you have the gift of sight. He believes you can read the signs clearer than anyone else around here, that you are destined to be a druid diviner. You will show me where Caracalla will make camp." The chief headed towards the horse enclosure near the entrance to the hillfort. "We will ride out; it will be quicker that way."

Show him? Aran was dazed. How could he possibly find a place when he was nearly two thousand years out of his own time?

Seonagh ran up with Brian and Fianna at her heels. "Do you wish the others to have mounts too?"

"No, girl, I do not," barked her father. "I only need the warrior here. We are not going on a raiding party. I want only to see what this stripling can show me."

Aran jumped in at the deep end hoping Tuadh wouldn't be too angry with him as he mounted the horse indicated by the chief. He needed Brian with him, just to be sure of his facts. "Brian has great skill in reading the landscape."

The chief sounded irritated by any possible delay as he headed off towards the other end of the horse pen. "Then they had better come. Find mounts quickly."

Seonagh led them to a horse handler by the gate.

"That one." Brian pointed to a spirited looking pony.

The handler chuckled. "That little black pony is a difficult creature, lad. You would be better served with this one."

Putting his fingers to his mouth the young warrior whistled softly. Immediately an obedient creature whinnied over to him. Aran could see Brian loved her on sight.

"You are a fine filly," Brian whispered, stroking the horse's muzzle, clearly desperate to ride her.

By the time they all joined Tuadh, who was strapping a gleaming axe into a leather sheath attached to his waistbelt, four other warriors were mounted alongside—one of whom was Tyrnan.

Fianna preened alongside Aran.

"Not again." He'd had enough of Fianna's fawning over the scary warrior and now her side glances showed she fancied Seonagh's brothers as well.

"Which way, lad?" Tuadh shouted.

"I must speak with Brian first." Aran hoped he sounded confident.

"Do not be long," the man barked, his impatience increasing by the second. "We have no time to idle."

Aran urged his horse away, beckoning Brian to follow him.

"I'll stay here with Seonagh." Fianna's wink told him she was going to hang around the young warriors.

"Tuadh's ordered me to show him where the Romans made marching camps."

"What?" Brian was aghast. "How can you do that?"

"Not me, buddy," he grinned. "You're going to show him."

"No way! I'm not putting my head on the block for you, pal. Do your own dirty deeds." Brian pulled his horse away.

"You've got to help with this. I need you to identify the landscape with me, just to be sure I'm thinking straight. Mapon's convinced Tuadh that I can tell him things. Remember what Callum said?"

"Share your knowledge wisely, or something?" Brian nodded, still looking unsure.

"Close enough." Aran grinned again. "I need you to help me find Deer's Den."

Brian's freckle-decked nose squirmed around a bit. "How?"

"Remember Bennachie?"

Brian's head bobbed up and down though he clearly didn't know what he was referring to.

"We need to find our bearings from the view of Bennachie that we'd get from our bridge at Kintore—I mean the view that we'd normally see."

"Aran, in case you've forgotten, we're not in our own time." Brian reminded him before a penny dropped. "Hey, that's neat! Our local tiny hill in Kintore is called Tuach Hill and Seonagh's father is called Tuadh – though they say his name a little differently here – more like Twaach."

"You've only just realised that?" Aran grunted wondering how Brian could be so intelligent and so slow at the same time. "Can we get back to planning this trip? Tuadh already looks mad at the delay."

The chief surged forward calling the boys to heel, like the faithful hound already at his horse's hooves. He was not a man with abundant patience. "Where to, lad?"

"The riverside." Brian's response was firm.

"Follow." The man cantered off with his warriors at his side leaving Aran, Seonagh and the twins to take up the rear as they wound down through some trees to the meandering flat riverbed.

Brian swivelled around when they halted near the water's edge.

In the distance was the feature Aran had hoped very much to see. The conical peak of what he recognised as The Mither Tap soared above woods on the foothills.

"Definitely Bennachie." Brian agreed with Aran. "So what next?"

"The village of Kintore is off to our left and mostly behind us—would that be correct?" Aran confirmed their position, imagining what it was like in the twenty first century.

"Yep."

"Okay, so Tuach Hill must also be behind us on our left?" Aran deduced.

"Correct." Brian confirmed as they turned around and took note of the only small hill nearby.

"That has to be Tuach Hill." He pointed to it. "Now Brian, imagine the road into Kintore from Aberdeen. Deer's Den is off to the—"

Brian finished for him. "—left, just after Tuach Hill on the right as you travel northwards. Though only after the Torry Burn."

"Yes. There's just one tiny problem, though, about Deer's Den."

"What's that?"

"Archaeologists believe the Roman camp at Kintore was set down in Agricola's time back in AD 84. They're not absolutely sure about Severus using it."

Brian was thinking his way through this minor dilemma. "Wouldn't Severus have used the site of an older Roman camp rather than find a new place?"

Aran was impressed. "That's pretty good thinking. The Romans did re-use old sites, and that's what the last archaeological Deer's Den survey concluded."

"You're planning to tell Tuadh you know the Romans will camp at Deer's Den?"

"Yes. But it'll be more difficult to find the site at Durno."

"We have to find Durno as well?" Brian turned to look way up the river towards Bennachie. "To get to Durno we need to follow the River Don to where it meets the River Urie. Then if we follow the Urie till we're directly in front of the peaks of both The Mither Tap and Oxen Craig…"

Aran took up the thread. "Good thinking, again. See, I did need your geographical skills. You can be my landscape advisor. Now all we have to do is work out how to tell Tuadh those details."

The chief didn't look at all happy with either the delay or with their hilarity when he called them over. "Well, what have you divined?"

Aran pointed towards Tuach Hill. "There will be a Roman Camp on the far side of that hill."

"Roman invaders made camp there a long time ago, though Severus did not tarry there last Lughnasadh." Tuadh confirmed.

Brian beamed.

"They will use it soon for another short term occupation," Aran added.

"How many? There were thousands on this Taexali land the last time." The man barked like an angry hound.

Aran was slower to answer for fear of saying something wrong. "Ten thousand men, or even more…" He broke off remembering that Kintore's Deer's Den site had a larger and a smaller camp. "…if they extend the camp boundaries used the last time."

Tuadh's fingers strayed to his droopy moustache. "We make no dwellings on that land. Our gods do not permit occupation of such a despoiled area. The stone circle and burial place of the ancients overlooks that place it but we do not venture there."

Aran swallowed hard. He'd read that for centuries Deer's Den had remained deserted after Roman occupation and was only partly resettled on during the late nineteen hundreds.

Tuadh turned to his warriors, a sharp and heated discussion taking place. "How many of our Balbathan scouts patrol in that direction?"

"More than enough warriors guard there to give us early warning of the arrival of so many enemy troops." A warrior whose name Aran didn't know gave the definite reply.

"Send more warriors further afield," The chief bellowed before he turned back to Aran. "And the other place?"

"That is not so close to here."

Tuadh's teeth gritted with displeasure. The chief's fingers fretted on his axe handle making Aran regret what he'd set in motion. "Get on with it, lad. Tell us where to go."

Looking up the meandering little river, his gaze fixed on the sight of Bennachie, his focus inward as he imagined how to describe it. "We'll have to follow this river till it meets with a smaller river." He pointed upstream.

He got no further before a tetchy Tuadh interrupted. "Aye, lad, I know of that meeting point and after that?"

"You need to follow the smaller river…"

"Are you certain?" Seonagh's father had run out of all patience and finesse.

"The smaller river." Nodding his head, Aran confirmed more forcefully. "Follow the smaller river till it flattens out at a place where…" He pointed towards Bennachie's The Mither Tap. "…that peak is directly facing you when you look to where the sun sets in the west."

"I am with you, lad." Tuadh indicated that he was following. "And then?"

Aran took a deep breath since it was getting harder to describe. He didn't think he could use the terms right or left; and he wasn't so sure of using north, south, east or west either. "Follow the river bed till the hillfort on this side is flanked by another high peak, about the same height, to this side." He signalled with his two hands.

"The peak that's hidden from view right now?" Tyrnan questioned edging his horse alongside.

"Yes." Aran nodded again. "The hillfort will be on this side and the other high peak will be on this side." Again he used arm signals to make his point. "You will be standing at the place where a small burn meets that smaller river.

"The Gadie!" Tyrnan roared and slapped Aran so hard on the shoulder he almost shot off the horse. "The boy is correct. He describes the Gadie waters as they run into the River Urie."

"You tell me the Romans will camp by the flat bed of the burn and the river?" Tuadh looked unconvinced of that.

"No. That's not where they'll camp." Aran hastened to make his information clear. "They will make camp on the slope directly opposite the hillfort." He closed his eyes and again used his arm pointing behind him to make his vision seem clear. "The hillfort is here…and the other peak is here." His arms flailed to reinforce his description. "The Roman camp is here…" He pointed directly behind him. "It will be up the hill where the land flattens out and before the level ground ridges with another one."

"He's right. I know where Aran is describing." Fianna's enthusiastic outburst surprised him as much as the assembled warriors when she moved her horse closer. "It's a great place for a Roman camp."

"What do you say, girl? Are you also a seer?"

The incredulous glare from Tuadh had Fianna tugging her horse back a bit but not before she chipped in with, "I just mean that the view is very good from up where Aran describes and it'll be easy for you to spot the Roman armies."

Inside Aran groaned. How was he going to smooth over that one?

Before the gaff got any worse, thankfully, one of the warriors spoke up. "There is level ground above the place he describes."

Having got over his surprise at Fianna's interruption, the chief's habitual terse wave of his arm was sufficient brush-off to have her trot her horse back to Seonagh.

"How large a camp?" Tuadh was fixated with numbers.

Aran was reluctant to divulge what he knew, though he owed it to answer the best he could. "It will be a very large camp."

"Ten thousand, as at Deer's Den?" The chief was becoming extremely agitated, his restless mood transferring to his whinnying horse which snickered and fretted. Aran's grimace caused him to change the numbers. "Even more than that?"

He gulped. "The camp might shelter as many as thirty thousand men…" Tuadh's sudden bark hastened Aran to complete his bad news. "… if reinforcements join them from their ships."

Tuadh burst forth with a torrent of words that he didn't understand since they were so quickly spewed out, but he was pretty sure he didn't need to understand them.

"Mapon spoke true." The chief eventually calmed down, his need to soothe his horse greater than his own comfort. "Though it may go ill with us, we must make a stand against these usurpers who will kill and scatter our remains. The hill behind the Urie would indeed be a good place for the Romans to survey the land, but I was told our Roman enemy likes to camp on lower ground. Why not below?"

"They need the flatter land for amassing their troops in a stand of strength."

"They would easily see our warning beacons from the summits. From our hillfort." Tuadh peered into Aran's face. "What makes you so sure of this, lad?"

"I can only say that I know what I know!"

"Will we battle by the River Urie? Do you see that in your waking dreams?"

"I don't know." Aran knew his last words didn't satisfy, yet he had no other answer, since that was way beyond any facts that he'd read, beyond information uncovered by archaeologists of the early twenty-first century.

What seemed like an age later, but wasn't actually, he sidled his horse next to Brian's mount. The mounted group had cantered along the valley following the River Don to the point where it met the River Urie. Tuadh halted and had a word with his sons.

Fianna was to go back to the settlement with Seonagh and Thain. Aran didn't want Fianna to be so far away from him and Brian but the chief was adamant. He no longer listened to Seonagh's soft spoken reminders.

"Thain must warn those at Whiterashes. Our outlying roundhouse tribespeople will be safer at Balbath." Tuadh was firm. His order was given.

Thain trotted off with the girls, Fianna giving him a cheeky wave and showing she wasn't bothered about being separated. He watched them turn on to a different track—not the same way they had come from.

"Do you think Fianna will be okay?" Brian sounded concerned.

He had to believe so. Even more than that, he had to make sure his best mate believed it. "Sure. Our armbands would have warned us if there was any danger to her."

Brian managed to send a grin in his direction. "You mean Callum would have sent us an O.O. H. signal?"

"Yeah." It was a stretch of the imagination but it seemed to make Brian feel better about being apart from his twin.

Thick trees blanketed most of the view on both sides of the small river. If Aran hadn't already given his description from his mind's eye below Balbath, he knew he'd never have been able to describe where to go now. Brian's expression indicated his thinking wasn't much different.

Tuadh was not to be denied though. Using Aran's earlier directions the chief determined to plough on towards the Gadie Burn. Aran couldn't believe just how much the River Urie twisted and turned and, depending on the banking and the heavy tree cover, at times Bennachie totally disappeared from sight.

Without warning Tuadh halted after they rounded yet another bend in the river.

A huge sigh escaped. Aran now had a clearer view along the riverbed, making him feel much better. The hillfort on The Mither Tap was startling, the solid stone construction something he'd never seen in the same way before. An impressive complete stone wall ringed the summit, the tops of some roundhouses just visible above the barrier. He was so glad to see it since Tuadh's glower had increased with every last tree-shrouded curve.

The chief pointed way over to his right. Mixed woodland dotted parts of the slope but the bit Aran knew of as the Durno Roman camp was easy to discern, the ledge of land visible above cleared slopes. "Up there?"

Aran nodded.

Without warning, Tuadh whipped his axe free of its leather sheath and hurled it towards an unsuspecting hare which bounded between rocks near the scrubby riverside. Flipping over and over the weapon whomped through the air before the blunt edge smashed the poor creature's head to pulp against a nearby rock.

Aran gasped. What an incredible aim… and what an incredible power the chief wielded. No man, or larger beast, receiving the sharp end of the axe blade could possibly survive.

At Tuadh's nod, one of his warriors calmly set his horse to trot off—to collect the hatchet and the prey.

The huge lump at Aran's throat couldn't be swallowed down. Messing about with the chief of Balbath wasn't an option. He'd heard about a horror film called *The Axeman Cometh.*

Tuadh of Balbath would never need to rehearse for the part.

He felt the grin spreading but couldn't catch Brian's attention. Had he just solved the mystery of the hill?

After returning the axe to its pouch, Tuadh stared for a while at the scene before them. Eventually, heeling his horse around, the chief drove his animal hard, back to Balbath, his entourage hot on his heels.

Chapter Eleven

"Where are they all?" Brian was grinning like a Cheshire Cat.

Aran wasn't grinning. He was miffed. Having been grilled again by Tuadh about the Roman marching camps at Deer's Den and Durno, on their return to Balbath, meant that he'd missed opportunities to show off his spear skills on the training ground.

Happiness wreathed Brian's face because he hadn't needed to pluck up a sword or a spear.

Close to, Aran could only see one warrior supervising some of the smaller kids who were sparring with wooden swords. However, in the distance, the far end of the huge field seemed much busier.

"Warrior Aran of Durris!" The call came from one of the horse-handlers who approached from the side. He pointed his spear down the field. "Seonagh requests that you join her."

As the boys jogged their way over the cropped grass, four chariots raced across their sightline towards a finishing point. Closer to the action, Fianna rushed up to them beside herself with glee. "I had a shot at riding in Seonagh's chariot. It was absolutely cool. She says she'll let you two try as well, but that it might have to be tomorrow."

"What else did you do while we were away?" Brian sounded mildly interested.

"Before we rode her chariot, Seonagh had to visit the old herbs wifie. That was a hoot. I knew the names of some of the plants since Jennie has been teaching me about them." She grinned, her green eyes sparkling with merriment. "I thought I'd be bored stiff, but I wasn't."

"Was she a cre-e-py old crone?" Brian faked an eerie scary tone, his hands making weird spell-like motions.

Fianna slugged him on the shoulder. "No, she wasn't. You eejit."

Aran joined in. "No witchy incantations and evil smelling cauldrons then?" He pretended to be disappointed when Fianna made faces at him.

"She wasn't like that at all. She was a nice old woman. It was about having enough of the right herbs for concoctions to make people better if they're sick. They were also talking about things they had to add to their food stocks to keep people healthy because they don't have much stored grain left. The Romans burned the fields last summer before they could even do any harvesting, so they've only got some grain left from the year before in their grain pits. They'll be adding dried berries to it to make porridge, and things like that. Now I know of more healthy things to plant with Jennie when we get home." She looked at him in horror as the thought struck her. "But we're not going home yet?"

"Do you want to?" He hoped she didn't because he felt he still had a lot more to do to help Tuadh.

"No!" Fianna squawked. "We can't go before the feast."

"What feast? Have you wangled an invitation to something that we haven't?" Brian nudged his twin's elbow.

"How can they have a feast if they've hardly any food?" Something about it didn't make sense to Aran.

Fianna looked at him as if he was stupid. "There's

a humungous party tonight. Some of the warriors have been out hunting in the forests this morning while you were off gallivanting with Tuadh. Apparently, the hunting is allowed by their god, Cernunnos, because it's for a special feast. Seonagh says they only hunt wild animals for food every now and then because they don't eat meat every day."

"They don't?" Brian was disappointed. "I love venison burgers."

Fianna socked him in the arm. "No burgers, here, brother. Seonagh says it's one of the four big feasts of the year when they celebrate the coming of the better weather and when they pray to make the crops grow healthily. Sounds like magic. They sing and dance round big bonfires." She danced around them flinging her arms about.

"Don't talk rubbish." Brian pushed her aside.

"It isn't rubbish," Aran told him. "They celebrate the seasons."

Fianna's gaze lit up. "They make the cows run through fires."

"Have you gone scatty?" Brian pressed his face in front of his sister. "Or are you just trying to wind me up?"

"I'm not." She glared because he was spoiling her fun. "Seonagh told me about it. It's to make them have lots of calves and to survive the next season."

"And how is burning them in a fire—before they're even slaughtered—going to make them healthy?" Brian was totally scathing, his expression indicating his sister was a complete numpty.

"They did do that, Brian," Aran kept his voice calm, to keep the peace between brother and sister. It was the tone that usually worked, and fingers crossed he hoped it would work again since he didn't fancy having a Fraser twins blow up.

"There are rites later on in the wood near here but that's only for the adults." Fianna's tone was huffy as she started off down the field. "I could have shown you where the fires will be, but you don't sound too interested."

Aran had had experience before of Fianna's sulks but he had to give credit where credit was due: she'd found out quite a lot about what was going on at the hillfort.

With Brian reluctantly at the rear, they trailed after her. Large bonfires a few metres high had been stacked up in two rows, tribespeople still arriving with more wood to add to the piles. They had created a large channel between each row of stacked brushwood.

"This is where they make the cattle run between the fires." Fianna ignored Brian and concentrated on Aran. "That'll be after a ceremony at that far end, Seonagh says."

"Is Seonagh pulling your leg?" Brian still made cheeky faces at her.

"Did Seonagh think you were pretty dumb not to know anything about it?" Aran wasn't convinced about Fianna's discretion.

She shrugged, not put out by his question. "I didn't give the game away if that's what you mean. I pretended to know what she was talking about." Fianna looked about her, watching four chariots wheeling around in the distance. "Hey! They're going to race again."

Brian stared at where she pointed. "How can you tell that?"

"Which one is Seonagh?" Aran couldn't work out which one she was, since the challengers were still quite far away.

Fianna jogged off towards the race area, her eyes dancing in anticipation as she upped the pace. "The black horse. That slight rise is where they start and finish from because the area isn't level. The girl with the white horse is Duhlain's sister Maga. She's really good. Just watch her."

There were two other horses and chariots driven by other girls.

"Is Seonagh the best?" Brian's question was breathy as they drew closer to the race.

"Not from what I've seen today." Fianna halted at a prime spot for viewing, claiming it was close enough to the end. Her breath came in short pants after their run. "Tyrnan's sister is with the chestnut horse; she's called Tasca. She was very good earlier, though I think Maga is the best today."

Aran watched a spear soar up into the air, a signal for the race to start. The light two-wheeled chariots hared up the length of the field in front of him, neck and neck, their occupants standing proud till they came to a bumpier section with slight rises in the surface. Wheels lifted off the ground for a second or two making it very difficult to control the landings at such speed. The riders were unsettled as they flew up high, again and again, though none fell out and no chariots tipped over. The break in stride was just enough for Maga to gain the edge on Seonagh and the other two, as all the chariots slowed into a turn at the far end of the field. Clouds of dust and chaff flew up making it difficult to see clearly but he could tell the turns were executed skilfully. Once they were all back onto the straight and heading for the home stretch, bit by bit, Maga streaked ahead.

A few tribespeople gathered alongside to cheer on their favourite contestant, friendly banter going on as a half dozen boys and girls cheered for different people. The finish line, in the distance, was marked by two rows of spears making a gateway, the chariots having to pass through to win. Aran itched to have a go, his fists controlling imaginary halters.

As soon as the chariots had all passed them, the Balbath children took to their heels in pursuit, calling to the lead horse. Aran, in turn, took off after Fianna who squealed Seonagh's name over and over.

"Come on, Seonagh. We want to see you win today. Faster. Go faster, Seonagh" He had no breath left but Brian wasn't too puffed, his mantra more measured to his thuds on the earth.

"Seonagh. Seonagh. Seonagh."

Brian's calls were echoed all around. The favourite of the children of Balbath was obvious.

As the chariots neared the spears, the chants of the Balbathans suddenly tipped the balance in favour of Maga. Aran thought that a bit odd. The kids who were running alongside him seemed to have changed their allegiance, and were now calling for Maga. If that was what they did at Balbath, then it was quite different from home.

In the lead, Maga was three chariot lengths ahead of Seonagh. Aran got it. What they were doing was quite neat. It wasn't that they'd changed allegiance – he realised that it was just their way of acknowledging the stronger candidate.

As someone who was always fiercely competitive and reasonably confident, he'd have been be miffed if his backers suddenly changed their support but he acknowledged that what the crowd around him was doing was actually much fairer.

The race over, the clutch of children took to their heels again and scattered across the field, back to the fire stacks.

Aran and the twins hared up the rise and along the flat to where the horses had eventually stopped. Seonagh was conceding her defeat well. Jumping down she clapped her hand on Maga's shoulder, congratulating her. Her fellow competitors likewise acknowledged the winner, horse handlers having appeared to take control of the horses, calming the beasts down.

"You bested me in three out of three, Maga," Seonagh groaned, yet still grinned. "I need lots of practice with my foot being so weak, and my injured arm causing me some pain, but soon I will be winning again."

Maga nodded, her expression inquiring when Aran felt her gaze fall on him. "What about the new Taexali warrior? Can he handle a chariot as well as I can?"

"'Course he can."

Aran was amazed to find such immediate support from Fianna.

Not to be outdone Brian chipped in. "Aran's the best horseman I know. You want to see what he can do with the Clydesdales on his dad's farm."

Aran was relieved when he didn't need to intervene. Seonagh did that for him. "I have not heard of this type of horse you mention but you may race with us, if Maga is agreeable?"

"Go, Aran. Show them what you can do. They're great fun to ride. You'll scoosh it." Fianna's laughter was tinged with sass. She knew he'd never tried one of the Celtic chariots—unlike her.

He was desperate to have a go but this was jumping into an icy bath! A weird fear of failure slipped down his spine when the Balbath girls made comments of disbelief.

"There are no better horsewomen than those of us at Balbath. We are the best." Maga's grin was haughtily convincing.

Aran absolutely couldn't lose face when one of the other riders, Tasca, offered her chestnut mount and chariot. A tight smile pinned in place, he gripped the leather rein handed to him, the harness and simple bit at the horse's mouth not much different from what he was used to.

"Follow!" Seonagh commanded as she clicked her horse into a slow walk after springing back up onto the flat bed of her chariot, Maga heading the same way.

Sheesh! Aran's pulse thumped. These Celts didn't hang about.

Jumping onto the light chariot he prayed to a goddess he'd read about. "Epona? I think that's your name. Keep me from making a complete arse of myself."

The little filly wasn't much more than a pony but it was strong and was used to pulling the chariot weight—though from the jiggling Aran could tell that the frame actually wasn't heavy at all. He found that controlling the horse after the first few seconds wasn't much different from horses pulling the little carriage on his dad's farm. His mum ran 'riding for the disabled' classes so he was used to helping her drive the vehicle. What was entirely different was standing on the low flat bed of tightly placed planks. The chariot sides were made from woven wicker and only covered him to thigh height. They were basic protection and not much else, though maybe they were only meant to be decorative? He wasn't sure.

Keeping balanced on his spread feet meant totally different skills from sitting on a bench seat. The chariot jounced its way down the field as the horse made its way to the start point. While he covered the distance, he worked out strategies for keeping his balance, creating just the right distance between his feet for best grip and flexibility. He pulled to a stop up alongside Seonagh as she slowly manoeuvred her vehicle. On Seonagh's other side Maga whooped when he eventually moved into place.

He wished he'd had a chance to try a turn on the run but understood that the horses had needed that short walk before racing again.

Last. Even to get into place at the start point.

Resolve firmed his chin. He'd show them what he could do.

Way down the field Brian and Fianna waved and jumped up and down like loonies. He wouldn't let them down either.

One of the horse handlers, standing nearby, gripped his spear vertically in his fist. Too soon, the spear rose aloft before Aran was quite ready, the other two contestants surging into action. Following on behind, he encouraged his horse to gain speed to catch up with Seonagh who was now a couple of lengths ahead of Maga.

"Come on, you beauty. You can do it."

Thundering down the field, he focused on the lead horse. Maga was closing up on Seonagh but he was still a good ten chariots behind both of them, and he couldn't blame his horse because she was a game little filly.

"Faster little one, faster."

The other two spurred their horses ahead using only the simple bridle. He continued to cajole his horse but he couldn't seem to make her speed up. His competitive spirit was to the fore, his lungs bursting, yet he was still way behind.

He absolutely refused to be beaten by the two warrior girls in front of him.

His mind worked furiously to find a way to catch up. The turn area was looming up ahead but he had no strategy for circling the vehicle. He didn't dare go too tight into the manoeuvre in case he crashed into one or both of his fellow riders. Pulling to the side, he went wide just as Seonagh and Maga made super fast turns. Losing time on the wider turn was inevitable but he had no other choice.

He was still going too fast to control his vehicle when the horse suddenly made the decisions for him. Too late to angle his weight properly, he flew up into the air when the filly yanked herself around. Almost wrapped around one of the wicker sides he struggled to keep himself inside the chariot, the rein slipping through his fingers.

He couldn't lose control on a simple turn. He absolutely wouldn't!

By the time he regained his feet, his little horse was well back into her stride and pulling forward as though nothing odd had happened. Gripping the reins more firmly he rebalanced himself. Sweat ran down his forehead and into his eyes as the chariot galloped down the straight.

If he didn't do something soon he knew he was definitely going to be last to the finish line of spears, now easily visible to him. A small crowd of tribespeople had gathered beside Brian and Fianna, their cheering heard over the thumping of the horses on the cropped field.

"Aran. Let the horse do the winning!" Up ahead of him Fianna was jumping up and screaming. "Let her fly."

Easing off his grip, just a little, he realised Fianna was absolutely correct. Allowed its head, the filly knew the field better than he did as she swayed here and there to avoid bumps he couldn't anticipate.

"Yes! You can do it."

Adrenalin surged in his veins as he drove on. Now only two chariot lengths separated him from Seonagh, with Maga only one length ahead of that. Exhilaration thrummed, his tangled hair flying out behind him. The current of air at his face was cooling and that was just as well, since sheer excitement had him seriously overheated.

Without warning, his horse veered to the right, avoiding a confrontation with the back of Seonagh's chariot. Scrabbling with the rein Aran overbalanced and ended on his knees, his chin slumped over the wicker side.

"Aran. Aran. Get up. Keep going!" Brian's screech penetrated the fug he was in as he scrabbled to get back control of the horse.

"Nay!" The cry in front of him was agonised. Maga's black horse suddenly lost speed, her chariot lurching over to one side. It all happened so quickly she slipped off the back and thudded to the ground. One wheel had come loose and was careering off at an angle.

Seonagh tugged to the opposite side to avoid crashing into the remains of Maga's chariot just short of the finish line and veered away from the row of spears.

It was a no-brainer for Aran to let his little filly ride through the finish line to huge cheering around him. Even if he was on his knees, and still wrapped around the wicker side of the chariot.

Slowing the horse down was easy too, because the horse knew exactly what to do without any instructions from him as it came to a stop. Back to his feet he turned the chariot around with no mishaps, jumped down and then walked the horse back to the finish line. Adrenalin still surged as he regained his breath. He grinned like mad as the twins rushed up to him.

He'd won by default. He hadn't fallen off—even if he had made a pig's ear of the riding.

"You were absolutely pants." Fianna crowed, her grin splitting her face. "But I knew you could do it."

He was the winner!

Chapter Twelve

"Have all the outer guards trebled."

Aran could hear the man bellow before he could even see him. Peeping out from behind the stall hanging, he watched the chief bluster his way up the roundhouse calling for his washing water. The man was in a foul mood. Again. Two warriors scurried after him listening and arguing with him. At his stall, Tuadh turned to the men and pointed a finger.

"Double the inner guard with our youngest warriors. We will have our Beltane rights in peace. See that it is done well."

Disappearing inside his cubicle, still muttering to himself, Tuadh left the two men at his doorway. The warriors charged out of the roundhouse as though a hive of bees chased them.

Fianna crept into the boys' stall. "Any idea what that was about?"

"Don't reckon he was too happy." Brian edged along to make room for his sister on the cot.

"Something's upset him for sure, but then he always seems to be in a grumpy mood. Guess it must come with the territory." Aran sidled further away from Fianna who was now sitting centrally between them.

Her face screwed up. "Whose territory?"

"The job. My dad says that if somebody is a big boss then he, or she, is always moaning about the responsibility."

"You're the one charged with our responsibility, and you're doing plenty moaning right now." Brian cackled, nudging him off the bed.

"Yeah, well we haven't exactly been successful with the tasks Callum set for us."

They had only recently returned to the chief's roundhouse, Seonagh having told them to wait there for her.

Fianna was quick to answer. "We have."

The look on his face must have had her doubting her answer.

"Well, we've covered a few of them."

Aran didn't feel so certain. Brian didn't look too sure either.

She continued. "You two have helped Tuadh by pointing out where the Roman camps are going to be. I don't think I've been nosey enough yet, and that's why I want to stay a bit longer."

Brian started to recite their list of objectives. "Where? We know we're at Kintore. When? We think it's AD 210. Who? They're the Taexali Balbathan tribe. Threats? The Romans are about to come and smash them to pulp."

"Nicely put, Brian. This is the sticky bit. We don't know yet if we need to give Tuadh more information to help his people."

"Don't forget the nasties." Fianna's heels drummed on the wooden support struts of the cot. "We're supposed to help them as well, and before you say anything, Tyrnan isn't one of the baddies. He's just very serious about his job of keeping an eye out for Seonagh. Seonagh says he's the best guard she's ever had."

"I'm warming up to Tyrnan but if he isn't the baddy, then who is? We don't know that yet."

Brian sounded sure. "That Roman Severus guy. It has to be him. Hey, sis. Maybe you're supposed to nosey around the Romans?"

"Sure thing, brother dear. If that's the case, how am I going to do that? Do you see me walking casually out of Balbath and wandering down to the Roman marching camp at Deer's Den? Am I going to find Severus and tell him that I've been sent to help him? I don't think Tuadh is going to let that happen."

"Evidence." Aran tried to diffuse a twin argument from developing. "We need to think about what the visual evidence might be that Callum needs. Maybe if we focus on that, we'll be successful with our other tasks, like we have been with the name of the hill."

Before Aran could say anything else, Orla entered the stall looking very fine, her young daughter Caitlinn accompanying her. Grabbing Fianna's hand Caitlinn dragged her off the bed chattering like a bubbly jock. The boys stood up, too.

"Come. We must not miss the beginning." Caitlinn was in a hurry.

Orla held the door curtain open. "It is time to go, though you must remain close by me. Wear your cloaks. After dusk falls, it will be cool."

Outside the roundhouse was a revelation. Many torches burned in high stands like the flambeau he'd seen on Caribbean holiday beaches, giving the growing dusk a festive air. People milled around chattering excitedly.

The unearthly beating of skin drums cut short the hubbub, the signal sound sending everyone scurrying towards the settlement opening. Aran sensed the restrained excitement around him as he and the other two trotted after Orla who clutched Caitlinn's hand very firmly with one hand, a lit torch brand in the other. Apart from a sizeable number of young guards who were left at strategic places, everyone followed the drumbeats, surging outside through the zigzag walkway and on towards the training ground. Burning flares at the far end of the field beckoned the crowd.

When they reached the area, the brands he'd seen were markers indicating where the stacks had been laid. He grinned at Brian and Fianna, all of them caught up in the general excitement. It was the same sort of anticipation he always felt when he stood around the local bonfire. He was desperate to see what would happen since this was Guy Fawkes Night with a huge difference.

The swell of people came to an abrupt halt well before they reached the stacked wood; waiting for something. It wasn't long before the crowd parted to allow someone to pass forward to the stacks.

Tuadh. A splendidly dressed Tuadh whose gold torque gleamed in the flare of his torch brand, the hilt of his sword and his unsheathed axe twinkling below. When the chief got to the first of the bonfires, he raised his arms high above him and began to chant. Though the words were difficult to make out it seemed he was incanting a spell to each bonfire as he approached it. One by one, he lit each fire, each flickering into action as the dry tinder ignited. When each was lit, the marker torch was cast into the flames making the corridor between the fires even wider. Soon eight roaring fires lit up the darkening blue dusk, four to each side of Tuadh.

To more ceremonial drumbeating, Aran watched the elders of the tribe proceed up the now well lit walkway towards the chief. Eventually coming to a halt, they arranged themselves alongside or behind Tuadh, a few rows deep, facing the awaiting tribespeople.

The drumbeat changed very slightly.

"Follow me!" Caitlinn in her firm grip, Orla moved through the noisy clutch of people and gradually made her way along the fire corridor, to her hearth-husband.

Aran and the twins towed at her heels, among the many people who now surged through the fire curtain. It seemed to be the turn of important warriors, those of high rank but who had not reached the status of being an elder of the tribe.

Orla whispered to Tuadh on reaching him. After the chief nodded, she turned back to Aran.

"Follow."

Orla was a woman of few words. The twins at his side, he trailed after her and Caitlinn as she went to one end of the row of elders, the bulk of the important tribespeople now clustered alongside the chief.

"Stand next to me, Warrior Aran."

Another order from the chief's wife but Aran wasn't too bothered since the view was good. Fianna stood next to him, Brian on her far side.

Tuadh raised his hand, the torch brand held aloft. He said nothing, yet at his signal, the crowd at the far end quietened till the only sounds to be heard were the fires. They burned brighter and brighter as the flames licked their snaking tongues to the topmost wood. The sparks flew high, and the cracking and popping filled the now deepening dusk. A column of puffing smoke rose majestically from each blaze, since there was no wind to speak of. The wood smells were unmistakable as damp fiery debris floated into the air around their cheery brightness.

Anticipation was palpable, an edgy strain circling all around. Aran just knew something fantastic was about to occur. Then, as though no mortal person started it, a different thrumming rippled around him. From somewhere he couldn't see, the low beat of the skin drums rumbled through the air—sending an even deeper expectancy over the throng. Eventually, when the tension had become almost unbearable, the faraway crowd silently parted and from out of the inky blue dusk came the strangest, most alarming figure he had ever seen. It walked with the body of a man, though the head was a huge stag with glittering rings adorning the twisted full-grown antlers.

It was fantastic!

It towered over the mass of people who parted to allow the figure to be visible by Tuadh.

Aran shared a quick glance with the twins. Fianna looked beside herself with glee. Brian all but hopped in his enthusiasm, as well. Nobody else grinned around him, though. Whatever was happening was a serious business to the people of Balbath. He suppressed the smirk that wanted to escape; his stomach flutters of pure exhilaration and expectation.

At the far end of the fire corridor, the figure stopped in all its splendour.

Fianna gasped alongside and he felt her trembling fingers clutch at his cloak. Her eyes glittered. Though it was an unearthly looking figure, he knew it was a real live man underneath the strange helmet. Mapon was long gone, but he'd said his acolyte would remain and what a substitute he was. The figure was magnificent. In the tense hush around him, he truly appreciated the difference between seeing something similar in 3D on a screen, and what he now experienced in real live, seeing, smelling, touching... living.

Callum's interactive story was incredible.

He realised that he'd actually forgotten about it being a story, being so drawn into the life at Balbath. Right that moment, he was so glad to be experiencing it.

The druid acolyte carried a strange staff, not unlike Mapon's, but this one had a shining silvery animal head atop the shaft. Huge twisting antlers made it easy for him to recognise the head as that of a full antlered stag, which matched the figure's magnificent headdress. The staff-top glittered malevolently in the firelight as the acolyte held it aloft, the weight needing both his hands to hold it high. The billowing robe he wore trailed around as he headed for the fire corridor with long strides.

When the druid's footfall passed the furthest away fire, a carnyx shrieked its terrifying resonance alongside Aran, notes that lingered in the gloom. The tension amongst the multitude was so powerful he felt it ripple through him. It wasn't a frightening feeling: more of an extreme exhilaration. Any of these objects—staff, headdress or carnyx—would be incredible evidence to take back to Callum. How could that happen though?

Without looking down, he became aware of Caitlinn who'd slipped from her mother's grip. Sneaking in between him and Fianna the little girl bristled with anticipation. Orla nodded her approval when he glanced her way to indicate he was aware of her daughter. When the last resonance of the carnyx could be heard no longer, the acolyte's voice replaced it from that furthest away fire, carrying mournfully up into the cloudless, now star-studded navy sky.

"Cernunnos, Lord of Darkness..."

Brian nudged Aran in the ribs as he mouthed, "Cernunnos strikes again." His toothy grin shone white in the flickering firelight.

"Shut up and listen!" Aran whispered in his friend's ear, wanting to be respectful.

The druid intoned a deep boom across the moonlight.

"Go with thanks. Yet come with blessings. With the mother-earth, Brighde, bring energy to our fires."

The sounds of his chanting sent creepy shudders through Aran. Fianna dug her nails into his arm, her trembling transferring right through the fabric of his tunic. Caitlinn snuggled in even closer to him when the druid slowly paced his way up through the fire passageway, his eerie incantation increasing in volume as he walked towards them. Lamenting the passing of the dark winter moons his dirge was now addressed to Brighde, the name sounding a bit like the word bride—the name Aran knew to be the mother earth goddess. The acolyte came to a stop in front of the chief and his elders, and thumped the bottom of his staff to the ground.

So close now, Aran could see the mouth and chin of the mask had been cleverly cut away to allow the druid's voice to be heard clearly. The man's fierce eyes stared from eye sockets that had also been carved out. A soft hush came from the gathering then they all started to intone very softly in unison after he began to chant again.

"Healing fires. Burn brightly. Burn! Inflame us with your fiery strength. Bring us forth your fruitful blossoms. Let your sun shine brightly on us."

The chant repeated itself as the trainee druid's arms opened wide, first pointing dramatically to the right and then to the left. At the far end, the crowd parted. Still chanting, some of them moved off to the left and others to the right behind the fires leaving the far end of the walkway opposite Tuadh totally empty.

Aran looked around him. Everyone chanted quietly with only the smallest of children not joining in. Pretending to know the words Aran mouthed silently. Looking at Fianna and Brian he was thankful to see they tried to do the same. Better not to look too suspicious since it looked like they ought to know the words.

When the tribespeople were all settled well behind the fires, the high ranking warriors of the tribe came out and drove their spears into the ground, purposely set closely together like a barrier, alongside the staff of the druid. The line of weapons made a wall in front of Tuadh.

The people no longer chanted solemnly. Their pace had quickened, the verse growing louder and louder till it became a deafening roar. Yet, again, the sound of the shrieking carnyx stopped its momentum.

Into the immediate and dead silence came another disturbingly strange noise. Through the darkness, from beyond the rise at the far end of the training ground, came the loudest protest of bellowing animals that Aran had ever heard. The yelling of the farmers was impressive as they herded the poor beasts into a long funnel at the far end of the fire passage, a funnel created by a wall of warriors. The animals, clearly terrified of the flames and smoky smells ahead of them, lowed and snorted and bucked as they tried to evade their fate.

Standing in front of his staff, the druid's voice roared above their din.

"Brighde, mother goddess, giver of life, purify our animals and bring bountiful fruit. Bring your sun's energy to them through our conflagration."

The crowd repeated the chant three times then stopped. They hushed again and waited for him to finish his entreaty. This time the druid's voice was different. Not a chant any more as a druid, but the warning of a mortal man.

"This Beltane must be different, people of Balbath. Let your animals be sacrificed again rather than yourselves."

The crowd's low moan was eerie. All around them Aran and the twins could feel the alarm of the people of Balbath…though they could also see determination in their faces. Were the animals going to be sacrificed on these fires? Aran felt Caitlinn burrow in closer to his leg.

"Are they going to burn these poor cows, Aran?" Fianna whispered in his ear.

Aran's head shaking was her only reply as the druid returned to his prayers. In actual fact, he hadn't a clue what was about to happen.

"Let these healthy animals aid us to fight our foe as they did last Lughnasadh." After the druid warned another time, he walked to one end of the spears and gestured to the people ranged behind the fires on that side, his arms waving towards the sky in a wide circular movement.

His silent signal didn't make any sense to Aran. It still made no sense when the druid walked to opposite end of the spears and made the same gestures.

Returning to his staff, his arms and stag's head

rose skywards in open supplication. His voice reached epic strength as he bawled a prayer to the heavens.

"Oh, mighty Taranis, from your realm above, give our animals your blessing!"

On the last word, the corral of warriors holding back the cows began to split open. The first of the animals was lashed into movement, forced to launch itself down the avenue of fire towards the druid. The thwacking of birch switches, and the cries of farmers alongside the terrified beast, kept it in motion as it howled and screeched through the fire corridor. The rest of the animals surged forwards into the walkway on the hooves of the first. Running alongside the lowing beasts, to keep them in order, the farmers kept up their hollers.

It was like a mini-earthquake as the cows thudded their way up the glowing orange and red channel. Aran watched the people of Balbath kneel down at their place behind the fires as the beasts proceeded through the fire corridor. The tribespeople touched both hands to the earth below them to feel the pounding of the beasts. Women pulled down some now screaming and howling infants as the great charging of hooves rocked the soil beneath them, the reverberations rippling below the whole arena. Aran felt Caitlinn pull him down, Fianna and Brian following suit mimicking the tribespeople, since the elders alongside him had knelt to the ground as well.

The terrified cattle reached Tuadh's end of the fire corridor. One by one, they hurtled themselves right or left when they were confronted by the line of spears. Once they had turned, they loped away from the crowds to disappear out into the darkness, where other warriors waited ready to quieten them. Aran understood the significance of the druid's arm gestures now. The druid had been ensuring the space was cleared for the beasts' exit.

When rounded up, the terrified cattle would be taken back to their enclosures.

As the last few animals started their charge, a huge and totally deafening roar went up from the crowd, drowning out the thunder of the cows as the people heralded the end of their cleansing ceremony. The few cows that remained bucked and swerved, here and there, trying to run off but were completely distracted by the human clamour around them.

One bewildered animal escaped the handlers and swivelled between the last two fires instead of completing the journey along the whole fire corridor. Terrified shrieks rent the air as the beast trampled over two men in the front row, pounding them into the ground, smashing limbs to pulp as the creature blasted headlong for the darkness beyond the kneeling people. Panic set in as the throng scattered in all directions away from the snorting and crazy beast. Not knowing which way to go in its headlong flight, it constantly changed direction.

"Flee!" Orla cried as the beast whirled towards them.

Aran felt his cloak yanked back as he leapt to his feet, the warrior behind him dragging him away. Brian's shout indicated much the same was happening to him as he, too, cried out.

"Run, Fianna!"

Caitlinn whimpered in front of Fianna, too transfixed to even get to her feet. Scooping her up by the shoulders Fianna whirled the little girl out of the animal's path, throwing her aside like a Frisbee and straight into the arms of a warrior who rushed to help them. Her back now to the animal, Fianna began to run but she'd only taken a couple of steps when its head pounded into her, pitching her high into the air like a rag doll before it charged off into the now cleared space around her.

Fianna thumped to the ground.

Chapter Thirteen

"Fianna!" Brian shrieked, rooted to the spot.

He watched Aran rush over to an unresponsive and completely motionless Fianna. Slumping to his knees, Aran grasped her wrist.

Caitlinn howled; her reaction to what happened having just set in, yet Orla's scream nearly outdid her daughter's as she rushed over to the warrior who had caught the little girl. Tuadh, and a bundle of others, set off after the terrified animal to make sure it didn't trample any more tribespeople.

Brian wailed when he eventually reached his sister. "Fianna! Tell me you're still alive or Callum will never forgive me."

"She's still alive. Her pulse is quite strong." Aran sounded sure of it as he glanced up to him, but Brian noted that his mate kept two fingers in place to check another time.

Orla came gasping over to them, a sobbing Caitlinn clutching her like grim death. "Fianna, you have saved the life of my daughter since she would surely be dead but for your quick thinking." Her voice rose upwards to the stars above as she implored, "Brighde! Earth-mother! I plead with you to make this girl well since she has saved my child."

The chief's hearth-wife moaned her way through more prayers to the earth-mother as Brian watched Aran gently feel Fianna's upper arm bones to see if there were any obvious fractures. He was no paramedic, but he'd watched enough TV programmes to know Fianna shouldn't be moved till she'd been thoroughly checked. As Aran's hands moved down

Fianna's forearm, she regained consciousness, her eye-lids fluttering open.

"Fianna!" Brian pleaded. "Can you tell us if you think you've broken anything?"

"Don't know," she croaked, her pupils rolling a little as she adjusted her focus.

Brian realised he was bent so close she must be able to see his tonsils.

"Can you wiggle your fingers? Try this hand first." Aran touched her right hand. She managed to move all of them, thumb included. "Okay. That's good. Now let me raise your arm at the elbow."

Her right arm was certainly not broken since there was no protest as Brian watched Aran manoeuvre it about very carefully, ensuring the rotations of her elbow and shoulder were comfortably easy. Then Aran tried her left one. No problems. By then she was struggling to sit up, protesting that she wasn't really hurt at all. Aran made her lie down again till he checked her legs and ankles. Since all the sockets seemed to rotate without any screeching of pain on Fianna's part Aran stopped his examination.

She was talking well, so Brian knew her breathing wasn't affected. He bent down and felt all around her neck and shoulders. Nothing seemed to hurt her. That was good wasn't it?

"Let me up! I'm fine," she moaned, but through embarrassment rather than pain. A little crowd had gathered around them.

Nothing was going to stop her from sitting up.

"The fuzziness in my head is disappearing," she whispered as he felt all around his twin's head and neck. Fairly sure all was well; he helped her to her feet.

Once standing, Fianna gingerly rubbed her backside.

"You are hurt?" Orla still wept.

"A sore bottom, but nothing's broken." Fianna croaked again, and tested all around her buttock area. "Is Caitlinn all right?"

"Yes. Thanks to you. You have saved her life, tonight."

"Is my daughter well?" Tuadh's voice bellowed as usual when he thrust his way through the little crowd. Pulling Caitlinn out of Orla's arms, his hug was fierce.

Orla now grinned, her tears spent. "By the goodness of the earth-mother, they are both safe from harm."

The chief's hand patted Fianna's shoulder, his respect clear in the unusual smile on his face.

"My heartfelt thanks go to you for saving my little daughter. She is as dear to me as all my children are. You have the heart of a warrior, young woman of the Durris Taexali."

Tuadh's voice was husky, full of an emotion Brian had thought he wasn't capable of. After another brief hug for Caitlinn, the chief was back to business.

"Now that I know you are both well, the next rites must begin."

Brian was surprised when Fianna dared to ask the chief a question. "The men who were trampled? Are they badly hurt?"

"You have concern for those men?" Tuadh sounded taken aback that Fianna should think of them. "They will live. They both have broken lower limbs but with the bounty of our earth-mother, they will not limp. Now we must move on and put this behind us. We must complete our ceremonies."

Brian put his arm round Fianna's shoulders, seriously pleased with his sister, maybe for the first time ever. "You were absolutely ace, Fianna. I'm so proud of you." he beamed, though he whispered in her ear, not quite ready to make a huge public declaration quite yet.

"Warrior Aran!" Tuadh beckoned, back to normal. "You will remain with me for the rest of our Beltane rites. Take your place beside Seonagh and follow me."

His order issued the chief strode off, a magnificent figure in his fine tunic, his thick torque glinting in light shed from his firebrand. The elders trooped after him.

Aran darted a hasty look at him. Brian knew Aran had no choice in the matter. Tuadh expected Aran to join the group of adults.

"You need to look after Fianna. Make sure she's okay."

Brian nodded but then blurted out, "Should we be separated? Aren't we best to stay together?"

Fianna shrugged away from his shoulder grip, looking pretty certain. "I'm confident our armbands will warn us of real mortal danger. Look what we've done already in terms of death-defying exploits, without any warning messages. Besides maybe it's time you took centre stage, Brian. You've still got to survive some dicing with death."

Though she was joking, Aran only had time for a nod before he scurried towards Seonagh who beckoned him to catch up.

Brian stared as Aran caught up with the file of elders following Tuadh. The chief strode between two rows of warriors standing at attention, their spears forming a colonnade. Illuminated by the torchlight of the warriors, the elders glittered in their finery—torques gleaming and arm bands glinting on bare arms. When Tuadh reached the end of the warrior escort column, Brian could just make out the imposing figure of the druid stepping from the side to head the line up, his tall staff held aloft. Gradually they all disappeared into the darkness towards the forest that stood to the north, beyond the plateau and the training ground.

Brian sighed. Whatever was about to happen to Aran wasn't something he was going to share. He looked to where Fianna waited with Orla and Caitlinn. His twin rubbed her butt cheeks and had that look on her face that always meant she found something painful but was determined not to wimp about it. He grinned when he noticed her stroking strands of little Caitlinn's hair back from her face. Being proud of his sister was quite a weird feeling.

A shepherding of children snaked their way back into the settlement, some of the stripling warriors flanking them. Orla led him and Fianna to the large roundhouse where they'd eaten the evening before.

Maga came forward. "Come and sit by me. I am in charge of this children's gathering tonight since Seonagh is with the adult warriors."

"Are you staying here, Orla?" Fianna asked.

Orla settled Caitlinn down by the fireside. "Nay, Fianna. It is my duty to check on the warriors who were wounded by the rampaging cow, but it would please me very much if you will take care of Caitlinn? That is, if you feel well enough?"

Brian was pretty sure that had to be some kind of an honour.

"I feel fine and I'm very pleased to look out for

Caitlinn." Fianna bent down to the little girl. "You'll be happy here with me, won't you?"

Caitlinn's answer was a great big hug. Brian noted the wince on his twin's face. Though her bones hadn't been broken, he now reckoned her bruising was on more than her well-padded butt cheeks.

"Why isn't Seonagh here?" Fianna asked after Orla had scurried away out the roundhouse door.

"Seonagh's time has come to join the ceremony tonight, for the remainder of the Beltane rites.

"For the usual rites?" Brian tried not to seem dumb, yet he wanted Maga to tell him more about what would happen to the adults.

"Seonagh is now able to join the warrior branded at the Sacred Grove. What she does will be very solemn but we can celebrate here in a cheerful way, as can the other children of the tribe." Her grin indicated which she preferred.

Brian wasn't sure what she meant, his question blunt. "There are other gatherings only of children, in other roundhouses?"

Maga seemed surprised he'd asked. "Aye, indeed. We have many children at Balbath. We cannot all gather in one roundhouse."

"What can I do to help?" Fianna was eager to get started. Brian knew by her tone of voice just how much his sister reined in her curiosity.

"Before we feast, we challenge!" Maga's eyes glowed in the flickering firelight.

Brian groaned, his gut telling him he'd be rubbish at their challenges. Playing childish games while Aran was doing adult stuff wasn't funny. Leaving Balbath to go back home right away sounded just perfect—but they weren't together. His thoughts turned glum.

He didn't dare press the ejector seat since he wasn't in the least hint of danger. Thinking how to avoid any roundhouse capers, a sudden brainwave sloshed him, his goofy grin hard to suppress.

"Are you sure you're all right, Fianna? Don't you think you should rest for a bit? You might be concussed," he said, hoping against hope she'd say she needed to lie down. Then he'd have an excuse to get away.

"I'm fine." Her glares meant she was now bothered by his over concern. "Don't bug me. No worries. Okay?"

Brian made a back-off face. "I was just asking. Keep your hair on."

Maga clapped her hands for silence, the children gradually quietening down. "Let the challenges begin!"

Thumping of hands on the earthen floor was thunderous, the children making a deafening sort-of drum roll for a few seconds, though at Maga's signal they halted.

"Who states the first challenge?" Her gaze roamed the room.

A tall boy around Brian's age stood up. "I challenge Duhlain."

"Duhlain?" Maga asked. "Do you accept Dughall's challenge?"

Duhlain looked ecstatic about it as he leapt up to his feet. "I accept."

"So be it," Maga decreed. She scanned down the seated children, her gaze stopping at one particular boy. "Torcull will judge."

Brian nudged Fianna, whispering in her ear, "Do you know what they're about to do?"

The tiniest of headshakes was her response.

Duhlain looked confident as he faced his opponent in a space that lay cleared, well away from the fireside. Brian watched carefully. After a short nod of acknowledgement, each contestant to the other, the boys balanced on evenly spread feet. Torcull approached and stood between the two contestants, facing Maga. Gradually Torcull back paced till only his outstretched arm separated the challengers. The drawing of his arm high into the air was the signal to begin. Immediately, both boys leapt forward to grip each other by the shoulders.

It took only a few moves for Brian to see that the challenge was a wrestling match.

Soon the competitors were locked together in an almost impossible position. The shouted names of both wrestlers echoed around the room as first one, and then the other, gained some advantage—all the assembled children encouraging on their favoured combatant. One particular boy cruelly taunted Duhlain and urged Dughall to make some dirty moves, his jeering echoed by a minority who sprang up at a simple nod and joined him. Brian watched the boy sensing the bully in him.

"Garath." Maga named the nasty lad. "Be seated. Be fair, or do not comment at all. The same goes for the rest of you who seek to dishonour."

Brian turned his attention back to the two boys grappling together on the hard earthen floor. They were good, though their moves were very simple. The referee rarely needed to intervene since both seemed to follow clear rules. Eventually a particular neck clutch ended in deadlock. By then both he and Fianna were bawling for Duhlain to win.

Torcull, the judge, held up his hand for silence. "As judge I say Dughall is the winner because he has had three successful holds out of five. Does anyone doubt my wisdom?"

"Dughall, Dughall, Dughall." The assembled children all accepted the wisdom of the judge as they chanted. Duhlain grinned, a bit out of puff, even though he wasn't the victor.

"Don't you mind not winning?" Fianna seemed amazed at his cheerfulness.

Duhlain slumped down beside her. "Nay, I make no mind, Fianna. We wrestle every other day, and every attempt I creep closer to winning. I thought it would be this time, but the gods have willed that I train harder."

He lay back on the ground, sweating hard as Maga continued. "Dughall is seasons older than Duhlain, though soon Duhlain will have the better power because he grows from sapling to strong tree much faster than Dughall."

As she spoke, a few other boys stood up to challenge each other. Maga chose the pairs of wrestlers and the new judges each time. It was satisfying to see the opponents were well matched.

A good bout just completed Garath stood up and called over to Maga, "I challenge the new boy."

Brian's groan fortunately couldn't be heard above the boy's boasting.

Garath continued his jeer. "We have seen no evidence yet of how well trained they are at his settlement. I challenge him to anything of his choice."

He inwardly grunted even more. Anything?

Garath's little cohort of followers chanted his name, feeding the bully's confidence.

He had a feeling he knew what he could and couldn't do but wasn't going to boast about it. "Anything?" He faced Garath head on.

"Did I not just say that?"

Garath advanced on him in a threatening manner, but Brian refused to give the boy any satisfaction. He determined not to show any fear, even though Garath was of a much sturdier build.

"Two challenges!" Brian declared after he got to his feet. Not a hint of doubt showed in his face; he projected only sheer confidence and bravado.

Fianna looked up at him as if he'd lost his mind.

"Two challenges? The new boy is ambitious. Name them." Garath's sneer around the room dared all to doubt his superiority.

"First, a bout as conducted by the other challengers tonight." Brian folded his arms across his chest.

Garath rudely interrupted before Brian could continue, his scorn even more pronounced. "You really intend to take up my test? You, with your puny strength? Ha!"

He didn't allow himself to get riled. "If I win the bout of the body, you must take up my second challenge of the head." His index finger tapped his forehead to emphasise his point.

"What can you mean by that?" Garath's mocking encouraged the room to support him, though fewer looked as though they wanted to.

"My second challenge will be music, or storytelling."

Brian felt a lot more confident when the brash colour receded from Garath's cheeks. Then the bully's feet shifted around uncomfortably, his scan of the room furtive.

It was exactly how he wanted the boy to feel; guessing that all Garath could do was make physical threats. He was confident that very few in a tribe would have been taught an instrument, or would have learned the tribal stories by rote.

"Do you accept the double challenge, Garath?"

Brian was sure that Maga struggled to contain a smile. Having her on his side would be a big bonus.

"I accept. I will easily win." Garath's grunt was nasty as he looked all around him, his eyes challenging the gathering to say anything against him.

Brian sweated wildly while he readied for the bout. What if he couldn't outmanoeuvre this disgusting bully after all? His face might end up like mashed pulpy strawberries. His freckles might be so squashed together he'd look like one huge splodge. He felt terrified, but he loathed and detested bullies. Removing his torque and his tunic, he carefully placed them down beside Maga, desperately wishing he looked cool about the whole affair.

Thank Taranis he hadn't eaten yet because the food would be fighting to exit right about now. He glanced down at his bare torso and remembered his shiny armband. It would be impossible to wrestle wearing it. Garath would use it as a means to overpower him. Brian's thoughts were frantic but there was no time for long thinking. Garath was already in place, his torso bare.

He stared at his twin willing her to help him. Callum had told them to wear their armbands all the time, but he'd also said to do the right thing when it cropped up during the story. It had to come off.

On Fianna's positive nod, he removed the

gleaming silver and put it safely into her hands.

"Go to it, brother." Her confidence radiated from her twinkling eyes. "My money's on you any day. That bully braggart doesn't know what he's in for. You give him it good, brother mine!"

Brian knew Garath's muscles were packaged round a stupid empty brain with little more else than a loud mouth as he faced him in the cleared wrestling space.

Maga chose the judge and the bout began. In no time at all, Brian found he was held in an arm lock he knew he'd have difficulty breaking without coming out of it needing a plaster cast. Better to give up on this first one were dismal thoughts as he rubbed his shoulders, the judge having ordered them to separate. Garath incited his audience to call support for him, his raised palms making them clap and shout his name.

While Brian regained his breath, he was pleased to note that only a few followed Garath's lead. Of course, the opposite side of the coin was that no-one rooted for him.

He almost lost ground in the second round as well, Garath's strength nearly too much for him. On the point of almost giving in, a rousing cheer encouraged him. Fianna's bellow was fit to beat Tuadh in volume.

"Come on, Brian. Use your *Sooyang Do.* Show him you're a brown belt already."

He whipped Garath's feet from under him and was upon him in a blink. A few squirms and he had the advantage. Second round to him. Garath wasn't a happy chappie as he slunk around flexing his shoulders and biceps. The third round threatened to go the other way, Garath's upper body strength much greater. Brian found himself clutched from behind by

Garath's arms till he used a few more of his martial arts strategies, *Sooyang Do* built around defensive moves. Both he and Fianna went to *Sooyang Do.* They were both good but it was one of the few things that he did better than his sister. He was confident about what he'd learned; Fianna often too impetuous.

"Aaie…hah!" His upward arm swing broke apart Garath's flexed arms, thrusting them aside like scrawny little sticks. He whipped around, one fist protecting his face. Hooking his leg behind Garath's knee Brian's reverse swing kick threw his opponent off balance, much to the amazement of the audience because before they could blink Garath was on the ground with him standing triumphantly above him, his foot pinning down Garath's chest. Bully-boy was furious. Garath struggled up complaining to the judge that the new boy had cheated, that he'd made some kind of illegal move.

"You wanted to know how we do it at my home, but now you don't like it when I show you?" Brian now did the taunting. Justifiably, because although Garath was complaining some of the underhand moves the bully had made weren't ones anyone else had used.

Another round ended with him appearing to be outmanoeuvred till he sneaked in a few different defensive strokes. Once again, Garath tumbled to the ground, this time face down, one arm held firmly to his back. Their judge ordered them to separate declaring another win for Brian.

Garath was even more furious when he stood up. Without warning two fists pummelled into Brian's stomach. He bent doubled over, the blood draining from his face.

"Garath! Leave him be." Maga rushed to help him. "Do you want to stop?"

Only one more round was needed to have a clear winner declared.

"Never!" He was adamant he'd not let this bully get the better of him. "I'll finish him this time," he vowed straightening up his aching body.

The decider went on forever. As soon as Brian got the advantage, Garath managed break the grip. Garath pulled some sneaky moves Brian knew must be totally illegal, though they happened so quickly the judge didn't pick up on them. His stomach really ached and he was tiring fast. There could be no unobtrusive moves now. He took up his fighting stance.

"Come on, Brian," Fianna shouted into the now deadly silence around him. "You can do it."

"Aiee…" Brian's cries were fearsome as his hands whipped in front of Garath's face, intimidating but not contacting. "Aiee…ha!" Springing forward he hooked his opponent's legs once again, grappling around for a second or two till off balance by the speed, Garath fell like a stone. He had the bully pinned to the ground before the audience could believe it.

"Yes, Brian." Fianna squealed. "You did it. You beat the bully!"

His name echoed around the roundhouse.

Garath snarled, rising to his feet. "You won tonight, but I'll beat you some other time." Sidling away from the fireside, towards the doorway, Garath was followed by a few of his cronies.

"Nay, Garath." Maga was firm. "You will remain. No one leaves tonight without my permission, and you are not granted it."

Brian was glad her word ruled. The children quietened down as Garath and his followers slunk to the back of the room.

"Aren't you forgetting something?" Brian shouted at their backs while he casually pulled his tunic over his head, ignoring his aching stomach muscles and the smell of genuine sweat.

"What?" The question came from one of Garath's spiteful hangers-on.

"Garath agreed to my two challenges," Brian reminded the bully. He fixed his torque around his neck before he took the armband from Fianna and slipped it up his arm.

Maga suppressed a grin. "Will it be the story? Or the music, Garath?"

"You know I cannot make music. Nor can he," Garath accused.

"I make music well enough, though I'd need something to play upon." Brian secretly hoped somebody could produce a harp like Mapon's, but was sure he'd manage a tune on anything they could produce.

One of the older girls stood up. "Old Ailish would not mind the stranger trying the Pipe of Netherdaugh. I know where she keeps it, Maga. Should I fetch it?"

Brian felt interest stir when Maga informed him that old Ailish, Seonagh's grandmother, was keeper of the strange little pipe, though no-one in the tribe had been taught how to play it.

"Aye, bring it to Brian and we will see what he can do with it."

Maga declared a small time of talk around the hearthside while the instrument was collected.

A rounded disc-like instrument was soon popped into Brian's hands. He heaved a sigh of relief knowing he'd be able to get a tune, of sorts, out of it.

It was an ocarina.

"Thank you." Brian nodded to the girl who had carried it so carefully. "I'll look after it well." Turning to Garath he held it aloft. "Can you play this?"

Garath scowled, refusing to answer.

Pulling the pendant cord over his head Brian held out the instrument to admire it before he put it to his lips. Made of polished hardwood it was beautifully carved, inlaid with bright enamels in snaking patterns at the centre of which a green stone glittered. Maybe an emerald? He wasn't sure of the stone but was confident that it was revered by the tribe. It was larger than his own ceramic ocarina, though the finger holes, and what he called the exhaust hole, were similarly placed around the bowl.

The first blow was gentle. A clear deep sound rang free as he removed first one finger then another to test its pitch. Some children clapped to hear the sounds though he hadn't even played a tune. Maga held up her hand for silence.

Into the dead stillness Brian played a tune he knew that was the closest to the kind of Gaelic music he'd heard the bard play the night before. The sounds of the only Gaelic tune he knew—*Brochan lom, tana lom*—filled the air. He played it slowly at first, and then gained in speed when he'd mastered the holes, ending with a fast and furious version that had all the children clapping, drumming their feet and diddle-doodling like Fianna did alongside.

"More, more!" the children squawked when it ended. Brian looked to Fianna for suggestions, his mind suddenly gone blank. His gaze fell on the sneering Garath whose face looked like his scowl was set in concrete. Grinning at Fianna his head bobbed in Garath's direction as he started a new tune. He played… *For he's a jolly good fellow.*

Fianna giggled like mad. The others in the roundhouse didn't get the joke at all, but it didn't stop the little ones jumping up and down in glee.

After he entertained them with a few more songs, Maga stood up and declared that it was time to eat. This went down even better than Brian's music. The older girls set to, ladling soup from the cauldrons into bowls, some of which they set aside to cool for the smallest children. Chopped chunks of bread and pre-cut meat were passed around along with wooden goblets of water. After all were served, Maga held her hand up for silence and then solemnly thanked the goddess Rhianna for the food.

Fianna stared down at her bowl. "What do you think it is?"

His bread had been dipped in as soon as Maga had given the command to get tucked in, his answer around a huge wet mouthful. "Do you actually care? I'm hungry enough to eat a hairy mammoth, except they were extinct even now. Tastes like vegetable broth with bits of yummy meat floating in it."

Everyone gobbled and chatted, sometimes staring down the hearthside at him which made Brian self-conscious yet amazingly self-assured at the same time, which was weird. Hoots of enjoyment echoed around the room till a sudden cry made a totally different kind of sound.

"Flee!"

Chapter Fourteen

"Oh, my Taranis, or whoever." Aran wasn't sure how he felt.

Though excited, almost beyond measure, he also felt weird. Standing beside Seonagh he shuddered at the scene in front of him, having a good inkling of what was about to happen. His staff held aloft, the druid acolyte chanted into the night air. When the acolyte stopped before a huge tree, a warrior stood at his side with a flickering torch to ensure more illumination. Aran realised that the space had been created by man; it was not natural to have so empty an area in the heart of the woods. He stood mesmerised as the young druid knelt before the ancient oak, its silhouette distinctive against the moonlit sky.

Seonagh tugged at his arm to make him kneel down along with the rest of the assembled crowd. The druid's mournful drone continued, a second warrior stepping forward to flank the acolyte, both angling their torches to the bole of the tree. Aran gulped, biting down his surprise. Surely they weren't going to set the tree on fire? As the flaming brands got closer to the bark the breath stopped in his throat. The trunk of the tree bore the unmistakable shape of an animal-man. Talk about wood carvings?

Totally fantastic and very scary.

"Cernunnos?" His question was the merest whisper.

The body was a seated man, the head was once again a magnificent stag, yet the face was a very frightening human one, the penetrating eyes staring out at all who viewed it. The carving was so cleverly done that the antlers grew out from the tree itself, the whittling of the figure sunk deep into the trunk – yet the tree still looked very much alive as the branches above the figure shushed in the faint wind and the movement of the night air.

A soft hooting and the faraway sound of a wolf howl accompanied the druid's chanting. The hair on Aran's neck began to prickle as the man's sounds grew more and more animal like as he pleaded for Cernunnos to hear his most loyal worshippers. The crowd of adults didn't move a whit when the druid got to his feet once more, to step to the side of the tree. All eyes followed the druid's passage as he approached a stone table that Aran hadn't noticed before, since no torch-light had yet fallen on that area. Now the two warriors stood sentinel at each side of it, their torch brands silvering the glittering granite surface.

A terrified squealing came from behind Aran. He heard the approach into the clearing of one of the tribesmen who led a loudly protesting sheep, the farmer literally dragging the beast before the table. Aran's breath hitched. He felt his increased heartbeat begin to thud in his ears. The prickles he'd felt earlier were nothing compared to what he now felt slide down his back.

Sacrifice!

He was about to witness a real live sacrifice right in front of him, yet the terrifying thing was not the poor animal's approaching death. Aran lived on a farm. He was well used to animals being bred for slaughter.

What if the animal was only the first kill of the night's sacrifice? Would humans be sacrificed too?

Those skulls in the chief's roundhouse? Had they been sacrificed at this very same table? He was a stranger to this tribe. Could he be the next victim after the terrified animal whose squealing meant it had probably guessed its fate? Animals were like that. They acutely sensed imminent death.

Oh, Cernunnos... or Taranis... or Brighde... or whoever.

Brian and Fianna might never know what had happened to him. The earth trembled beneath him, worrying him more than a little, till Aran realised it was no earthquake—it was his own knees quivering and that made him shudder even more.

The druid's voice level increased when the farmer lifted the little sheep onto the altar, its head dashing back and forth as it writhed. A swift twisting of a cord had it tied down in an instant.

Oh, friggin' heck! Aran whimpered inside. Yet, some part of his paralysed brain weirdly applauded the speed and skill of the warrior's knot craft.

Unsheathing a large bladed knife the druid held it to the night sky beseeching the lord of the darkness to aid the fertility of the tribe and of their animals.

"Accept our offering, Cernunnos," he screeched. "Let the blood of our sacrifice be our season's strength."

Swiping the knife across the animal's throat the druid killed it instantly. One of the warriors drew forward a shining metal bowl from under his cloak to catch some of the life blood now spurting from the neck. Before handing it to the druid he bowed his head over it.

Aran shuddered. Were they going to drink it? Oh, yuck! What if they asked him to do it too? Or what if they drew him out to lead him to the table? Absolutely horrible thoughts flittered through his mind. The torque round his neck began to throttle him as he watched the druid lift the bowl skywards invoking the powers of the earth-mother to waken and hear their pleas. Then, just as the druid threw wide the arm holding the bowl, scattering the blood over the kneeling crowd, Aran looked up just at the wrong possible moment.

Some of the animal's blood splashed down onto his cheek as the droplets landed all around him, landing on the still bent heads of the tribespeople while they chanted their own prayers, adding to the imploring noise of the druid. When the smell of the blood hit his nostrils, Aran felt nauseous, right there in the forest, in front of all these people who attended these rites regularly, and who didn't flinch at all from its cruelty and horror. Then the sudden uproar from behind made him even more alarmed as a guard charged into the clearing, hollering for all he was worth.

Tuadh leapt up, brandishing his freed axe in an instant, his eyes even wilder than usual as he looked round at him.

Flippin' Taranis! Was Tuadh about to behead him?

"Romans attack Balbath!"

The assembled crowd rose up, the chanting abruptly ceasing.

"The Romans are heading for Balbath? We will be besieged."

"How can there be a Roman raid, at night?" Tuadh roared at the young warrior. "We trebled the guard beyond Deer's Den. How can this happen?"

"They are approaching us from Oschie Hill, from

the sea. The clear moonlight is giving them all the guidance they need to cross into our terrain," the man shouted.

"They must have come directly from their ships. That has to be why we have had no warning of their approach till now." Tyrnan's voice rang out across the clearing.

"Auxiliary forces from their Classis of vessels?" Tuadh cried.

"They'll be intending to join up with their main forces after dawn." Aran interrupted, having set aside the fanciful notions of Tuadh taking his axe to him.

"Can the children still flee the settlement if we hurry?" Tyrnan was already over beside Seonagh though his question was directed at the news bearer.

Aran was horrified: the cruelty of the sacrifice gone in an instant and replaced with a different dismay. The adults had taken ages to get to the clearing in the woods.

What was happening to the twins? He was supposed to look after them!

***

The young guard bawled again. "Flee! Get out of here, now!"

Brian grabbed Fianna, who in turn grabbed Caitlinn. The youth's urgency put the fear of death into all the children in the roundhouse as they scrambled to their feet.

The guard's sweeping arm movements urged greater speed. "Collect only your cloaks, if they are in here. Flee the settlement by the nether. Once outside, run up the hill towards the Sacred Grove."

Panic set in as the children rushed from the

fireside and ran towards the door, squealing and hollering.

Maga cried out over the clamour of alarm. "Why must we leave?"

"The Romans attack Balbath. Collect all little ones Maga. We must flee the settlement. They approach now, but you must hurry, or we will not get the children away."

The guard was barely older than Seonagh, dread showing on his face as he rushed a whole group of the smaller children over to the doorway.

"By the nether?" Maga gathered one toddler into her arms, and grabbed another by the wrist to drag him along.

"It must be by the nether. The Roman file has circled the hill and now approaches the main entrance to Balbath. The Roman raiders are too numerous for the warriors we have posted at the main gate." The guard's voice disappeared into the night as he fled with a bunch of children.

Brian's heart thudded against his ribs as though it were desperate to get out.

Maga yelled at his twin. "Fianna. Look after Caitlinn. Go. Collect your cloaks and any furs you can carry. I must make sure the babies are out from the other roundhouses. Leave by the nether."

Her disappearing back jerked them into immediate action. Children still scattered all around them, some dragging their mantles behind them, having scrabbled around the pile of cloaks in the corner to find their own. Brian scooped up some furs from the fireside while Fianna picked up the last of the cloaks. Grabbing Caitlinn up into his arms, she snuggled into the furs. The little girl looked terrified, yet she didn't even whimper. They rushed out of the roundhouse as fast as they could but it was to find no children near them. None at all, though they could hear plenty of screaming from the direction of the latrine area.

"We must get out of here," Brian shouted at Fianna who looked as lost as he felt. "But Seonagh didn't show us this nether place when we toured the settlement."

"Brian!" Fianna squealed, looking behind him. "There are Romans inside the main entrance."

The pounding feet and the noises of jingling metal armour were unmistakable. Clashing of swords, metal hammering on metal, squeals of agony and bloodthirsty cries rent the air as the guards continued to defend the now almost empty settlement. Taking to their heels brother and sister fled in the direction of the midden heap.

"Brian!" Fianna's shout was cut short as she fell headlong into the dust, the pile of cloaks having tripped her up. The thudding of heavy feet drowned out Brian's agonised squeal as he twisted down to help his sister, little Caitlinn still clinging to his neck.

A dark shadow loomed behind him…

***

Aran pelted after Seonagh and the warriors of Tuadh, male and female, as they bolted down the hill and back towards the settlement. The older and more infirm of the tribe remained up in the Sacred Grove since it was the safest place for them to hide. As they got closer to the settlement, Aran could see files of kids fleeing from a side entrance that he hadn't noticed before.

"They escape by the nether," Seonagh shouted.

"The guards have managed to get the children out of the settlement."

Tuadh separated his warriors, his orders barked in typical fashion. He sent half of them to the main entrance, and the others to enter by the gate the children were fleeing from.

The youngsters were shepherded up the hill, mothers looking for children and *vice versa*. Aran and Seonagh sped past a long line desperately seeking Fianna, Brian, Orla and Caitlinn.

The twins were not among those who'd got out of the hillfort.

Frantic, Aran checked again, up and down, hollering out their names into the general hullabaloo, since the night was full of cries of desperation. Callum had made him promise to look after them. Though how could he when he didn't even know where they were?

Should he terminate the experience? Should he press the 'ejector seat' clock icon? He didn't know if it would work for all of them if they weren't together. He couldn't risk it. He couldn't go back alone and leave them stranded.

Should he press the question mark help button? Loads of questions peppered his mind, yet he couldn't make decisions. He hadn't a clue what to do. Things weren't looking good for Balbath right that moment, but he personally wasn't in immediate danger of being killed. Sure, he could hear the clamour of fighting nearby, though there wasn't a Roman in sight that he could fight.

Good gods! Taranis, Cernunnos or whoever.

He didn't have a weapon—not even his measly little knife, because nothing had been returned to him.

How could he defend himself without a blade of some sort? He had to get back into the settlement, get himself to the armoury and get kitted out. Then he had to find Fianna and Brian and get them out of this precarious situation.

Seonagh was almost beside herself screeching next to him as she reached the walls of the hillfort. "I have to find Caitlinn and Orla. They must still be inside."

Her thoughts were for her own family: it was quite evident she'd forgotten about the twins.

Just inside the nether gate, a small exit behind the latrine area, a woman struggled to support a badly-limping brawny warrior. The wooden staff under his armpit helped a little, yet the man was clearly almost spent with pain. It was one of the warriors who'd been trampled earlier by the stampeding cow, and the woman helping was Orla.

"Where is Caitlinn?" Seonagh cried as she reached her father's hearth-wife.

Orla's answer was feeble; she was so taxed. "She is with Fianna and Brian."

"But they're not outside yet." Aran shouted over the din of confusion and battle that was not so far off. "We double checked all those already out, and they're not among them."

Some of Tuadh's warriors launched in from behind to help Orla, cradling the injured man in their crossed arms. Once they had their patient supported, they carried him out of the settlement. Others helped two older women who struggled to carry someone stretched horizontally in a makeshift litter of a blanket. The effort had really been too great for their frail bodies, yet they'd persisted in getting out the second injured warrior from the cow charge. He, too, was soon whisked away and up the hill.

Seonagh and Orla sped off to the roundhouse where the children had feasted. Aran headed for the armoury, remembering that it wasn't far away: weapons of some kind a must. The sounds of battle deafened his ears, but he knew from the way the noise carried in the night that the action took place in the direction of the main entrance. In no time at all, he'd located a suitable long knife, since the first swords he found were too heavy for him. Then he grabbed up a few small rapier-like knives and a bunch of spears that he could grip tightly because, as Tuadh had ordered, all useable weapons lay in ready piles.

Where to go now was his next question? Where would he find the twins? He raced towards the children's gathering place, yet could see that Orla and Seonagh had had no luck there, because they charged back towards him. The clamour of weapons got even louder, the battle cries of the Celts fierce and terrifying. Aran knew that the senior Balbath warriors must now be defending the main entrance but Brian surely wouldn't have gone there.

A sudden screech rent the air.

Fianna.

Aran knew that particular howl only too well. She wasn't screeching out of fear, but out of sheer fury. Running between two roundhouses he could see her frantically kicking up at a single Roman soldier who was bent over her, his sword poised and ready to strike. Brian dangled from the soldier's back and pounded away at the auxiliary's helmet with his free fist, trying to dislodge it, his other arm a vice around the auxiliary's neck. Little Caitlinn cowered nearby in a huddle of skins and cloaks.

Thank Taranis it was just the one soldier, though he thought it was unusual there was only one Roman auxiliary in the vicinity.

Aran daren't use his spear this time because he'd likely kill Brian or Fianna. Instead, he whipped out the long knife from his pouch. Brandishing it in front of him, he charged forward, shrieking his own challenge. The soldier whirled around, attempting to dislodge Brian as the man forced himself upright to investigate what the howling was behind him, Brian's arm still wrapped around the Roman's neck. Aran watched as Brian slipped off and rolled away, the momentum tipping the auxiliary backwards. Aran lunged with his long knife, the blade heading for the soldier's bare arm.

Th…whomp. Huumm. Twaaang!

This time it was Aran who felt the singing passage of the spear go right past his ear. By Taranis, it was terrifying! The contents of his stomach lurched up as quickly as he'd lunged out with the long knife. Once again, Tyrnan's spear hit the mark, but this time not the ground. The Roman soldier lay pinned to the earth; the spear a direct hit through his throat, having precisely landed between the long earflaps of the helmet. The Roman Auxiliary's death gurgle was a feeble blood-bubbling mutter since the man truly didn't know what had hit him.

Aran slumped to his knees willing himself not to vomit—though he was so close. The soldier beside him, prostrate and pinned to the ground, was likely dead but he couldn't bear to check. A rush of something like gratitude flushed through him because it hadn't actually been his blade that had killed the Roman soldier. Not his. It had been Tyrnan's spear.

What if Tyrnan hadn't turned up? Aran's stomach rebelled for real as he puked up the contents of his stomach with a few violent heaves at the side of the soldier. As the last of the vomit emptied out, he knew he would have driven his long knife into the Roman auxiliary if it meant that Fianna would be safe from the Roman's gladius, the sword now lying alongside the body. Playing in a game, killing the enemy seemed so easy but in real life it was sickening. When he'd stopped heaving, through the fug of his shock, he eventually heard the plea beside him.

"Hurry." Tyrnan urged them all as if nothing of note had happened. "Get away from here."

Adrenalin kicked-in in good time as Aran struggled to his feet. He swiped a hand over his mouth before he passed Fianna one of the spears, and a sharp little knife. He felt in limbo: a place where he imagined all that had just happened. Brian lurched to his feet and picked up the gladius, as though fighting a Roman soldier was an everyday occurrence. It was all incredible.

None of them commented on the fact he'd just heaved his guts up.

Tyrnan scooped up little Caitlinn, and they rushed towards the nether. He followed on still rickety legs. As they approached the exit Seonagh and Orla headed towards them from another direction, their cries of relief and joy a delight to behold when they caught sight of them.

"By Taranis, I am so pleased you are all safe!" Orla bawled her head off.

Only when they were well up the hill did Tyrnan relinquish a silent Caitlinn to her mother's arms, ordering them to rush to the safety of the woods.

"Seonagh and Taexali warrior, Aran!" he cried. "You must defend the people of Balbath who shelter in the Sacred Grove. There may be only a few branded warriors up there, so the care of those up there lies in your hands. Do not fail them."

Tyrnan sped off back down the hill leaving Aran open-mouthed.

Chapter Fifteen

"Sleep, Aran."

Seonagh's command was firm, yet Aran wasn't sure he could do anything but stare.

The Sacred Grove was full of Balbathans, and the druid who still mournfully intoned at the altar—though almost silently. The tribespeople were hushed too, apart from the occasional baby whimper. The flickering fiery brands now pushed into the soil beside the altar, no longer seemed spooky. Aran felt that after what had just occurred he could face anything. Fianna and Brian were also quiet alongside him, the attack on Fianna still too fresh for them to speak of it. All Fianna had said, when he asked if she was okay, was that she was dealing with it. He was finding a lot more to respect about her than he used to. She was handling the surprises on this mystery adventure a lot better than he was, and that scared him. His best mate was surprising him, too, because in Brian's grip was the sharpest sword he'd ever seen. Ready to be used. Brian had said he'd mow down any other Roman who came near his sister and Aran believed him.

Settled down on their spread out cloaks, the occupants of the grove were resigned to await their fate, their expressions from glowering to almost completely blank. They were either too young to help; too old and infirm; or wounded—none of them any use to the warriors defending their settlement down below. He easily empathised with them because he wasn't sure he'd have been any use if asked to join the branded warriors battling at the gates. That Tyrnan had sent Seonagh to guard the grove made him feel better. Although also a branded warrior, she wasn't in the fray down at the settlement either.

Seonagh had taken the first watch near the entrance to the grove, having strategically spread out some of the remaining female warriors and the eldest children around the whole area on guard duty.

"I will rouse you and the tamhas when it is your time to guard," she told him. "Sleep if you can."

Sleep didn't happen—except maybe for the youngest of the tribe of Balbath. Aran and the twins took their allotted places when the guard was changed. They were exhausted but no more so than all the others in the grove. The night was long but as the first rays of dawn peeped above the trees, Aran heard the faintest noise in the distance. It was no more than the tiniest twig snapping. Reaching over he tapped Seonagh's shoulder. She was napping right next to him at the entry to the grove.

"Someone's coming."

Instantly Seonagh was on her feet, her spear in one hand and her feet balanced for attack but the call of a lapwing had her relaxing so much she lowered the weapon and rubbed her eyes to clear the sleep matter from her lids.

"It is my father."

How she knew it had been his bird call he couldn't be sure but Tuadh and some of his warriors entered the grove.

"You may return now to the settlement," the exhausted chief informed them. "The Roman raid was small; no more than two hundred auxiliary soldiers who were foolish to attack our main entrance. Of course, they had no expectation of us being outside the settlement so the element of surprise was in our favour. My warriors attacking them from both inside and outside confused them. A few fled, but my warriors will rout them out since they have no camp nearby to scurry back to."

"Will they return?" The old woman who asked the question was very distressed; her voice almost a sob.

Tuadh's tone was surprisingly quiet. He looked deadly tired and maybe even dispirited because although his tribe had just won a guerrilla battle of sorts, Aran knew it had only been a small skirmish. "Aye, they will no doubt return with more troops but, with help from our gods, not till another day."

The Romans had mistakenly thought that the moonlit night would aid their progress, but the opposite had happened.

Tuadh explained further. "Some of us entered by the nether gate and drove them out of the settlement. My other warriors awaited them at the hillfort entrance where we forced them down onto the curving floodplain of the river, to the reed beds and soft mud that we normally avoid during the day. We had the Roman auxiliaries encircled and subdued before they realised what was happening to them. It was easy for us to vanquish them when they were knee deep in the mire."

"What of our younger guards?" Seonagh's question was concerned. It was a question Aran had wanted to ask.

Tuadh looked away before answering. He took a deep breath, his voice sounding a bit wobbly. It was the first genuinely distressed emotion Aran had seen the man express.

"Not so well. Many are maimed, others dead defending our gates."

The chief's fingers strayed to the axe hanging from his belt where dark splodges marred the shiny glint of the previous evening. Aran guessed the weapon had been well used.

Although Tuadh sent the tribespeople back to Balbath, Aran had a feeling it would only be for a very short time. If one ship had landed, others would soon follow. He remembered that the Roman Classis, the ships of the Roman Empire, tended to sail together in small fleets. He found his feelings were torn as he trudged back to the hillfort, supporting one of the elderly Balbathans who could hobble, though only just.

Inside him, there was a great excitement over the concept that he might actually see a whole amassed cohort of uniformed Ancient Roman soldiers who manned one of the larger Roman ships: perhaps a bit less than five hundred men. There was also an utter dread in him because what he had recently experienced was the fighting machine that each Roman soldier was trained to be. There had been nothing glorious, or stirring, in seeing that auxiliary soldier attack the twins, or in his gory death.

Brian chewed his lip, his legs swinging off the edge of the low cot where they were all sitting, back in Tuadh's roundhouse. "I'm not sure it's a good idea for us to separate again."

They all agreed on that one.

"Want to pull the plug and go back to Callum?" Aran asked.

"No!" Fianna cried, "It can't be time for us to go yet. I don't know why, but it doesn't seem like the right thing to do, and Callum told us we were good at doing the right thing at the right time."

Brian reminded them again of their tasks. "We've achieved almost all of them now, except the bit about helping those who seem to be the nasty ones."

Fianna's voice came out a bit squeaky. "Yeah. That auxiliary who attacked me was pretty nasty but I don't think we helped him much—except that we sent him to the afterlife."

The reality of the episode really hit home.

"I'm not sure we've learned anything to pass on to the archaeologists and we haven't got any visual evidence either," Fianna eventually broke the awkward silence that had descended.

Brian wriggled a hand down inside his tunic and produced the ocarina. "I still have this." Then he rummaged down under the cot they were sitting on and pulled up the Roman gladius. "And this. Do you think they qualify?"

"I know where the gladius came from but where did you get that?" Aran pointed to the instrument in Brian's hand.

"I think we've got some things to catch up on—like what you were doing before the Romans raided Balbath and how I got this," Brian answered.

Fianna suddenly squeaked alongside. "My armband is heating up my arm!"

Aran felt the same sensation just before the edge of his band pinged open.

"You're not done. The historians are not satisfied, yet." Brian read out the message just in time before the bands snapped shut again. "What's that about?"

"We must still have to find out something special about the people of Balbath that they don't know yet in the twenty-first century."

"Cool! I wanted to stay anyway," Fianna smirked.

One of Mapon's warriors arrived by late-morning with news. Tribespeople congregated outside Tuadh's dwelling to hear him. Aran huddled with the twins not far from the chief.

"A few Roman ships landed at the mouth of the Dee after first light. Hundreds of soldiers disembarked and are now marching towards us." The warrior was still out of puff from his fast gallop to Balbath.

"Have they attacked any of the nearby settlements?" Tuadh paced about.

"Aye. Flames have been seen rising from Connal of the Deemouth's roundhouses."

"Are there survivors?"

"The only one I know of was the messenger I found crossing onto our territory." The man accepted the beaker of bere that was handed to him and then slumped down the low stool placed near him.

"Do the Romans follow the line of the coast?" Tyrnan asked.

The man gulped down a long mouthful. "Nay. The messenger said they were headed inland. They have cut a swathe over the countryside and are heading towards the old Roman road leading to The Mither Tap hillfort."

"That cannot be the soldiers of Severus or Caracalla. They are surely still to the north of us?" Tuadh was confused.

Mapon's druid confirmed it. "These are not the legions of Severus, and not Caracalla either. The troops landed from ships which sailed up from the southern seas."

Tyrnan was furious. "Then we will be trapped

between the two Roman forces."

Aran felt Fianna clutch his cloak. When he looked round her eyes glistened with expectation when she bent in to whisper, "I bet they're coming to Kintore, first."

"How close are they?" Tuadh was agitated, his pacing around restricted by the amount of people around him.

"The first group have just breached the high hill near the standing stones of Clinterty."

Brian nudged in this time keeping their conversation just between the three of them. "Clinterty is near the Tyrebagger Hill, so they're only about six miles away."

"We must evacuate Balbath." Tuadh ordered an immediate withdrawal of all his people.

Tribespeople scurried about collecting what they could before abandoning the hillfort: the whole settlement vacated by the time the sun was high overhead in the sky. From the description given by Mapon's scout, Aran guessed that if the first Roman cohort, perhaps as many as five hundred troops, had already topped the Tyrebagger Hill then they would be approaching Tuadh's territory very soon.

Marching at a rate of four miles an hour with accompanying baggage carts was a doddling pace for a Roman legion but if the men had come from a ship then perhaps there were no baggage carts involved at all, since they would need mules or oxen to pull them. With no extra loads to haul, the cohort could move across the landscape speedily. The day was one with intermittent cloud cover though dry, which meant weather was not a factor which would hamper Roman progress either.

The small Celtic battle chariots from Balbath and some basic open carts were loaded up. Bundles of covers and clothing; meagre food supplies; hens; lambs; were piled as high as possible.

"Look at those." Fianna was awed by the sight. The truly infirm and injured tribespeople were piled on like sardines in a tin, one driver only aboard and the spearman running alongside. The horse handlers led all the other horses and ponies, some of these with small toddlers, older tribespeople and women with babies astride them.

Every possible weapon was collected, including those from the many Roman dead, and removed from the settlement. Adults and children were armed with what they could use and bear the weight of, most of them with many spears apiece, and numerous knives tucked into their belt pouches. As a branded warrior, Aran had been handed a Roman gladius that he wasn't sure he wanted. It burned a hole in his side even though it was in the leather sheath that had been rustled up for it, a similar sheath given to Brian for his sword.

Smaller children carried shortened sharp-tipped spears, and used them as walking sticks to help them keep up the furious pace. The adults bore burdens of portable food and children carried blankets and rugs. Animals were herded alongside them.

"My bundle's sliding."

Brian stepped behind to adjust Aran's sack which was dangling free of his shoulder. Food and rugs were crammed into folded cloth which had been twisted with rope into makeshift bags to hang around their backs.

A long snaking line of people towed after the

warrior leaders, their pace punishing. Only when they were well away from Balbath did the rate of progress slacken.

"I think we must be close to the River Urie." Brian huffed because he was already feeling the strain of the furious trot.

"Yeah." Aran agreed, also lacking breath. He'd thought himself fit before this interactive story adventure, but he was finding that wasn't the case. "Tuadh told me he's heading for the tribesmen who are already gathered near Scare Hill. Wherever that is."

Brian burst out laughing, a difficult job since he was breathing hard. "You don't know?" He gently nudged Aran with his spear end. "The great memory you have, and you don't know where Scare Hill is?"

"Well, I don't," Aran nagged. "Do you?"

"'Course I do, it's down at the bottom of Bennachie; it's the little hill close to Donview car park."

"Oh, right," Aran said, though he wasn't convinced. "You sure?"

"Sure," Brian answered. "My geography's always better than yours."

It was true. Aran had to acknowledge it. Brian was much better at map work.

Though Aran expected the people of Balbath to follow the River Urie when they came to it he was surprised to find the warrior leaders cut off to the west across the countryside, still roughly following the River Don.

"Aran of Durris! Where are you, lad?" Tuadh bawled orders as he and his son Liam galloped back down the file of people.

Aran wasn't sure he wanted Tuadh to find him from the look on the chief's face. Somehow it wasn't very reassuring.

"Move to the front of the line, now." Tuadh's orders came when he pulled up alongside. He looked closely at those all around shaking his head as though to clear his vision. "Where is Seonagh?"

Fianna was quick to answer. "She was near the back the last time I saw her when we stopped at the joining of the two rivers. She told me to go on ahead with Aran and Brian while she helped her grandmother."

"All of you to the front, now."

Tuadh disappeared in a flurry, shouting orders to Liam as he sped to the end of the file of tribespeople. Liam galloped the opposite way to the front of the line. By the time Aran and the twins had almost reached the leaders at the front, a hard-ridden chariot came back up behind them. Seonagh and her grandmother, Ailish, were in it, Tuadh riding alongside.

"What's happening now, Aran?" Fianna asked.

"Don't know yet!" he answered. "But we're getting closer to the foothills of Bennachie."

Tuadh issued orders to the warriors who were leading the tribespeople. "Head for Tullos. I've just had word from a messenger that Blairdaff and Delnabo have already made a temporary encampment there, so we shall also stop close by."

"Who are Delnabo and Blairdaff?" Fianna didn't need to be delegated to ask the question of Seonagh.

"Blairdaff is High Chief of the tribes of the Garioch, of all the settlements and hillforts that are within sight of The Mither Tap. My father has told me that High Chief Delnabo comes here as the spokesperson for all of the Caledon tribes of the western hills, though I have never met the man."

Aran had somehow expected that Tuadh was the high chief of the area, the man seeming so full of bluster and command. He wasn't sure if the knowledge that he wasn't made him disappointed, or not.

By the end of the day, the people of Balbath were settled near the Clachie Burn not far from the small roundhouse village of Tullos. The Balbathans constructed rudimentary shelters with branches, mosses and other foliage, foraging from the surrounding countryside. This was all the protection they had apart from their cloaks and blankets. Aran and the twins had pitched in to do their bit to help build the refuges where they could: learning how to do it as they went. In a way it had been challenging fun, but neither he nor the twins had dared to show any enjoyment in it, because the mood of the Balbathans was gloomy.

"This shelter of mine is cool, don't you think?" Brian sounded so convinced about his work of art.

Aran looked at the lopsided covering his mate had made between two bush branches, the sides so open a Double Decker bus could have driven through it. Cool indeed.

Fianna doubled over, suppressing a noisy fit of giggles. "Brother, it's absolute pants and you know it, but hey! I love how you've become so confident about what you can do."

Aran thought that a really nice comment—coming from Fianna.

"Aran." He groaned to find Fianna wasn't done.

"You know those hideaway island programmes on TV where they do survival skills? You'd get a fabulous two out of ten for yours."

He wasn't saying anything about Fianna's because hers actually did look like it would shelter her overnight if it rained.

"Just as well," she crowed, "that it's not big enough for three."

Sharing a tent with Fianna? He didn't think so. No sooner had that thought come, the rain started to spit. On second thoughts, it was easy to decide that sharing a dry shelter with Fianna would be okay if the rain got heavier.

The food that the Balbathans had managed to carry was limited, but it had been shared around. Small animals that had been caught during the march had been roasted and split amongst the tribespeople as best they could. It wasn't much after the feasting of the two previous nights, but with water from the Clachie Burn it was enough. After they'd eaten their meagre fare, Aran and the twins huddled around a small fire, sharing it with Seonagh, Orla and Caitlinn. Tyrnan was close by, still watchful, still guarding Seonagh.

Aran wasn't sure if the man was guarding them as well because the warrior's expression was again serious.

Tuadh sat at a larger blaze with the High Chiefs Blairdaff and Delnabo, a little way off. Some Balbath senior warriors and envoys from other local settlements made up the circle, as well. The talk between the seated men looked very intense. Aran was pretty sure the chiefs of the Garioch area knew their only hope of mass survival was to make a new treaty with the powerful Roman enemy—even though it wedged in their thrapples to do so.

He looked all around him. Misery and despair abounded. Thrapple was such a good Scottish word—it sounded so much better than throat when in context of all the awkward tension driven swallowing that went on everywhere he looked.

His thoughts were disturbed by a flurry of activity close to Tuadh's fireside as a couple of newcomers approached on the run. Tuadh had jumped to his feet clearly recognising his own scouts from a distance.

"What news?" As always, the man was impatient.

Chapter Sixteen

"Aran of Durris, you will come here now."

Tuadh's call couldn't be ignored. Aran sighed and got to his feet.

Brian slapped his leg as he passed by. "Get the information that we need and the evidence to take home. I'm getting bored of this lark, just sitting around on this wet patch."

"Oh, stop being such a damp squib," Fianna chided. "At home, you'd probably be just as bored. Go find out what the man wants, Aran, and come back with the juicy bits."

Fianna was getting better at tossing bits of wood on their fire. Aran smiled at her in commiseration before he headed over to the Big Guns' fire. Brian was his best buddy but he could be a bit of a pain, at times.

When Aran reached Tuadh, he stood where the chief indicated. He was behind, yet close enough to give information if needed.

"The Roman camp at Deer's Den has been re-established." The scout who spoke was winded from his trek.

"Just as the lad said!" Tuadh turned and slapped at Aran's knee, not able to reach his shoulder because Tuadh was seated.

He'd forgotten to watch out for that neat little trick and had swivelled off his feet before he could brace himself for the impact. Regaining his balance, Aran glanced back to see Seonagh and the twins scuttling closer to Tyrnan when the warrior joined their fireside group. He wished he was back with them. They were out of range of Tuadh's wrath—but he wasn't.

"Heed well to the information the warrior has gleaned and tell me what else you know, lad." Another barked order blasted his face.

"How many soldiers are there now?" Tuadh asked the scout.

"Perhaps five hundred men." The warrior sounded disheartened. "The detachment came down and across the valley in a huge swathe. They cut down the trees and bushes that hampered their way where the old Roman pathway was not wide enough for their file, leaving a cleared passage behind them."

The man stopped talking at Tuadh's abrupt signal. Some chiefs from other settlements that lay outside of the Garioch area arrived to share the news bulletin. A few of these leaders Aran soon learned were from the south and had already been displaced from their homes by Roman attack. Other chiefs had settlements to the west—not yet under threat—though that might still happen depending on where the Roman Emperor Severus chose to descend. Tuadh waited till they were all welcomed and settled around the fireside before he turned back to his surveillance scout.

"These Romans, now encamped at Deer's Den, have all marched from the same place?" Tuadh asked.

"Aye. They have come from the mouth of the Dee." The scout sounded sure of his facts.

"No additional forces joining them from other directions?" This came from one of the newest arrivals.

"We do not believe so, at least not before dusk fell." However, the scout claimed he could not be sure of what happened after dark.

Tuadh twisted around and stared at Aran. "What do you say to this information, Aran of the Durris? Will more men join them at Deer's Den even after darkness falls?"

He wasn't sure what to answer but he did know what the general sequence of events was during a campaign in foreign territory. "The usual Roman way is for the soldiers to build their temporary camp turf walls before darkness falls and then they shelter behind them till the following day. Gaining entry to a temporary camp overnight would be very unusual." He halted when one warrior interrupted and addressed Tuadh.

"We have been told that Roman troops attacked your settlement after dark."

Tuadh answered exactly what Aran was going to say. "Aye they did, but they had no camp of their own to flee to when we routed them from my roundhouses. We have come to the conclusion that they must have landed earlier than the other ships and lost their direction."

"Perhaps they were to set up camp at Deer's Den?"

It was an excellent question but Aran had no real answer. "Specialist engineering scouts are the ones sent on to set up camp, well in advance of the remaining troops, because it takes them a good while to build the fortifications and mark out the interior for the tents. Once behind their barricade the legion beds down to defend themselves. Roman attack on Celtic settlements overnight is not usual."

"That is the pattern they follow, indeed. The lad speaks true." Aran didn't like the suspicious look that came his way from Blairdaff which didn't match the man's positive answer.

"If the soldiers at Deer's Den came from the ships which landed at the Dee mouth they may yet be joined by more soldiers arriving by ship come the morrow or the next day." Tuadh's heated tones came and went in the night dark as he paced around the fireside.

Aran felt the tightly reined in fear around the circle of warriors. He could sense that it was deeply worrying to all the chiefs to have renewed aggressive activity from the Roman legions, yet they didn't seem keen to do battle either.

"What happened to the raiding party we sent to hamper their progress across the land?" Another local chief asked the second scout. "Was it successful?"

"Your warriors separated off some stragglers, and routed out the last of the Romans heading to Deer's Den. They have slain a few handfuls of the weaker soldiers."

Tuadh's scathing tone flayed the man who had given the information. "What do you call weaker?"

The tone was even worse when Tuadh turned to him. "Aran who knows much of Rome—would you call any of the Roman soldiers weak?"

Everyone stared awaiting his answer. He knew what he could say but wasn't entirely sure if he should tell the assembled men.

Blairdaff got up and stood right next to him, his face fiercer than before. The man wasn't nearly as tall as Tyrnan but was much bulkier; an intimidating presence to have right at his nose.

Aran swallowed hard. The urge to blink his eyes was huge but he didn't want to show any weakness that Blairdaff could exploit. It took another, hopefully hidden, swallow before he could speak. "Roman soldiers are not allowed to become weak in body. Emperor Severus has given orders to his legion commanders. If men of the cohorts become too ill to walk, or too injured to heal quickly on campaign, then they must die. If the injured, or sick, cannot be supported for a short time by a fellow soldier in their contubernium group then they are slaughtered."

A huge outcry erupted around the fireside. A number of the chiefs jumped to their feet to ring themselves around him. No one touched him, but they stared and stared.

"Again, the boy speaks true. Our southern Miathi brothers told us that they found dead Romans left at temporary camps when the soldiers have marched ahead on their campaign last Lughnasadh. They were dispatched by Roman hand, the cuts from a double-edged gladius."

"Why does Severus kill his own men?" The speaker was disgusted.

Aran answered because the man stared at him. "The army moves on. The ailing soldiers are killed rather than have them captured by the Celts who challenge the Empire."

"What ailed the weaker Romans who were killed earlier this day?"

The second scout was less intimidated by Tuadh's ire, his face wreathed in a malicious smile. The darkness and the firelight made his teeth look menacingly whiter. "We are pleased that some of the Roman scum have succumbed to a mysterious stomach sickness. They have been drinking tinkered water. It was easy to kill off those stragglers."

Sensing the anger of the men around him, Aran

wasn't sure he would have wanted to witness those deaths by the Celtic long sword.

"It sounds like my ploy went well?"

A little cheer went up as yet another chief stepped into the light of the fire. Aran could tell the man was popular when delighted greetings came so spontaneously.

Tuadh rushed over and clapped the man around the shoulders in his typical fashion. Aran was heartened to see that the brawny warrior hardly flinched. In fact he pummelled Tuadh back as good as he had been given. From the happier grunts, and battering arm hugs, Aran concluded they were the best of friends.

"Connal." Tuadh whooped; the happiest Aran had seen him. "I thought you had perished when no word of your safety arrived at Balbath. What happened to you?"

Aran listened to Connal's update for the assembled crowd.

"My settlement near the mouth of the River Dee was overwhelmed when three Roman ships anchored near my sands just after day break. The auxiliary soldiers jumped out of the vessels, to neck deep, before the vessels had even reached the beach. Hordes of them surged over the dunes to my settlement, slaying my guards. My tribespeople were next, those who had no time to make ready with their weapons."

Tuadh interrupted. "Did you manage to fell any of them?"

"My warriors killed a good few, but we were well outnumbered," Connal told them all. "Those like me, who survived, had no choice but to flee inland when they put my roundhouses to the torch."

"What is this ploy you mention? You have managed to thwart the Romans in some way?" Tuadh slapped his friend again in a gesture of solidarity and praise.

"Aye, indeed," Connal laughed triumphantly. "Some disruption was created as we sped away. We added a taint to the water supply—some dead Roman auxiliaries—upstream from where the Roman soldiers were likely to collect the water. To be even more certain the herb wife of my tribe added something noxious, which will be effective along that short stretch of water before it disperses into the sea."

"Will it taint the whole river?"

"Nay. The river flows too forcefully for that. The sickness will only last a day or so and will cause a fearsome gripe, but if they've been greedy, an agonising death may befall them."

Though the news cheered up the assembled group, Aran knew it was only one small delaying tactic. The fireside group around Tuadh grew as yet another local chief arrived.

"Carden!" Tuadh greeted the man and arranged space for him to sit alongside. "The lad and I must talk with you. We have news that you will not like."

Carden chose to remain standing and surveyed those around the fireside till Aran felt his eyes settle on him. "Is this the Taexali youth that Mapon sent me word of?"

"Mapon has already told you about Aran's knowledge?" Tuadh sounded amazed.

Aran was surprised, too, because everything he had told Tuadh had been after Mapon had quit Balbath. He wasn't sure he liked the look of this newest chief either. His penetrating stare made him feel very unsettled.

"What I know is that you have a young warrior who has great knowledge of the Romans," Carden answered before he eventually sat down. "What am I not going to like?"

Tuadh bent around, grabbed Aran by the arm and yanked him forward. Feeling very vulnerable, he stood alongside Seonagh's father.

"To all the chiefs around here I introduce Aran, son of Durran of the Durris. Durran has likely perished under the Roman gladius but he sent on Aran to us, through the Forest of Bendauch. The lad carried a message for us all. The Pin of Funach."

A low murmur rippled around. Aran couldn't fathom it. Distrust was there in the sounds, and the looks, but there were other sensations he couldn't quite identify. Fear—definitely. Suspicion was rife but there was also a repulsion he could almost taste.

"Mapon believes this young warrior has much wisdom to share," Tuadh told them. "Though he had not been there, he told me the Romans would camp at Deer's Den. We now know they have done this." A soft murmur of distrust hummed around. "He also has knowledge of another place where the Romans will shortly set up camp, most likely Severus or Caracalla's troops. This place he has precisely described."

"Not possible!"

"How can this be true?"

"Can we believe his words?"

Aran wasn't comfortable with the tone of the protests that echoed around him. Like his arrival at Balbath, he felt truly threatened.

Connal's soft enquiry was just as threatening as the shouted ones, maybe even more so as the tone was calculated to make Aran squirm. It was working.

"Mapon has every faith in him, and so do I." Tuadh was adamant, his fierce expression daring anyone to dispute him.

Aran was pleased to see that the chiefs calmed down again, even if they didn't seem to share Tuadh's opinion because Tuadh was also getting some very distrustful looking glances. However, he was less enamoured when Carden stood right next to him and almost buried his beard in his face. "What will I not like to hear from you?"

Aran refused to be cowed by the man, if fact he felt bolstered up by the fact that Tyrnan had separated himself from the huddle around Seonagh and now stood to his other side.

Tyrnan's voice was just as sure as Tuadh's had been as he added his own support. "Aran described a place to Tuadh where the Romans will muster their forces—near the River Urie and close to your settlement, Carden."

"The Romans will not overrun my settlement." Carden was livid. "Why do you believe this stripling?"

Aran felt Tyrnan's huge hand rest on his shoulder, though this time it was a squeeze of reassurance that he felt in the fingers.

"We do believe, Aran. Your people must come across the valley and join us, or they will be doomed." Tyrnan sounded so convinced.

A fierce barrage of shouting broke out amongst the chiefs around the fireside. Aran was really glad when Tuadh turned back to him.

"Go, lad. Those of us here have much to discuss."

Aran scurried back to the twins. Seonagh had kept the fire going with their meagre pile of brushwood, but Orla and Caitlinn were fast asleep, snuggled down into a pile of blankets inside Orla's shelter.

"I must check on Ailish." Seonagh nodded to him before she sloped off to see how her grandmother fared.

Fianna patted a space at the fire, indicating he should sit alongside her. "We couldn't hear what they were saying but I didn't like the way those chiefs stared at you."

He thought for a moment before answering her. "I know. They hate me and don't trust me but I don't know what more I can tell them." He felt dispirited and exhausted.

Fianna tried to cheer him up. "If you hadn't told Tuadh about the Romans at Durno then he might have told the people of Balbath to walk on up the River Urie before stopping for the night. If we'd done that, we'd probably be waking up to thousands of Roman feet tramping over us to get to Durno."

"You're right, Fianna," Brian agreed. "That's probably what would have happened."

"True." Aran thought she was spot on as well, though it didn't make him feel better. "Tuadh says he'll summon me tomorrow at dawn, but what else can I tell them?"

Brian chewed his nail, a sure sign he wanted answers. "What do you remember about Roman troop movements during the time of this Severus guy?"

"Archaeologists are sure there were over thirty thousand soldiers at the Durno marching camp. Agricola probably used it in AD 84 but they also think Severus, or maybe Caracalla, used it, too."

Fianna twirled a stick in the embers to liven up the fire. "Didn't you tell us yesterday that Severus had fifty thousand men?"

"Not up here. Remember I said that a lot of men died on the way north, before they even reached Balbath in AD 209."

"So how many do you think are with Severus and Caracalla just now?" Brian was hunched over, stretching his fingers to the meagre warmth.

"I don't know, but probably less than twenty thousand. The Severan marching camps that went all the way up to the Moray Firth were quite small camps. It sounds like it's those guys who are now marching south again."

Fianna tapped her burning stick on the ground making the tiniest of fire sparkles. "But if they've had big battles up in Morayshire maybe they've got even less men now."

Aran nudged her to make sure she didn't burn her fingers. "No big battles."

"How can you be sure of that?" She tossed the remnants of the stick in the fire before purposely reaching for another from the tiny pile of firewood, all that was left of their collection.

Brian fidgeted about on his bottom, not comfortable on the hard ground. "There's no record of a battle here in AD 210?"

Aran shrugged before he shook his head. He was sure he hadn't read anything like that.

Fianna rubbed her hands together, even though it wasn't that cold—her gesture like Fagin in *Oliver Twist*. "I bet the Romans bribed the Caledons by giving them lots of gold, so that Roman troops could march all over Scotland and back down south to England again without much blood being shed."

Aran gulped. Fianna had just twigged the thing that had been niggling. "You're right. Severus did bring huge amounts of gold to bribe the tribes when he came to Britain."

He leapt up and ran around the dying fire.

"Got it!"

Chapter Seventeen

"I know what it has to be!"

Aran mimicked a Canadian First Nations war dance: silently though, since he was aware of the situation around him.

"Spill!" Brian whispered clawing him down. "What can you tell them?"

The three of them huddled again.

"Some Roman historian wrote tabloid news stuff about Severus and his two sons. It was because of Caracalla and Geta that Emperor Severus came to Britain in the first place." Aran waited for the twins to absorb that. After he had their nods of understanding, he continued. "Well, the sons were a wild pair, up to all sorts of shenanigans. They didn't like their father, and I think they hated each other." He paused for emphasis. "Severus, being a soldier and all that, decided it would be a great idea to bring them on the campaign to Britain."

"I'd have thought he'd have been running miles away from them." Fianna sounded doubtful.

"Severus wanted them to stop their capering about. He'd already made them emperor stand-ins, jointly ruling with him, I think. Anyway, being in the army was supposed to make them knuckle down and be good Romans. Caracalla was a cruel teenager, and Geta wasn't much better, so their dear old dad brought them to Scotland."

Brian's eyes flickered in the firelight. "What was special about Scotland?"

Aran looked around to see if anyone, apart from the twins, was close enough to hear. "Scotland was the last bit of the west that wasn't properly ruled by the Romans. The people here were so fierce and said to be barbarian, that the Romans had never totally conquered them."

"But I thought Agricola occupied this area in AD 84?"

Brian's question was tricky to answer. "He did but not in a lasting way. Agricola and his forces left north-east Scotland fairly quickly after AD 84, when the Emperor Domitian summoned Agricola back to Rome, so the natives were never under full Roman control like in the rest of Europe."

"Forget that Agricolan stuff. That was ages ago." Fianna gripped Aran's arm in her excitement, "Tell me more about Severus' sons?" She was like a terrier gnawing a particularly juicy bone. "You know something awesome about these guys, don't you, Aran?"

Aran heaved a sigh. "I do. It's a huge burden having a memory like mine."

"Oh, my heart bleeds for you! Just get on with it," Brian joked.

"Okay. Well, I can tell you some stories about the sons—if you really want to hear about them?"

They did.

"Caracalla seems a weird name. I don't know all that many Roman names but that's not like the usual Julius. Give us that first." Fianna was impatient.

"Caracalla was a nickname. I read it was something to do with a new style of cloak that he designed…"

"What? He was a fashionista?" Fianna giggled like mad.

"Crazy, I know." He grinned caught up in her hilarity. "I don't know how true that was. His original name was Septimius Bassianus, the Septimius because that was his father's name and the Bassianus name came from his mother's family in Syria. But Severus changed his son's name to Marcus Aurelius Severus Antoninus Augustus when he became Emperor."

"What a mouthful. That's even weirder." Fianna was disbelieving as she butted his shoulder.

Brian was making fake retching faces. "Why would he do that?"

"Severus wanted the people to call them Caesars – like Julius Caesar – but their names weren't posh enough so he felt he had to rename the boys."

He went on to tell them a lot more about the sons of Severus.

"Wow." Brian whispered a while later. "That's pretty gross. Caracalla duffed them in? Snuffed out thousands of Geta's friends?"

"Not only them. Caracalla was the nicer of his nicknames. He wasn't called the *'beast'* because he was nice to his opposition."

"You mean his own enemies?"

Aran nodded.

Fianna crept even closer to him, her smirk displaying the opposite of her words. "I hate to ask, but what did he do to them?"

"It seems he was quite proud to be called a *'beast'*. Sometimes he seemed to make pacts for peace, at the end of battle engagements, but then he had thousands of the opposing army slain."

"How do you know all this gruesome stuff?"

"A guy named Cassius Dio wrote things about Caracalla and his murderous megalomania. But the absolute worst thing was what Caracalla did to his brother Geta."

The whispering went on for a good while.

"Double yuck!" Fianna was grossed out by the time he was finished. "Nasty, nasty guy. But…how do you think that will help just now?"

Aran shrugged his shoulders, his earlier euphoria gone. "I don't know."

"The Romans arrive at Durno!"

The cry rang around the encampments. It was a few hours after dawn and the whole area was abuzz with renewed anxiety as news was delivered.

"Who's just arrived?" Brian asked.

Fianna had been delegated to hover close to Tuadh's huddle of warriors to find out.

"It's Carden. Seems he went back to his own hillfort last night, after your warning was given. He's back again and is furious with you."

Aran was getting fed up of being regarded as the enemy. He hadn't like the man the previous evening and didn't think he was going to change his mind now.

Brian halted Fianna's agitated pacing by grabbing her elbow. "What's happened?"

"Roman soldiers have marched onto Carden's territory—but not Severus from the north or those at Kintore. It's kind of the same as what happened at Balbath. Troops came over the hillside at first light from the east and headed to Durno."

Aran's mind whirred. "Auxiliaries from more ships?"

"Seems so. They reckon the Romans were anchored off the coast last night and spewed out of the ship just before dawn." Fianna slumped to a heap at the newly lit fire. "Carden's people had warning enough to scurry across the valley to get here, but the man is not a happy chief."

"None of them are," Brian added after looking across at the cluster around Tuadh.

Fianna wasn't done. "It was the warriors up at the hillfort on The Mither Tap who saw movements at first light. They gave the alarm and a message was sent to Carden in time. Now those up at the hillfort are saying that they can see the glinting of hundreds of weapons in the morning sun. There are already lots of Romans over at Durno." She looked over towards the fireside of the High Chiefs. "Oh, oh. I think you just won the lottery, Aran."

"Is this the time for fighting?" Tuadh barked his question at Aran.

Aran squelched his misgivings but felt a duty to do the best he could. "No."

He drew a deep breath before he continued. The steadying presence of Tyrnan alongside him helped but the distrust on the faces of the chiefs didn't. "You have made good success during petty skirmishes with the Roman invaders during the last seasons but you cannot face the armies of Rome when they are here in their tens of thousands. The time has come to make a new treaty with the Roman invaders. If you do that, their presence will be less threatening."

The clamour was instantly deafening.

"How can you be sure of this?" Tuadh asked when some hard won silence reigned. It was so weird to hear the man sound calm and collected, his usual bellowing tone now absent.

Aran persisted. "Emperor Severus has you trapped. Caracalla's troops will arrive soon from the north, from the direction of Tap O'Noth. They will be followed by those of Severus himself and all will muster at Durno. The cohorts who are already at Durno are only the first of many fresh new auxiliaries Geta will send to this area via the sea, like those now at Deer's Den. Geta also has orders from his father to send even more land based infantry. Those soldiers will come up from the south, from Raedykes, and they will not take long to arrive here since their roadway has already been cleared by those at Deer's Den."

"The boy seems far too wise about Roman affairs. We may not like to hear him but what he states makes sense."

Aran had no idea who had just spoken but the man at Tuadh's fireside looked pretty important, the gold torque around the man's throat a major work of art.

The chief continued. "Our constant raids on the Romans deplete us. We cannot sustain more warrior losses."

Someone else made a plea to the company. "Should we turn tail and flee west, to the hills, like whipped curs to avoid this trap? Like our forefathers did when the forces of Agricola routed us in battle here at Beinn Na Ciche?"

Aran felt brave enough to chip in. "Severus will be delighted if you do that. He will send his troops to barricade all the mountain passes, like the Roman General Agricola did a long time ago and you will be trapped in the hills. Severus has legions of his soldiers on your doorstep and can command more to this area if he needs them. If you are forced to remain in the hills, your productive flat farm land will be available to him with no bloodshed. Your harvested grain crops would be very welcome to him for feeding his armies who are campaigning in far off lands."

"How will he reap our crops if we are gone from here?"

Aran thought it a stupid question but wasted no time in answering the man. "If you are all trapped in the hills, the Emperor might use his own troops to work the land. However, it is more likely that he will force Celtic farmers from the very far south to do the work. Those Celtic brothers have already been subdued by Severus and are now slaves of the Roman Empire. They have no voice of their own. You already know that the Emperor has many enslaved tribes to choose from."

The word slaves provoked a huge reaction, livid shouts deafening those around the fireside.

Carden almost exploded. "How many soldiers do you say will be over at my settlement?"

Aran held his head high, though he hoped and prayed to Taranis that none of the chiefs could see the crossed fingers behind his back. His twenty first century information could be wrong, but he didn't think so. "The temporary turf walls he will create can probably harbour more than thirty-thousand men. Perhaps not all will arrive today, but soon."

"We are doomed!"

Aran didn't know who shouted that but many of the outbursts were similar.

It took a while for everyone to calm down.

Aran tried again. "Severus aims to browbeat you with this great show of strength, but I can also tell you that he does not intend to be in this Garioch area for long. Soon, whether blood is spilt or not, he will march his troops south again when he is satisfied with new treaties that you agree to."

"How can you know all of these things?" Carden was ferocious.

Aran couldn't tell him how he knew but had to try to make the man understand that he did know a lot. "Severus will retreat to the lands of the Brigantes but he will leave Caracalla here for a while longer to ensure you honour the terms, and you already know how brutal Caracalla is." Aran particularly added that since Caracalla was a butcher.

Carden pointed his finger making Aran feel decidedly uncomfortable. "The boy knows far too much. Are you so certain Tuadh of Balbath that he is not spying for the Roman Empire?"

Tyrnan ignored the venom coming from Carden. "Mapon has great faith in Aran, son of Durran. You will do well to heed his wisdom."

After some more disgruntled mumbling, further questions fired his way.

"If we sign new treaties, how many troops of Caracalla will remain here?" The question came from Connal of the Deemouth.

Aran was amazed that the man seemed quite calm considering the chief had almost been killed that morning. He had to make a guess but knew it was as informed a guess as possible. "He will leave smaller units to enforce the treaties. Maybe half-cohorts of some two hundred men will be left in places around this area till the next snows come, but that will only happen if you honour any new agreements made with Severus. If you don't, I believe thousands of troops will remain in your lands."

Carden spat at the fire. Aran was glad that the yucky goo didn't come in his direction even though the poison in Carden's words did. "It sticks in my craw to deal with the Roman scum but it sounds as though we have no other alternative. We cannot fight against thirty two thousand well armoured soldiers and keep on fighting season after season."

Aran thought carefully about the next part before he continued. "You are the last conquest, the last Celtic peoples that Severus needs to defeat in his western Empire. Severus wishes news to go back to Rome, to his Senate, saying that his legions have conquered the Celts of the western fringes. His armies have already experienced huge losses at the hands of the Miathi and the Caledons during the last two summer seasons as he progressed northwards. The deaths of many soldiers in his legions do not make him look successful in Rome. He wishes for no more bloodshed losses of his troops. Of course, if you continue to challenge him, he will destroy every last one of you. If you sign his treaties, you will live and will have most of your lands as you had them before he marched north, and he will satisfy the demands of the Roman Senate."

"The terms of the treaties will not be so easy."

Aran tried to pacify the chief. "Treaties never satisfy everyone but they are better than most of your people being slaughtered by Caracalla"

Another chief shouted at him. "I think that Severus will want to kill every one of us before he retreats. Treaty or no treaty."

He waited till the noise died down. "Not true. Severus will give you a lot of Roman gold as part of the treaty settlement, but you, in turn, need to give him what he wants as well."

"He will give us gold?" Blairdaff's expression immediately lightened. "For what?"

Aran hadn't a clue what the Taexali and the Caledons could give the Romans so he hedged a bit. "Think hard about what you are prepared to give to Severus, in exchange for the large amount of Roman gold he will offer you."

After many more questions, and some extra difficult ones from Delnabo whose stares held such a lot of distrust, the Caledon leader pointed at him. "The boy must go. We have much to discuss without him."

"Leave us, but remain within sight." Blairdaff's order wasn't disputed by any other chief, not even by Tuadh.

Chapter Eighteen

Aran was glad to scurry back to the others who were desperate to know what was going on.

"You only won a tenner and not a million, Aran?" Fianna was her usual blunt self.

He was in no mood for her teasing. "They don't think too much of you either."

Brian was more matter-of-fact. "What's the latest then?"

"They're going to be talking treaties, but we've got orders not to move away from here." He wasn't sure he liked the open prison situation very much but it gave him the excuse to stretch out and rest his taxed brain.

"If we ding our escape buttons they wouldn't be able to stop us." For some reason Fianna thought that funny.

He stared at her.

Fianna tried her casual wander after a while, since the heated talk at the High Chiefs' fireside continued, but she was chased away.

Updates eventually came through Tyrnan.

"There have been skirmishes between Roman forces and the tribes who lie near the coast, on the far side of Carden's lands."

Brian jumped in with both feet. "That nasty Geta's sent more ships. I bet the Roman Navy is patrolling the whole of the Taexali coast and landing at different beaches."

Fianna was gruesomely fascinated. "Have lots of those rotten Romans been killed?"

"There have been deaths and many injuries on both sides, Fianna." Tyrnan was grim about that but was brisk about his next order. "Come. We will climb to the hillfort."

"Really?" Aran's smile widened. It was the first grin for ages. He was glad to get away from the gloom that had settled around the Balbathans. "Even though the sun is well over in the sky?"

The twins looked just as eager for a break. Their fireside had been lonely since Seonagh was with her grandmother and Orla and Caitlinn had gone to check on the injured Balbathans.

"What if Tuadh needs Aran?" Fianna's question reminded him of how often the man expected him to be at his beck and call.

"He will not." Tyrnan was positive. "He wishes you to see what you can from the hilltop before night falls. You are to tell him your findings when we return."

As they scrambled closer to the hillfort, at the peak of The Mither Tap, Brian's voice sounded awed. "This is so incredible. We normally climb over a tumbled heap of boulders and scree."

The stone wall that fringed the summit was higher than Aran had expected: very weird since the hillfort at Balbath had no stone wall or stone buildings.

"Who built this hillfort wall of stone, Tyrnan?" Fianna had been matching him step for step, asking a question now and again which the warrior didn't seem to mind answering.

An unaccustomed animation brightened Tyrnan's eyes. "Tribes of the Garioch. It took many turns of the sun to build these walls. The quarry for these stones is down below it but took great effort to draw them up to the top of the peak. It was done long before my father's time."

Aran wanted to know more. "Whose hillfort is it?"

Tyrnan laughed and that wasn't a common occurrence. "The defences belong to no individual tribe."

"How come it doesn't belong to the tribe who lives closest?" Brian ran his hand along the roughly dressed granite wall when they reached it.

"After the last great battle with Roman soldiers many generations ago, the local tribes decided we all needed better warning of invaders. The Mither Tap is the best vantage point of the Garioch for us all to share."

"So it's a communal facility?" Brian asked.

"If you ask do we share the roundhouses here, then we do exactly that. Tuadh sends warriors to do guard duty here—as do chiefs from the other tribes of the Garioch." Tyrnan went on to tell them more about the operation of the communal hillfort.

Aran could see the guards posted at strategic places, facing eight main compass points, though only their heads and spear points were visible above the wall.

Aran had never read anything about The Mither Tap hillfort and was intrigued about all Tyrnan could tell him. "Has it been worth the effort of building? Apart from this morning's warnings, has anyone ever had to inform the local tribes about other attackers coming?"

Tyrnan looked like the answer would choke him. "Aye, indeed. Last Lughnasadh we were all given enough warning when Severus made his first demands on our lands.

"Did you see the Romans coming?"

"I wish I could say otherwise but, aye, I did and so did Seonagh. We could see their hordes move towards us like a worm moving slowly across the ground. They were so tightly packed as they slithered across the flat valley towards Balbath."

Aran was awed. "I wish I had seen that."

Tyrnan was dismissive. "Wish not for that, it can only herald bad things." He broke off to shout to the guards. "Tyrnan of Balbath seeks entry."

Once through the gate, Aran could see the hillfort housed more than he had first thought. The cluster of roundhouses were smaller than those at Balbath and more tightly packed together but built in the same basic design.

After greeting a few of those posted around, Tyrnan led them along the built up platform that ringed the inner wall.

"Oh, wow! Look at that." Fianna had been first to jump up on the walkway.

The day was still beautiful, the sky very clear. The bustle of the camp over at Durno was a myriad of twinkles. It was impossible for Aran to see any people with the naked eye but the shining armour and weapons of Roman soldiers glinted and sparkled in the sunshine. It was a sight that he was sure he would never ever forget.

As the flashes continued Fianna gaped, "The glints cover a huge area."

"There are hundreds of them over there now, Fianna." The sight was both thrilling and terrifying.

"What if they're all as ferocious as the one that got killed the other night?" Fianna reminded him of the Roman auxiliary who had attacked her at Balbath.

Brian didn't really need to add his tuppence-worth. "They're all trained to be brutal, sis."

It was completely petrifying to think of all those Romans rushing at him at the same time. Gruesomely horrible. Aran wasn't cheered by his imagination, yet he felt a perverse excitement that the men opposite were real Roman legions.

"What will you tell Tuadh?" Tyrnan's question came in the silence that hung around them.

Aran walked round the parapet towards the north as he thought about what to answer. He sucked in a breath and stretched his eyes further, his stomach turning somersaults. "Is that what I think it is?"

"Flippin' heck!" It came from both twins at the same time who had circled close on his heels.

"That has to be Caracalla or Severus." Aran had got his wish, maybe too soon, because in the distance there was a faint serpent shadow on the far valley floor.

Tyrnan hailed one of the sentries, his voice fit to beat Tuadh. "When did you first notice them?"

"A while ago. We have already sent word to the High Chiefs."

Tyrnan turned back, satisfied with the answer.

Aran did a very slow circle of the wall. When he faced south-east, he spent time having a very good look. He could see the River Don meandering across the valley floor though the hillfort of Balbath was hidden behind a belt of trees. Near the vicinity of Balbath, there was some tiny movement. He couldn't be sure but guessed what it might be.

"What's that, Tyrnan?"

Tyrnan looked where he pointed and mouthed something Aran didn't understand.

Aran suppressed a grin. He might not know the word but he could work out what the context was.

"A group of mounted Celtic warriors would not glint so much, even armed with many spears. It has to be some of the fully armoured Romans from Deer's Den."

"How many horsemen would kick up such a stir on the soil, Tyrnan?"

"More than twenty. Maybe thirty horses."

"A turma, then."

"What is this word?" Tyrnan sounded interested.

"It means thirty-two mounted soldiers. That's the smallest fighting unit of light cavalry in the Roman Army."

Aran wasn't convinced that Tyrnan was impressed, the warrior was so serious. "You know so much about my Roman enemies."

Aran agreed. "I do, but you have also told me a lot about the Celtic Taexali and about this hillfort on The Mither Tap. For that, I thank you. It has all been new knowledge to me but I have one more question."

Tyrnan's brows furrowed after listening to his inquiry. "Nay! Tuadh uses his axe with great skill. That is why he has acquired his name, but killing a man using a rope around the neck in this way you describe would be something new to me. I have never heard tell of this on The Mither Tap."

The following afternoon, the measly little fire that was reluctant to light was making Brian grumpy. He'd been tasked with getting it lit and it wasn't playing along. He'd moaned about the fact that it wasn't fair that he got the day when it had been raining overnight and the wood was damp. "This is pathetic. Maybe it's time for us to call it quits and press the end button? We're all bored."

"What a wimp you are. The first little thing that doesn't go right for you and you want to quit?" Fianna pointed to the belligerent fire, a cheeky smirk on her face.

Her fire had been easily lit, especially since Seonagh had spent time the evening before showing her how to use the stick and hollowed piece of wood that she'd found in her pouch when they'd first time-travelled to the woods. The fire-making tools worked pretty well but Brian had refused to try them when she'd offered them to him: he was sticking to a stone bashing technique that wasn't playing strikes at all.

"Well, nothing much happened, yesterday." Brian still mumped.

"What? How can you say that when Duhlain spent ages teaching you how to use your sling? You're a bona fide expert now. I'm impressed with how accurate you were in snagging our dinner last night."

Aran snorted. "Yeah. The bird you caught made a great clear soup."

Brian threw a stick at him. "I was aiming for the hare."

While the twins had been playing, Aran had been summoned on and off to Tuadh, to tell him what he'd seen from The Mither Tap and that had been pretty scary. The High Chiefs' questions had been endless but in an odd way all about the same things—tell them what he knew about Roman battle tactics.

Aran felt a bit listless now but he didn't want to go home yet. "Do you want to quit, Fianna?"

"No way!" she declared. "I want to stay and make

sure that Seonagh and Caitlinn… and everyone else are safe from these nasty Romans. Don't you?"

Aran put it to the vote. "Okay then, let's vote. Go home now, or stay a bit longer?"

None of them got the chance to answer because their armbands vibrated.

"Oh, wow," Brian whispered. "It's doing it again."

Since the flap didn't open automatically, Aran pressed the knob. The others did the same.

'You have more to do.'

"That's definitely creepy," Fianna whispered. "These armbands are listening in to our conversation. Do you think it's Callum? Or someone else?"

Aran grinned, cheered by the message because he hadn't actually been sure what he'd have voted and by the fact that Callum was looking out for them. "Don't know who, Fianna, but we're staying put."

"What are they doing?" Brian nudged Aran. There was a lot of movement over at the chiefs' fireside.

Tyrnan marched over with news. "Mapon and his interpreter have arrived. Along with the High Chiefs, they are going along to the valley to meet the envoys of Severus, who is now across at Durno. The soldiers we saw were those of Severus and not those of Caracalla. The son is not expected to arrive at the Garioch before the sun is high in the sky."

"Why aren't all of the chiefs going?" Fianna was peering over at the men who were gathering their weapons.

"The first negotiations with the Romans need only High Chiefs down at the River Urie," Tyrnan told them. "You will remain here and will not wander anywhere." Though the warrior addressed them all, it was Fianna that Tyrnan stared at.

"Are we your prisoners, then?" Fianna's laugh was full of sass.

The warrior made no answer but sat down near their eventually lit fire. Aran tried to banish the thought but it truly did look as though Tyrnan was under orders to keep them close to him. They were maybe not under arrest but had no choice of movement around the area.

Brian tactfully changed the subject. "I don't understand why Mapon is getting involved in these talks, Aran. Didn't you say that the Romans always killed any druids they found in Britannia because they thought the druids had too much influence over the tribes? And that the druids were too good at being spies?"

"Yeah," he answered. "I've wondered about that, too."

Tyrnan enlightened them. "Mapon is also a high ranking brother to a chief of the southern Taexali and presents himself as the envoy of his tribe. His fellow druid is accepted as the warrior with the best command of the Latin tongue in southern Taexali territories. You will make no mention that either of them are druids."

The last comment was a strong warning. Tyrnan wasn't being nasty, or threatening, just quietly stating a simple order.

"Friggin' heck! Look at that. Are Mapon and the other High Chiefs on a death wish? The talks will be right below the Roman encampment at Durno. How can so few of the Celts face the might of Rome and expect to come back alive?" Brian sounded both scathing and impressed at the same time over the goings-on at the chiefs' fireside.

Aran laughed as Brian scratched at his head. He pointed beyond Tuadh's fire area. "They're not completely daft, Brian. There's a large contingent of warriors over there. They'll follow at their rear, ready to defend their leaders if necessary."

"The gold offered by Severus is generous." Caledon leader, Delnabo, spoke into the darkness round the High Chiefs' fire later that night. "Even when distributed amongst us all, it will make us rich beyond dreams."

Cloud cover meant no moonlight. The murky darkness had made it easier for Aran to slink close enough to hear the head honchos. Tyrnan had been summoned when the High Chiefs had returned and had been sent off somewhere. He hadn't reappeared which meant Aran was able to sneak across and listen in to the conversation.

"I say we should give the Romans the land they demand for their forts and guard towers in exchange for the gold," Blairdaff declared.

"Agreed, Blairdaff. Though what of their other stipulations?" A voice Aran didn't recognise answered.

"Aye! Who among us will be their pawns?" grumbled Carden. "How will that demand be fulfilled?"

Tuadh was amazingly quiet. "It has been usual for the Roman Emperor to do this with our southern Celtic brothers, but the thought of it makes me sick to the stomach."

Aran didn't think Connal sounded so cheered about the offer, either, when he spoke after a long pause. "Gold is surely something good to have but what of settlements, like mine, which have been destroyed? Will the gold of the Romans help me build a new settlement, if I lose more of my warriors?"

Someone else was just as unhappy. "The Romans overrun my lands so where would I rebuild? I heard nothing of that from the envoys of Severus."

Tuadh sounded dispirited. "Perhaps Severus or Caracalla will tell you. I have had enough talk and wish to rest now, even if my sleep is uneasy."

Aran scurried off when he realised the chiefs were calling it a night.

"Wake up!" He nudged Brian when he returned to his own fireside. His friend had been dozing where he sat cross-legged, his head almost nodding the earth. "A real Roman Emperor will be in position right across the valley tomorrow for more talks."

Brian wasn't that impressed. "So what? Severus is just a crippled old man from what you told us and his son is a delinquent youth."

"If Severus is as scary as his soldier was, I don't think I want to meet this man who orders his army to kill everything in sight." Fianna squirmed around as she settled for sleep in her nearby shelter.

Aran couldn't believe that his two best friends didn't get the enormity of seeing Severus and Caracalla.

Roman Emperor Severus.

It was like knowing your favourite band was doing an open-air concert and he wanted a ticket for the front row.

Chapter Nineteen

"What are they doing now?" Fianna mumbled her way through a yawn and stretched her arms high into the air as she came to the remains of their fire.

"I'm not sure," Aran answered.

He watched the morning bustle around the area of the High Chiefs become more intense. People came and went with information. The men huddled around and debated, fierce and low this time. No shouting—just quiet creepy talk that was accompanied by lots of them pointing around their circle. Eventually, it seemed as though they pointed at him and the twins even more often.

Tyrnan had been back as their informal guard since dawn, and had already warned him to stay close to his shelter. The man was fierce about it, so he did, but he sat and plotted how he could sneak another climb up The Mither Tap to see what was going on at the Roman Camp. He was startled when out of the blue Tyrnan was called over to Tuadh.

The talk between Tyrnan and the chief of Balbath looked angry. From the arm gestures and tense body language, what was going on didn't seem to make either man happy. When he returned to Aran's fireside, fury radiated off Tyrnan in waves.

"Seonagh! Go to Ailish right now, she has need of you."

Seonagh sprang up fearful that her grandmother was unwell. "I will see you all later."

When Seonagh had disappeared from sight Tyrnan turned to him, the anger still sparking in the man's expression. "Tuadh wants you now: all three of you."

Brian jumped up and reached for his gladius.

"Nay! You will leave all of your weapons here." Tyrnan bustled around gathering every weapon they had and stashed them in a pile.

"Give me your cloak!"

Aran unpinned his cloak ready to hand it over but something prompted him to re-clip the Pin of Funach to his tunic.

A short while later he was bragging to the twins. "By Taranis, this is brilliant. We're going along to the talks. Even if we have to stay well back we can say that we've been close to a real Roman Emperor."

"I'm not sure I want to see a decrepit old fogey. I'd rather stay with Seonagh and her grandmother." Fianna had none of his exhilaration. She hadn't liked the way that some chiefs had questioned them, and had thought their attitude nasty. "You could do the looking for us, except Tuadh's forcing us all to go."

"I'd be happier at the camp site trying to keep the stupid fire going, even though it's not my turn." Brian was reluctant about being dragged down the valley. He was siding with his twin and had said so quite emphatically.

Aran hopped around on impatient feet as the Celtic delegation got into place before moving off. At the front, in normal Celtic garb, were Mapon and his druid interpreter. Mounted in the next row were Delnabo who represented the Caledons, Blairdaff who spoke for the Taexali tribes of the Garioch, and a third Celt who was negotiating for the northern Miathi.

Tuadh accompanied the other minor chiefs who followed on foot behind the High Chiefs. Aran thought it pretty weird that although Tuadh was so important at Balbath, he wasn't important enough to be part of the main delegation which would interact with Emperor Severus.

Way over to Aran's left, a long irregular file of Celtic tribespeople was already heading down towards the flatland of the valley. They seemed to be shuffling but he guessed so many going down the slope had to be careful not to bump into each other.

To his right was a block of mounted Celtic warriors, the wedge stretching five or six horses deep. He'd glanced around when he heard them coming but it was hard to tell how many there were. The Celtic cavalry kept their horses subdued through quiet clicks and knee grips, the warriors ready with their spears but were no more threatening than that.

"Don't you think it a bit odd that those guys up ahead keep turning around to gawp at us?" Brian sounded so pathetic it made Aran laugh.

"No. They're just making sure that Tyrnan's behind us to make us keep up the pace."

Tyrnan would be able to hear his answer, the man being directly behind, but Aran wasn't bothering. In a way, the close guarding by Tyrnan was reassuring. He now felt the man was literally guarding his back because he had defended him on a number of occasions when around the grim looking Celtic chiefs. He was well used to Tyrnan's gruff and fierce faces which he reckoned were because the guy was a number one natural pessimist.

Nothing was going to stop Aran's enjoyment of seeing Severus—not the twins' and not Tyrnan's negative attitude.

The band of Celts set off.

"Keep yourselves a good step or two behind

Tuadh." Tyrnan was back to being bossy again.

It was a hushed walk down to the flatlands by the River Urie, only low murmurs being shared between the chiefs. When they got closer to the water, they halted and waited for the Romans to approach on the far side.

It didn't take long before Aran saw some awesome activity starting on the crest of the hill above the far bank. From Durno a swarm of Romans began to descend. A neat rectangle of legionary Roman soldiers paced its way down with a few mounted soldiers leading the way.

He could barely contain himself.

The Romans were coming!

To the right of the legionaries, were serried rows of auxiliary infantry and beyond them a turma of mounted legionary soldiers trotted down on the outside flank. The infantry and cavalry were mirrored on the opposite side.

"Wow! That chest armour in the middle is incredible." Brian couldn't keep the awe from his tone.

"Lorica segmentata."

"What?" Fianna looked pretty impressed, too, by the unbelievably shiny metal breastplates.

"It hasn't disappeared." Aran couldn't prevent a smirk from escaping.

"What's not disappeared?" Brian was answering automatically but, like his twin, he couldn't tear his gaze away from the magnificence in front of them.

"I read an article which claimed that type of segmented, plated armour wasn't often used in Severan times."

"What's the duller stuff that the other lot of

soldiers are wearing?" Fianna asked, pointing to the auxiliaries.

"Lorica hamata. Auxiliary soldiers wear chain mail and legionary soldiers wear the shiny breastplates."

He was just about to explain the differences between auxiliary and legionary soldiers when there was movement at the front line of Celts. Many heads swivelled around. He soon realised that they weren't looking at him and the twins; it was what was behind him that held their focus. Rows of Celtic warriors had arranged themselves up behind Tyrnan. Not everyone at the Tullos camp but a lot of armed warriors.

The sound of the carnyx, the battle horn of the Celts, rent the air. After the echoing tremors died down, Mapon and his druid interpreter trotted forward to the very edge of the water, along with the other High Chiefs.

"Look. Something's happening with those Romans in the centre section." Fianna prattled on, "The front rows of mounted soldiers have peeled off to each side. And so have more of the foot soldiers. What are they doing?"

It became clear that the Roman front lines had been a protecting wall. In behind them was a litter carried by about half a dozen men and seated on the couch of the litter was someone who had to be the Emperor Severus.

Walking behind the litter was a clutch of high ranking legionaries, all wearing the copper chest plates that were designed to mould around a man's abdomen muscles.

Brian whispered alongside Aran's shoulder. "Why have they brought us here?"

"Why shouldn't they?" Aran answered without

turning round because he didn't want to miss a single thing.

It was breathtaking. The files of Roman soldiers seemed so precise they looked drawn on the hillside as though an invisible ruler had been used. It was a magnificent show of strength flanking their Emperor.

"I think it's suspicious, too, that they've asked us to be here." Fianna backed up her brother. "Those chiefs haven't told us what the negotiations are all about, so why bring us?"

"Maybe it's because I helped them?" Aran didn't care what they thought; he was so buzzed at seeing real Roman splendour.

The litter was brought into place near the opposite banking and lowered to the ground after which Severus climbed out. The standard bearer with his legion's insignia moved to his right and another mounted officer flanked his left. As soon as the litter was removed to the side, the other high ranking officers moved in behind Severus.

"By Taranis or whatever they call him! Those things on that pole can't be real gold." Fianna's question was a mere whisper.

"The eagle on the top will be, but the discs might be something else like brass." However, they were certainly shiny yellow and looked the part enough to be real gold. He whispered an answer without moving his head. "His aquilifer—the guy holding the pole—will have been polishing those things for hours. He's got a really important job because that pole is the standard and it holds a huge superstitious significance. If the guy drops it, or if somebody were to steal it from him, it would be a very bad omen, a huge disgrace to the legion and that emperor over there is a super superstitious guy."

"Yeah. You told us about that already." Fianna wasn't being sarcastic, just stating fact as she absorbed the on goings of the delegations.

The Emperor might be old, but Aran found the man totally forbidding in full armour; his breastplate and helmet amazing.

A formal greeting from Mapon rang out across the valley; repeated by the druid interpreter.

Aran strained his ears but he was too far away to hear the conversation that followed. Severus spoke first, the mounted officer interpreting his words afterwards. In turn, via their interpreters, Mapon and Severus conducted the negotiations.

"That old guy's really something isn't he? Look at the metal jacket he's wearing. He looks so stiff necked that I bet he's got a pole up his backside to help him bear all that weight." Fianna's whisper tickled his ear.

He wanted to laugh at her comment but didn't want to break the spell of the momentous occasion because something was happening. Delnabo was interrupting and shouting over Mapon's interpreter. Mapon's hands came up to bracket his waist as he stormed back towards Delnabo. The Roman tribune was joining in the barrage of shouting as well. Back and forth the words went, but they were still too far off for Aran to hear.

In a very short time, the druids and the High Chiefs retreated to Tuadh and the other minor chiefs. A heated discussion took place amongst them all, their muffled voices unable to be heard though all around the area was dead silent except for the occasional neighing or whinnying of a horse. Tuadh's gestures were wild as he pivoted about, his arms reaching to the sky as though imploring his god Taranis.

The chiefs all looked over towards Aran.

Brian grabbed Aran's cloak to get his attention, "This isn't good Aran. Something's very off here."

"I don't like it now, either," Aran said.

After some rapid whispering and nodding of heads, Tuadh strode away from the delegation. The chief's voice was hoarse and he was unable to look them in the eye when he reached him and the twins.

"You are going to the Emperor Severus." The words were blunt.

"What?" Aran gaped at Seonagh's father. Any worry disappeared in the excitement of the moment. "That's fabulous!" He whooped with glee though no-one else around joined in.

"Tyrnan!" Tuadh ordered.

Aran thought some kind of silent message passed between the two men before Tuadh stomped away in a direction that was back up towards the temporary camp, the man looking fit to burst. It was odd, but Aran had no time to dwell on it because Tyrnan had his hands behind his back in a blink.

"What are you doing?" His yelling protest made no difference. The young warrior whipped a leather thong tightly in place around his wrists, a restraint he couldn't break apart and then Tyrnan pushed him forwards. It was like the first meeting with Seonagh all over again.

"Leave me alone!" Fianna could only manage a kick at the warrior who had her held tight by the cloak, another man securing her wrists.

Brian had fared no better. His restrainer was equally as big as Tyrnan. "Where are you taking us?"

"You are going to the Emperor Severus. It is as you desired, Aran of the Taexali." Tyrnan didn't sound thrilled with his news.

All of his earlier excitement gone, Aran looked at the warrior guard he'd begun to have a huge respect for. Tyrnan's eyes were blank, expression wiped away. The man wouldn't meet his eye but continued to force him towards the druids, the tightness at his lips as though he detested following orders.

Mapon called out across the water. "Receive your payment, Severus of Rome!"

Loud protests rent the air to Aran's left, the screeching and wailing pitiful to hear. The file of tribespeople that he had noticed earlier was being dragged forward towards the river.

Now he realised why they'd been shuffling down the hill. They were trussed up together along a long rope and kept in place by aggressive guards. Attempts to flee the column were useless; no escape was possible since they were held captive, just like he was.

Brian's moan alongside him was horrified. "Some of those people are from Balbath!"

"What?" Aran cried as Tyrnan shoved him towards Mapon.

One young boy in the row gestured wildly at Brian, his tied hands yanking on the rope as he pointed. "This is your fault!" His attempt to break free from the line was thwarted by a burly guard who felled him with one blow. The warrior snatched the boy up and forced him back in line.

"Who is he?" Aran was appalled at the mistreatment by a fellow Celt.

Brian was pale as a ghost. "Remember I told you about the bully I wrestled with?"

"That's Garath?" Aran whispered.

Mapon's voice rang out, "Emperor Severus!"

The druid interpreter translated Mapon's words and then continued what seemed to be a rehearsed speech in Latin.

Aran glanced at the twins: he wanted to press the red lips icon to understand the tongue of the Romans, but it wasn't possible to open his armband.

Mapon turned to him, the man as aloof as a stone statue. "Aran, son of Durran, you have the wisdom of the gods though you are still a boy." The druid shouted so that as many people as possible would hear him. "The gods now go with you. You will take your knowledge to the Emperor Severus. He has need of your divining of the future."

Blairdaff guffawed drowning out Mapon's next words as he leaned down from atop his horse. "The boy is not much of a diviner if he cannot see his own fate in front of him!"

His words pitiless, he grabbed Aran's golden torque and yanked him free of Tyrnan's clutches. Blairdaff tugged him towards Severus, increasing the horse's pace by using knee pressure alone. Aran dangled alongside, his feet skimming along the ground in uneven lurches.

"It is your moment now, boy. You can tell Severus we have no further need for any of you. He can kill all the hostages immediately, including you, if he desires to, since your use is now over." Blairdaff crowed when the horse padded across the tightly lashed planking of a makeshift bridge which had been set a across the waters of the narrow river.

Aran felt himself airborne for a few seconds before he regained his balance on the far banking, his toes stubbing against the ground. He struggled to get free but it was no use. The torque bit into the back of his neck when he was towed across the rough grass till the High Chief came to a halt. He was furious but Blairdaff was as strong as an ox holding him in place for the Romans to collect. It was too late to realise what the Celtic leaders were doing. It wasn't only the line of screaming tribespeople who were being dragged across the river as hostages to Severus. The treaty included bodies for slaves and he was one of them!"

The Roman Emperor Severus looked as cruel as the history books said he was. There was nothing forgiving in the Emperor's expression as he signalled for the hostages to be rounded up by his too eager auxiliaries.

Why on earth had he wanted to get close up to this murderous man? Aran now seriously regretted his earlier enthusiasm as he dangled by the torque, Blairdaff's grip not relenting till a fully armoured legionary grabbed him by the arm and whirled him about. The Roman wedged him in place by his tied wrists, his shield sandwiching his front. The man grumbled something but Aran couldn't understand a word.

Unable to do anything but ineffectively struggle, he watched Blairdaff circle around. In a show of bravado, the Celtic High chief urged his horse to jump the water avoiding the Roman made bridge.

Frantic about his imprisonment, he looked across to where Celtic warriors still held the twins. Most eyes were on Blairdaff's return but that wasn't what Fianna was doing. Taking advantage of her guard's lack of concentration, he watched her hook her leg behind the young man's knee and bend her shoulder in a push. The surprise on the young warrior's face, as she toppled him over, would have been comical if the situation had been less fraught with danger. In that split second, her captor was on the ground and Fianna was running towards the end of the file of people who were still being forced across the water.

She stumbled across the grass, her hands tied behind her, her furious words snatched into the air. "Seonagh's in that line!"

At the end of the long snake, Seonagh struggled for all she was worth. Not tied, yet, to the original line she was being restrained by two warriors before being added to the hostages.

"Fianna!" Brian's screech echoed along the riverside.

Aran watched Brian frantically fighting his guard to run after his twin.

"Stay together, you two!" Aran shouted.

When he pushed forwards to escape from the Roman legionary's clutches, the edge of the soldier's scutum was slammed against his temple, a glancing blow but a well aimed one. Someone nearby barked a loud command. He guessed it was Severus who was speaking but the voice got fainter and fainter. The last thing he saw before blackness descended was Brian being dragged across the water towards him, screaming and hollering like a banshee.

Chapter Twenty

"Stop! Let me untie you."

Fianna knew the voice but didn't dare stop running.

On reaching her, Tyrnan had the knot undone in a second before he sped off towards Seonagh, his long legs covering the distance faster than Fianna could since Seonagh was already almost hauled over the River Urie.

"You will not send the daughter of Tuadh as hostage!" Tyrnan was the angriest Fianna had ever heard as she watched him struggle with one of Seonagh's restrainers who wasn't pleased at the interference.

"Leave her be! The daughter of a minor chief is essential trade with the Romans. The treaty demands high ranking hostages and she is one of our best." Keeping his hold on Seonagh who was struggling like fury, the man tried to placate Tyrnan.

Tyrnan ignored the words and heaved a mighty blow at the guards jaw but one punch was all he could get in before more warriors surged around to prevent him from freeing Seonagh.

"Seonagh! I did not know this is what they intended for you. Please believe it…" In seconds, Tyrnan was overpowered by Celtic warriors who should have been his allies. When the hilt of one attacker's sword made the almightiest crack on Tyrnan's skull, his attempt to free Seonagh was over. Huge though he was, Tyrnan toppled like a felled tree trunk.

Fianna grabbed Seonagh's hand and dragged her

away from the banking, pulling her up towards The Mither Tap. Her intention was good but her treatment was little better than what Tyrnan had received. Only a few paces into the run she was brought to the ground in an easy tackle. Protesting and squealing, she was bodily lifted from behind and clutched in an unbreakable arm grip.

The gruff voice behind her sounded resigned. "We have no choice. You must also go to Severus. The gods have spoken, so accept what must be."

The man's brawny forearm muffled her next cries. "They're not my gods. Let me go!"

Handed from warrior to warrior three times over, Fianna was passed across another temporary bridge that had been slapped into place by the Romans and set on her feet at the end of the file of hostages. Seonagh was already in place in front of her, restrained by two of the shiny breast plated Roman soldiers. Fianna might have been admiring their gleam a short while ago but she found being clamped against one was a different thing entirely. It wasn't in the least comfortable and she let the legionary soldier know just how furious she was. One effective stamp on his leather sandaled foot earned her a slap at the jaw which almost dislodged her from his grip, never mind the teeth in her gums.

"Fianna! You must stop. They will hurt you. I will make them keep you with me. My status will give me advantage."

Seonagh might mean what she was saying but Fianna wasn't convinced. There was nothing she could do to break free right that moment anyway as she and Seonagh were locked into iron manacles and attached to the chain that bound the whole line of tribespeople. After they were secured, they were dragged past a whole rectangle of infantry and up the hill.

Lots of words were flying around her ears but she understood none of them. The translator? Handcuffed to the chain her fingers were useless—there was no way to reach it.

For every three or four Celts there was at least one Roman soldier herding them. Though she concentrated hard on the ground in front of her as she was pulled and hauled, she couldn't work out a way of opening her armband. Her mind whirled. Maybe she could get Seonagh to help open it and only tell the girl what she needed to know about it? If she did manage that, should she just get Seonagh to press the lips so that she would be able to understand the talk of the Romans, or should she ask Seonagh to press the 'eject' thing? That sounded way too dodgy since she was separated from Brian and Aran.

A worse thought occurred. If someone else was doing the pressing and not her, then it wouldn't be her fingerprint. What would happen then? Would the whole armband connection stop working? Oh heavens, or Taranis, or whatever! That was unthinkable.

She worried her head off because she knew Aran had been taken directly over to Severus. She'd seen that before she'd set off to help Seonagh but when she'd looked over from the end of the slave line he was being dragged behind the huge swathe of legionary soldiers that flanked Severus in the middle block of Romans.

Not knowing what to do for the best bugged her but what worried her most was Brian. He had to be okay. Surely, she would know? They sometimes thought the same things at the same time but they didn't really have the major emotional thing going on that some other twins had.

Seonagh turned back to speak to her when the line eventually came to a halt. "They will come and remove us from the other tribespeople, Fianna. I'm sure of it. I am the daughter of a chief."

She thought Seonagh was a bit deluded but nodded to reassure her. Looking around at the huddle of imprisoned Celts, she could taste the despair. These people had an idea of what being a slave was like having heard about it happening to the southern Celtic tribes. What she saw stamped across their foreheads wasn't any kind of tattoo but a sense of utter dejection.

It wasn't long before one of the posh helmeted Romans came her way with another soldier, one wearing the chain mail kind of armour. She couldn't understand any of their words but they seemed to be talking about Seonagh, if the looks and finger-points meant anything.

When the auxiliary soldier spoke a form of Celtic, Seonagh had no trouble understanding. Fianna found it much more guttural, different from the way they spoke in Balbath, but similar enough for the translator to function.

"Aye. Tuadh of Balbath is my father," Seonagh said.

The auxiliary asked a few more questions and seemed satisfied with her answers. The red crested officer reached for Seonagh's manacle and gave orders that it should be opened before he dragged her free of the line.

"Nay! You must also take Fianna. She has to remain with me." Seonagh was adamant about it, while she struggled to free herself from the man's clutches.

Fianna felt Seonagh's fingers tighten against her wrist clamp so that she was pulled along, too.

"Is she also a daughter of Tuadh?" The auxiliary pointed to Fianna's bronze torque, making the officer aware of it.

Fianna was about to say she wasn't but was glad when Seonagh answered first.

"She is as a foster daughter to Tuadh, so, aye, she is his family."

Before Fianna could draw breath, she was unlocked. Yanked along by the auxiliary, he dragged her all the way past many lines of soldiers and up the crest of the hill to the Durno camp. By the time the Roman officer, who similarly tugged Seonagh up the hill, stopped at a larger than usual tent Fianna thought her shoulder must be pulled out of its socket, the pain was so acute.

The sentry stationed outside the tent exchanged a salute and a few unintelligible words.

Bundled into the tent after Seonagh, she scanned around. There was a little free space around a low cot and a wooden post rack with bits and pieces of clothing hanging free of the ground. The tent didn't hold much else apart from a table set near the back with a stool behind it. The table was littered with wooden ended scrolls and a few bits of stick that she guessed were quills and styli.

The officer's head popped inside and gave orders they had no hope of obeying since they hadn't a clue what he was shouting. Fianna got the general message, though—stay in here, or else, seemed to be the gist of it.

Seonagh was close to tears when she sank down on to the low cot, her hands cradling her face.

"Don't worry." Fianna made herself sound more confident than she felt. "I'll get you out of here, somehow."

"I do not think there is much chance of that, Fianna. There are thousands of Roman soldiers here in this camp and every one would stop us if we tried to escape."

"I agree, but that shouldn't stop us from trying."

Slipping to the back of the tent, Fianna pretended to look at the scrolls. Seonagh's head had slipped down into her hands, despair oozing from her.

The talking outside became louder, increasing to shouting point.

Taking the advantage of the moment Fianna slipped her finger on the knob of her armband. The minute the flap opened, she located the red lips icon and pressed.

"Caracalla will decide what to do with the higher ranking hostages but they must remain here till then. You are responsible for them!"

She couldn't be sure but it sounded like it was coming from the soldier who had dragged her up the hill, the one who had done the translation for the officer.

Caracalla? From what Aran had told her, Fianna didn't want to ever clap eyes on the disgusting guy. She cursed a blue streak when she realised that the conversation outside had made her miss part of a message on the armband. "*...give Severus what he needs.*"

"What the heck does that mean?"

Seonagh looked up just as a soldier entered the tent. "Are you ailing, Fianna?"

***

The words around Aran made no sense. Voices came and went as he resisted opening his eyes. He knew someone was bent over him because warm breath was wafting at his nose and it was rank. He was flat on his back but had no memory of lying down.

More talk.

Latin!

He remembered what had happened before he passed out. He couldn't speak the language but if he could reach his armband, he'd be able to understand. That thought prompted another. Why hadn't his armband given some warning that he was going to be knocked out with a Roman shield?

A hand pushed at his shoulder, the voice impatient. The sudden whack of a broad palm at his cheek sucked back the breath he'd just drawn. Disappearing in an instant was a great idea but it wasn't going to happen so he knew he'd have to face up to whatever was in front of him.

He flickered his eyes, just enough to get an idea of who was bent over him. Red feathers stuck up from the helmet in a wonderfully thick arc fanning from ear to ear. A centurion!

Multiple fingers dug into him when more than one soldier yanked him to his feet. The talk continued as he was swirled around to face the Emperor who was now seated on his litter.

Looking at the man, he truly did get his wish of earlier. The armour Severus wore was fantastic. The muscled bronze breastplate was polished to a mirrored gleam. Just below throat level was the gawping maw of a lion cast in gold, matching other embellishments around the armour.

Jaw-droppingly cool! The most spectacular breastplate he'd ever seen.

The deep bark of unintelligible words that came from the Emperor was as noisy as Tuadh could have managed, but it all meant he-haw.

Raising his eyes even higher he couldn't help gasping. The man's armour was amazing but the helmet he wore was even more so. It wasn't like anything he'd ever seen on the internet or in books. The helmet was tight to the skull with slightly shorter earflaps than the one the centurion wore but it was the gilded decoration that was stunning. At the forehead was a raised crown-like decoration trimmed in gold with a little rampant lion statue behind it. The white brush of clipped feathers and horsehair behind the statue went right down to the back neck piece and was part of the skull cap, not like the centurion's red plume which fanned out from a raised band and went from ear to ear across the top of the helmet. All the decorative elements were incredible to look at but Severus' helmet also had a lot of little dents in it as though the man had taken a lot of hits in combat. Although the man was old, he knew Severus had been an incredible military general long before he became the Emperor.

More grunts fired his way.

Staring at the Emperor was easy, answering the man was impossible.

Aran gulped a very painful gulp. His throat and neck were really sore: back and front. A lot more painful than when Tyrnan throttled him less dramatically than Blairdaff had just done. Unfortunately, the swallowing crumpled his forehead and he wished that hadn't happened either. His forehead wasn't feeling so good. He had that sense of having a huge egg up there, the bruising feeling a bit splotchy. He reached up to soothe everything—his throat first.

His gold torque wasn't there any more! His fingers slid down to his tunic. Neither was the Pin of Funach.

Horror had to be suppressed. Had the Romans removed his armband as well? He'd no idea how long he had been unconscious. He rubbed his upper arm surreptitiously feeling for it. A wash of pure relief flooded him when he realised the band was still there. It was only then that he grasped that his hands had been untied and guessed that had been because they'd needed to lay him on his back.

The centurion's hand shook his shoulder as though to make him answer whatever question Severus has asked.

"What did you say?"

His plea was met by a flick of Severus' hand, dismissing him.

Dragged to the side, he was able to see what was going on. Severus engaged in a rapid conversation with a legionary soldier positioned just behind him. Judging by the uniform that was fairly similar to Severus', but with a lot less gold on it, Aran guessed the man was either the legatus—the commander of the legion—or a senior tribune officer.

The officer stepped forward to come abreast of the Emperor.

"Did your father, Durran of the Taexali at Durris, give you this fine torque?" The man spoke halting

Celtic, pointing at the torque now held up by the centurion.

Aran nodded. He wasn't going to tell them how he came by it.

"The druid interpreter claimed that you are a seer who can tell the Emperor many useful things. Are you?"

"It is true that I do know information that others do not." Being truthful didn't seem to gain him any favours. At a nod from the Emperor, the centurion literally slapped him back into place in front of Severus.

"Tell the Emperor three pieces of your knowledge."

It was like being interrogated by the Celtic chiefs all over again. What on earth could he tell a superstitious old man like Severus was said to be. From the sour expression on the Emperor's face, he had about as much patience as Tuadh. Scrabbling around in his memory banks, he plucked out some innocuous facts he'd absorbed and took a moment to work out how to express them. Some of the things were a huge risk but so was being battered to high heaven. He felt his forehead. Although it wasn't hurting as much as his neck, there was a good growing bump at his temple. Glancing at his fingers, he was glad to see no traces of blood.

A second wallop from the centurion reminded him he was taking too long.

"I know where the Emperor will meet his death, though it will not be for a few more seasons. He—" The centurion halted his speech with an imperious hand held high in front of his face, so that the other Roman could interpret his words. Maybe that wasn't the best thing to start with but he'd committed himself.

After the interpreter went silent, he resumed. "Emperor Severus should also know that the soothsayer he has already consulted speaks the truth in all matters discussed." After another pause during which time he managed to think of a third thing, he chanced his arm. "The Emperor was wise to bring all of his gold to Britannia, since it will take even more to pacify these northern Celts."

He watched the old man's eyes flicker with sheer temper, yet it also seemed to him that Severus' shoulders slumped after one imperial hand brushed him out of sight. The venomous splurge that came from the Emperor's mouth wasn't pleasant and neither were the yank at his tunic and the nipping fingers at his elbows when he was dragged away past all of those in the centre section of Romans. When his captors continued uphill he was pretty sure he wasn't being treated as an honoured guest.

By Taranis! He was getting used to mouthing to the god of the Celts.

If Severus didn't kill him first, then Callum was bound to. He was supposed to look after the twins and here he was, yet again, separated from them and unable to do anything about it.

Half-run half-dragged, it seemed no time at all before he was facing the turf walls of the temporary camp at Durno. The fright he'd been feeling as a prisoner was replaced by that treacherous excitement again. He'd stood at the very same part of the land in the twenty first century when all there was to show for a Roman temporary camp was a bump in the field. What faced him now was incredible.

On the far side of a shallow ditch was a wall of sharpened stakes at the top of the banking that formed the outer wall of the camp—a temporary palisade. Behind it he could just see the worn leather of many sizeable ridge tents. He knew that a contubernium group of eight men shared each tent, but when he was marched in through a tightly-lashed wooden gateway the sight of those tents was even more impressive. Precisely packed behind the earthworks were rows and rows of accurately positioned shelters with clear walkways between them—town streets full of tents.

Aran found himself shoved into the opening of one of the tents but he knew it was no ordinary accommodation. The above man-height rectangular tent reeked of officer status. There was a table set close to the far wall with a mound of scrolls upon it. A low cot was positioned at one side of the tent flap. Heaps of bits and pieces lay on top of low trestle tables and items of clothing and weapons hung from racks.

An order was barked into his face. He guessed it wasn't the man telling him to make himself comfortable and there wasn't much chance of escape during the daylight with Roman soldiers crawling around like ants in an anthill. Unfortunately, he wasn't sure it would be better when darkness descended either.

The man who had frogmarched him into the tent stood talking to the soldiers.

Latin!

Aran reached for the tiny nub on his armband knowing that it might be his only opportunity to use the language function. The second the flap opened, he depressed the red lips icon. When a message scrolled across the tiny display, it was a huge surprise. *'The others are safe. You will be reunited soon. Do nothing rash meantime and learn what you can.'* Catching the words moving along the panel was an art because they fed along at a spanking pace.

It seemed he had to sit tight and work his way through the next stage of this weird adventure. He wished the twins were with him, yet he'd no time to dwell, or make plans, because someone was coming back in. He snapped the flap of the armband shut wondering why he still had it.

Chapter Twenty-One

"Get off me!"

Brian felt himself propelled towards the river till he was just centimetres away from the banking but he couldn't dig his heels in to prevent himself from tipping into it. The grip at his tied wrists and the push at his shoulder were too strong. Over on the other side of the water, he could see Aran struggling with a Roman soldier and then in a blink of shining armour he watched his best friend plummet to the ground.

"Aran!" His cry was cut short when the grip behind him suddenly slackened.

"Let the boy go!"

"Nay. He goes to Severus as part of Carden's share."

"It will not be this boy. Carden can find his own body forfeit."

The tussle behind Brian escalated, his handler being set upon by someone whose voice he vaguely recognised. Struggling to work out who was trying to free him, he was unprepared for the thwomp at his ear that sent him flying straight down into the river. As his feet slipped and slithered down the banking, he was pretty sure the punch hadn't been for him, but the almost idle thought didn't help him make a nice soft landing.

The water was no more than a couple of metres deep, but his tied hands meant a painful jarring of his tailbone on impact, his splashing entry almost horizontal. He wasn't in the water for very long, just enough to be soaked in what was nippy water for the beginning of May. A few hands grabbed his cloak and hauled him up like a sack of soggy potatoes before they dumped him onto the banking. The knife that flicked through his bindings stung his skin but he wasn't caring about a tiny nick. His rescuers had him up on his feet and running, hauling at his cloak before he could spit out all of the water he'd gurgled down.

"Run faster!"

He was trying but his wet braccae were flapping against his calves and his boots were squelching with every slap on the ground. "Where are we going?"

His question wasn't answered till they had cleared the block of warriors who had allowed their passage through the rows of gathered Celts behind Mapon. It seemed clear that those warriors hadn't liked him being used as part of the trade, either. He was ushered past so quickly he could barely glance at the men but he had a strong feeling that most of them were from Balbath.

"Liam?" Brian had remembered the young warrior was Seonagh's brother. "What are you doing?"

Liam slowed the pace only a little as they skirted the back of the amassed lines of Celtic Warriors.

"That traitor Carden changed the plans made by the High Chiefs last night. My sister was never intended to be one of those tribespeople in the trade with Rome. My father realised something was amiss when Delnabo interrupted the dealings between Mapon and Severus' tribune. That was why Tuadh stormed away from the chiefs and went in search of Seonagh."

"But Tyrnan was the one who came and told her to go to Ailish."

"Tyrnan did not know what Carden and Blairdaff had arranged. Delnabo decided that Seonagh was the highest ranking princess of the local tribes and that worm Carden agreed. They organised her exchange without telling my father and Blairdaff was delighted to hand over Aran."

"And now our sisters are both over on the Roman side of the river."

Liam didn't need to answer. They'd come out at the far end of the rows of warriors and could see that the slave lines had been marched well up the hill to the Durno camp.

"How do we get our sisters back from that horde of scavengers over there?" There was no point in wailing but that was how Brian felt as he viewed the thousands of precise Roman auxiliaries and legionaries stepping their way back up the slope.

"We need to find Tuadh, but first we will locate Tyrnan's body." Liam took off on a trot,

Brian puffed between Liam and the large group of Balbath warriors who had joined them.

That his clothes would dry more quickly on his body was the only positive he could think of at that moment.

By the time they found Tuadh, the negotiations were well over. The chief of Balbath was making himself very unpopular with the High Chiefs. He called them all sorts of deceitful liars and other names that Brian could only guess at because the translation was weird. When Tuadh threw a punch at Delnabo, Liam and Thain jumped forward to restrain their father.

Mapon banished a still loudly protesting Tuadh from the fireside of the High Chiefs who were haggling over the sharing of Severus' gold.

As Brian followed after Tuadh's men he could

hear Delnabo mump and moan. "My Caledons need to be certain that their portion is a fair one."

Carden complained even more than Delnabo. "Why do you grumble? I cannot return to my settlement till those Romans leave my territory. I do not even know if I have roundhouses to go back to. You can leave now and go back to your untouched villages in the high hills."

The talk of the High Chiefs was getting fainter as Brian moved further away but Mapon's words made him wonder what the druid could mean when he said, "Enough! Your portions are all fair ones and this bickering must cease. My time here is waning. I leave now with my fellow druid. I will return to this place, but by then only Carden needs to linger. The rest of you should go home after daybreak."

Tuadh was silent and it worried Brian even more than when the man bawled and shouted. Liam declared they needed to make a new fireside out of sight of the High Chiefs. Tuadh had curtly nodded and added that he wanted none of the pestilent Roman gold but vowed he wouldn't budge from the Tullos area till all had been done to rescue Seonagh from Roman clutches.

Along with the file of Balbathans, Brian trekked past the old fire area he'd shared with Fianna and Aran, Orla and Caitlinn still waiting for them. Brian collected their weapons which had lain wrapped in Aran's cloak—the things still in the place where Tyrnan had dumped them.

"We will work out some way of rescuing the girls," Liam muttered later that night at the new fireside. Unfortunately, Brian didn't think Seonagh's brother sounded all that convinced about it.

"Yeah." He wasn't sure either. He couldn't think of a single way to make it happen. Getting up from the small blaze, he wandered away. Only a few steps but still within the light of the fire because the night dark was dense, the cloud cover very heavy.

His worry increased. It wasn't only his sister who needed to be rescued.

He hadn't a clue where Aran was, either, so that meant no pressing of the stop button or using the ejector seat. Rescuing them from the clutches of more than thirty thousand Romans was laughable, yet there had to be some way to do it.

It almost scared the crap out of him when his arm tingled and the flap popped open, but that was all that happened. He waited. When no message appeared after a few seconds impulse ruled. He pressed the help button. Guidance was definitely needed.

Shielding the armband with his cloak, he read the eerily lit display as the words scrolled over the screen.

"Fianna is with Seonagh. Aran isn't. The sea is the place after dawn." The flap pinged shut.

"The sea is what place? What does that mean, Callum?"

Brian waited but the armband remained cold and motionless. More clues weren't going to happen.

Back at the fireside, Thain was arguing with his brother. Quietly, but still arguing, he sounded determined. "After dawn, I am going up that hill to free Seonagh."

Liam was firm. "Think wisely, my brother. You will not even get across the river. We must think of a way of snatching her when there are fewer Romans at Durno. Perhaps Severus will head south after dawn and only the forces of Caracalla will remain."

A dark shadow loomed towards the fireside. Tuadh looked up at the interruption. “If you have a way of bargaining my daughter free again you may remain. If not, then you are not welcome.”

Mapon’s head shook. “I have news but what you do with it may lie in the lap of the gods.”

Liam was more amenable than his father. “Tell us. Please. And give us some hope.”

The druid sat down, Meriel at his back, though Brian was sure that the harp had not been played for some nights. “The last of the negotiations are now over. The High Chiefs had one last meeting with the envoys of Severus after I sent you away. Tuadh, believe me; I tried to regain your daughter. It was never my plan for her to be in the settlement, but Severus has refused to return her. Seonagh is his highest ranking prisoner and he will not relent. For some reason I do not understand, he offered the High Chiefs even more gold to settle the matter. She now seems to command an even higher bargaining price. I have your portion of it here.”

“I want no Roman gold.” Tuadh sounded so quietly determined. “But I do want my daughter returned to me.”

“Will being worth more gold make any difference to what happens to her?” Brian asked.

Mapon was doleful. “I do not believe so. All of the prisoners will be sold to the slave traders come dawn. Seonagh, and perhaps your sister if she is held in the same esteem as Seonagh, may have a few privileges that others will not have but they will still be sent to the slave markets of the Empire.”

“At first light, I am going to the nearest sea beach,” Brian declared. “Is there one of you who can help get me there as fast as possible? Please?"

"The sea? Why would you go there?" Mapon wanted to know. "The slave traders will set their new slaves on the Roman road in a southerly direction as soon as the haggling is over. Many households just south of the stone wall will be very happy to buy fresh Caledon and Taexali slaves. That is what happened to captured Celts of the north, last Lughnasadh, when Severus first came here."

"That's not what will happen with Seonagh and my sister. They will be sent south in a Roman ship."

Mapon stared at Brian till he felt red as a beetroot. "I do not know how you can know this, Brian of Durris, but I am of a mind to believe you. You are a very knowledgeable young warrior with gifts that come from the gods. Your friend, Aran, is part of my destiny though he may not yet know that. Sleep well, young tamhas, because you must remain vigilant come dawn, if you are to rescue your sister."

Brian wasn't buying the bit about the gods but he supposed his armband contact was a sort of gift. For the next while, he and Mapon worked hard to convince Tuadh that his warriors needed to head for the coast at first light.

"Remind me about the latest news from the coast?" Tuadh still seemed too preoccupied about Seonagh's imprisonment to concentrate properly.

A groggy voice answered from the far side of the fire. "Three Roman ships were berthed at Baile Mheadhain, though the local tribe had ceased to skirmish with the soldiers who had been left to guard them. I heard about that before I got on the wrong edge of a sword hilt."

Brian nipped around to help Tyrnan sit up. The

man had slept for a long time after they had found him and brought him back to Tuadh's new fireside.

"Wow! That's a cracker of a goose egg that you've got there!" Brian grinned.

"If you mean do I have a sore bump then you are very correct, young warrior of Durris."

Tuadh piped up, looking more animated than he had for ages. "You will live. My warriors are made of strong constitutions but what more of these ships?"

***

The tribune, who had spoken Celtic, strode in with one of the other men who had been riding behind Severus. There was no polite greeting. "You will tell Emperor Marcus Aurelius Antoninius everything you know!"

The posh name didn't fool Aran. This was the Emperor's son?

Aran wasn't that impressed. Caracalla was probably taller than Severus but not quite as tall as him. It felt fantastic to look down very slightly into the round face with a heap of black tight curls but Caracalla's eyes and mouth looked evil.

Should he continue with the pretence of not being able to understand Latin and allow the tribune to translate for him? It took only a fraction of a second for him to decide it might not be a bad idea to keep them in the dark for a bit longer.

Again, he was prompted. "What can you tell him about his father?"

Aran stayed mute but it only got him a slap across the ear which rocked him off his feet. The tribune didn't hold back from dishing out another one when Aran refused to say anything.

When Caracalla stepped behind him, he wasn't feeling so chipper. The Emperor's son was smaller but he was as strong as an ox. When the arm locked around his neck and the bronze muscled breastplate dug into his back, he decided maybe saying something was okay. Though what?

In Latin he croaked, "What would you like to know?"

"Let the boy go!"

Aran hadn't heard the Emperor come in to the tent having been a bit preoccupied but he was glad of the interruption. Immediately the tension at his shoulders eased.

"The boy knows nothing!" Caracalla bawled and stomped out of the tent.

Aran guessed the son didn't like his interrogations being cut short by his dad.

Severus menaced right up to him "I think that there is much that you can tell me."

The nod from the Emperor to the centurion who had come in with him wasn't encouraging. Aran realised he'd just exchanged one problem for another.

"It seems that you can speak the tongue of Rome." Severus' beady eyes confronted Aran, a clenched fist jabbing painfully at his stomach. The Emperor got in another good dunt before he felt the centurion bracketing his arms in a tight clasp behind his back. Severus then propped himself on the edge of the desk as though his legs wouldn't support him any longer. Unfortunately, for Aran, the old man's fists still worked pretty well.

"Will these new treaties be upheld?" Severus demanded, his tiny nod a signal for the centurion to do a little torturing.

The good guy had just become the bad guy again so Aran decided on a compromise. Maybe there was a thing or two he could tell Severus from the jumbled storage in his memory banks. Blanking out the pain at his shoulders and wrists he grunted, "The Miathi will give you peace near the green wall and you will be able to build your forts there. As many as you please."

He was pretty certain he'd read that there were a number of forts built across central Scotland around AD 210 for maintaining control of the area.

"More." Another jab at his stomach from the Emperor wasn't friendly at all. Aran clenched his teeth to prevent the agony escaping.

The Emperor slumped back again, but his observation was still too acute to be comfortable.

While Aran gained composure, he thought about something that Severus had become famous for. "Your triumphal arch at the Forum in Rome will be admired as much in two thousand years from now as it is today. So will the one that you have built at your birthplace of Leptis Magna. You will be famously known for your fabulous buildings as much as for your military career."

That seemed to please Severus, enough for the nod to the centurion to release him.

Bit by bit Aran remembered some other useful things to say.

The grilling gradually slipped into more of a chat but then changed again when Severus demanded that Aran tell him more about the intention of his sons. That was a dodgy one to answer since Severus' boys weren't nice lads. Aran was hesitant until the centurion thumped at his back once again, the man's breathing down his neck very unnerving.

"Your sons both want to be emperor, very badly, after your death."

Back came the heavy hand of the centurion around his neck. This time the grip was so intense it made Aran squirm in pain but he continued—Severus wanted more rather than less information.

"You need to be careful when your elder son is near you. He is really volatile and, sometime soon, he will try to stab you in the back. You must warn your Danubian guard to be vigilant or your son may manage to kill you before your allotted time. Your death should not be this summer season but more like a moon's turn after the festival of Janus. Your soothsayer has already warned you of this happening at Eboracum."

Severus again signalled for the centurion to back off. "When will my son try to slay me?"

Aran had no answer. All he remembered reading was that it happened during some kind of low key negotiation. When Severus slipped behind the desk to sit down he asked some questions of his own.

"You've taken my torque and my cloak pin? Where are they?"

Severus scattered a pile of scrolls to reveal what was beneath. Holding up the torque and pin, Severus spat out an answer. Aran groaned when he saw the flick of an eye at the centurion, an indication that more pain was coming his way.

"None of my scouts who can decipher Celtic Symbols can give an answer to the riddles written on these. What do they mean?"

Since Mapon hadn't told him what they meant, he hadn't a clue. Fed up with the grilling and with the pain inflicted on him Aran did a bit of spitting out himself. "Only a druid can give you those answers."

Severus wasn't finished. The finger he pointed to Aran's armband was as shaky as the voice was sounding. It seemed the Emperor's strength wasn't all that good after all. "What meaning is there to those marks on the new ring?"

"On my armband?" Aran was stalling. He didn't know what they meant either. "They herald a warning."

"Those fire-flashes came from Jupiter?" Severus looked momentarily terrified.

"Flashes?" Aran bit back a grin. "Who touched my band and was burned?" Trying to sound stern was nearly impossible. Callum must have been sending him a message.

The old finger pointed to the centurion. Aran hadn't realised that the other man had now backed himself up almost to the tent flap. He looked petrified as well.

Aran found it was a great pleasure to chance his arm. "I can send much more damaging lightning bolts to both of you, if my torque and my pin are not returned to me."

Severus threw the jewellery at him before a command barked out. "Tether him outside, out of my sight!"

In the blink of an eye, Aran was shackled to a stake outside the tent.

Soldiers came and went for hours but it was as though he was invisible. Ignored by the two-man guard who flanked the doorway, he'd stopped pleading for his release since the sentries stuck to their orders unflinchingly. No conversation happened, apart from them always asking when entry to Severus' tent was sought. The Emperor didn't seem to sleep very much as the flow of soldiers visiting continued through the hours of darkness. The Danubian guards were changed regularly but all of them guarded their emperor zealously. All night long.

With no cloak to cover him, the night was cold and very lonely. Aran worried about what was happening to the twins and felt a real failure. During this adventure he wasn't supposed to end up separated from the twins. He was supposed to learn new information he could tell the twenty first century historians but he didn't think he'd learned anything new. Fulfilling the quest bit about helping the enemy was a real tricky one. He wished he could be sure he'd done that because there was more than one enemy in this story.

Severus was a nasty man, as was Caracalla but so were Delnabo and Blairdaff. He certainly didn't want to help those Celts ever again.

He needed to rub his neck, Blairdaff having dragged him like a rag doll, but his tied hands made it impossible.

Chapter Twenty-Two

"Someone is going to pay highly for a slave like you. Our Romans in the south of Britannia like the idea that they are being waited on by sons and daughters of Caledon chiefs."

Fianna thought that the Roman legionary who was speaking was a nasty piece of work. He stood looking at Seonagh with complete disrespect, his persistent jibing at her continuing even though his talk obviously meant nothing. Seonagh still sat on the bed.

Fianna pretended she couldn't understand either when the guard's gaze turned to her and ogled her bronze torque.

"That will fetch a few denarii at the market."

She bit back an answer. She was certain her lovely bronze choker was worth a lot of denarii but she wouldn't give him the satisfaction of annoying her. An insipid smile cracked her cheeks as though he had just complimented her.

"But it may only be the torque that gets as far as the market. You are both going to see Caracalla and when he is finished there may be nothing left worth sending to the slave market." The guffaw was even more spiteful as he headed back to the door flap where he stopped and deliberately turned back. "Come here, now!"

Neither she nor Seonagh moved.

The command was repeated one more time before the guard popped his head out to get the assistance of other soldiers.

"Take them to Caracalla!"

Fianna gave up the struggle quite quickly. The ox

of a man who had gripped her arm was too heavy to topple easily and she decided she might need her strength for later. "Leave me alone. I can walk without your help."

She was relieved when Seonagh whispered to her, "That was wise, Fianna. For now, I fear, we must do as they demand."

The relief was because she hadn't been sure how the language translation was going to work. She didn't want to let the Romans know that she could understand them and hadn't wanted to lose the ability to speak the Celtic tongue.

After being marched along a fairly wide flattened-grass street, where there were leather tents on both sides rather than buildings, the guards stopped them at a much larger higher than man-height tent, the flaps of which were wide open.

Inside was one man seated at a side desk. Fianna recognised what he was doing as the metal stylus busily scratched across the surface of a wax tablet. When he heard them arrive, he looked up and then got to his feet, a salute passing between him and the legionary in front of her. She couldn't decide who was the most senior of the two because the gestures made seemed very similar.

The secretary soldier put down his stylus and came forward. "Caracalla is with the Emperor. Who are these two?"

"Seonagh, daughter of the local chief Tuadh of Balbath, and his foster daughter Fianna of Durris."

"Then they'd better be kept apart from the others. Caracalla will want to question them when he returns. He's very interested to know if the local chiefs around here will stick to the agreement they've just made, or if they will also rebel come some new dawns. His recent experience with the Vacomagi tribe has not been a completely favourable one. That's what delayed his arrival here or he would have reached this Garioch area long before Severus." The secretary returned to his table and lifted a wax tablet. After using a tool to clear it he picked up his stylus again. "Seonagh of Balbath?" He pointed at Seonagh and waited till the legionary nodded. "And the russet one is Fianna of Durris?" Another nod was shared before the secretary jabbered on again.

Fianna guessed he was recording some more details about her and Seonagh. In between scribbling, the secretary carried on talking. "Those deceitful Vacomagi agreed with Caracalla during the hours of daylight and then attacked us when the next darkness came. None of these Celts are to be trusted."

Throwing down the stylus, he jumped to his feet and padded around her. Fianna didn't like the way he assessed her and Seonagh as he circled a couple of times.

"These two females will be suitable for the first batch that will go south come the morrow. That is if Caracalla doesn't kill them first. That man is in a murderous mood, though I am not sure who he hates most—the Celts or his father."

Fianna nudged Seonagh a few minutes later. They were chained to a post near the tent but the guard was talking to someone nearby. She kept her focus on the ground and her voice low, so that their conversation wouldn't be noticed. "I'm going to tell you something that will seem strange, but first I want you to believe that I am not a spy for these rotten Romans."

Seonagh's answer was equally quiet. "I am certain

you are not an informant, Fianna."

"I know what these men are saying. I can understand their talk."

Seonagh's squeak was squelched by Fianna's loud coughing.

"How can you?" Seonagh stared at her.

Fianna scrabbled for a credible reason but could only come up with, "I am able to master many foreign tongues. Caracalla is going to come and question us. He's probably going to torture us as well. He is a very bad man and known for his vicious streak."

"What do I know that he will want to prise from me? What does he not already know?"

"He'll ask you about Tuadh. He wants to know if your father will honour the treaties."

"But I cannot speak the Roman tongue!" Seonagh was agitated. "And I cannot even answer such a question. My father did nothing to prevent me from being forced into the hostages' line."

"Was that why Tyrnan sent you to your grandmother? Wait a minute, though, he said he didn't know what was planned for you. Who would have chosen you to be part of the slave numbers?"

"I am certain Tyrnan did not know what was planned for me. I am sure he had no idea that Delnabo's warriors were waiting for me. I did not even get as far as my grandmother and now Tyrnan might be dead." Tears hovered on Seonagh's eyelids, her mouth twisting in her effort not to cry.

Fianna hoped not. She'd sometimes been annoyed with Tyrnan's constant watching presence but she mostly thought him a great guy. "I'm sure his skull is hard enough to take a few knocks. He'll be fine."

"You can divine that he is healthy?" Seonagh

sounded hopeful.

"Sorry, I'm not that gifted."

Their conversation was abruptly halted. The tether was untied and they were bundled off along another of the streets in the camp. They passed tent after tent and made a right turn before arriving at another of the larger structures, one that was even higher than the last.

"You will only speak when the Emperor bids you."

Seonagh stared at him. Fianna thought the soldier an idiot—he'd already been told they understood nothing.

"Bring them in!" The imperious command came after what seemed like an age.

Pushed and hauled around was becoming the norm but Fianna decided not to make an issue of it when they were plopped just inside the tent opening.

A first glance inside the space robbed her of the breath she would have needed for protesting.

One splendidly uniformed soldier stood alongside a table set at the back of the tent, a couple of officers with slightly less sparkle on their breastplates flanking the other end. Like the previous tent they'd been in, the table surface was littered with scrolls to one end and piled wax tablets at the other. A low bed had colourful covers draped over it and a clothes stand kept a number of garments neatly off the ground. A small side table near the cot held some goblets and a small pitcher on a gold tray. Another man-height stand was for draping armour. It presently stored a fabulously shiny helmet balanced on top of the pole with a shield propped at the bottom. A sheathed gladius hug from a large hook near the top, ready to be grabbed quickly. Other bits and pieces of shiny metal were dotted around the room—a silver washbowl and what Fianna guessed might be a copper mirror alongside bone combs with metal backs and handles.

The old man who was seated at the desk had to be the Emperor.

Aran had said he was ancient and this guy certainly looked pretty worn. Grey wispy hair was dotted around his skull, the sort of fuzz that's left from hair that has been formerly cork-screwy and thick. Small beady dark eyes stared at her, the expression on the face not particularly happy looking.

"The daughter of Tuadh of Balbath wears the silver, or the bronze, torque?" Fianna could understand the man's Latin though it sounded a bit odd, a bit like a foreigner speaking English.

The guard shoved Seonagh past her and set her right in front of the table before speaking. "This one is the offspring of Tuadh."

Severus wasn't impressed. Fianna watched the man look at her and then at Seonagh as though assessing their clothes and comparing them.

"Why then has this one been brought to me?" Severus pointed to her but looked to a dark haired man at his side for an answer.

"She is said to be the foster-child of Tuadh and, as such, will also be valuable slave material. I have not yet had time to question them." The man stepped in front of Seonagh.

Caracalla?

The young guy, not more than twenty, she reckoned to be Severus' son though she could see no resemblance between him and the seated man.

The questions came thick and fast from Caracalla but Seonagh couldn't answer. The man paced around her, his open palm slapping at her shoulders, back and front, to make her lose her balance. His ugly expression stuck right into her face was designed to intimidate the girl and it worked too well. Her tears, falling like a burn in spate, would have choked Seonagh anyway since she got into a hysterical state. Fianna found her earlier plan to pretend not to understand wasn't a good one because she couldn't bear to see Seonagh suffer so much.

Taranis? Let me speak Latin now. She sent up a prayer to the only Celtic god she could think of before she let rip. "Leave her be! She doesn't understand your Latin."

The seated man's eyebrows rose up at her outburst. He looked at Caracalla. "I thought you said they could not understand the tongue of Rome?"

Fianna suppressed a little thrill. What she'd just uttered was yet another new language that she'd never spoken before this weird adventure.

Brian and Aran!

How could she have forgotten about them?

The clamps around her arms immediately brought her thoughts back to her own present danger. Struggling against one Roman soldier wasn't easy but one on each arm was impossible. Dragged forward to the desk she came face to face with the man Aran had been so keen to meet.

"Who taught you to speak the language of Rome?" Severus might look old but the man didn't sound like a weakling.

"I just learned it recently." That was a bit lame but all she could think of.

A while later lots of questions had been asked which she had no direct answers for. She was fed up of being slapped and prodded like Seonagh had been earlier. Caracalla was a nasty piece of work. His prowling around her made her feel trapped and very angry, and she'd had enough of his badgering. Remembering something Aran had told her she decided to see if it would shut them up. Instead of answering Caracalla, she looked directly at Severus.

"You've given the Caledons and Taexali so much gold that your treaties will be upheld for a while, though I can't see why you are so bothered about the Celts of the north. You should be concerned about getting yourself back down to Eboracum before the festival of Janus because you know what is going to happen after that. Your soothsayer has already warned you about it."

Severus looked horrified, his face turning puce which was peculiar on his slightly darkened skin. His words were a squeaky whisper. A wobbly finger pointed at Caracalla. "The other one from Durris knew this too. The gods must have sent them!"

Fianna groaned and didn't bother to hide it. More people who thought they were envoys of the gods. She looked at Seonagh but the Celtic girl was still in the dark about everything.

Mmm. Fianna was thinking on her feet. Aran had said Severus was incredibly superstitious. Maybe she could make this situation be to her advantage. Squaring up her shoulders, she boldly confronted Severus again.

"The goddess tells me many things. You must return to Eboracum very soon or you won't have time to set up the huge new supplies base that you intend to build at the Tay mouth, on the land that the southern Taexali just granted you last night in the settlement. I talk of the place you have decided on that is about four days march from here. The location that is perfect for berthing and beaching the ships of your Roman Classis. If you don't get that fort built at Carpow, you won't be able to keep the Miathi under your control. And, naturally, if you can't control the Miathi then you won't be able to send supplies up here to control the Taexali and the Caledons. And let's not forget about the Vacomagi of the northern firth coastline—those Celts who have already breached the initial agreements with you."

"How can the girl know that?" Caracalla demanded, his grip of her elbows tightening.

Severus' even more trembling finger shook at her, his eyes staring. "Which goddess is your mistress? I must know who to entreat to."

Ah.

Fianna came unstuck for a second. She couldn't think of a single goddess except the Roman goddess Diana and she didn't think 'Diana the huntress' was the one to pray to right now.

"You will find out soon—but first Aran of Durris must be freed." She was chancing her arm but what else could she do?

Unfortunately, Caracalla literally did twist her arm and that made her furious. Turning to him, she spat in his face so that he wouldn't misunderstand her. Low and venomous her words were mainly for him alone. "And you had better think about how you treat your father. I know what you intend to do to the Emperor. Your father has many enemies but he also has some very loyal soldiers. Think about that when you feel impetuous."

The huge wallop at her cheek knocked her onto her backside. It hurt like fury but she wasn't done. Crawling back to her feet she managed another jibe. "Geta is your father's son just like you are, but he doesn't deserve to have a murderous brother." The next whack sent her crashing onto the desk edge.

Seonagh's shouts kept Fianna focused on staying conscious. She'd been knocked out cold once already during this bizarre adventure and she was determined it wasn't happening again.

Fingers tugging at her neck and arm had her squirming around, kicking and punching, but she couldn't prevent the grasping fingers from snatching off her torque and armband.

"No! You can't take them."

Caracalla's response was a backhander across her crown that sent her flying into Seonagh and crashed them both to the ground.

Seonagh's thin silver armband and thin silver torque dangled from Caracalla's fingers, along with Fianna's two precious bronze items, when they were heaved out of the tent.

Chapter Twenty-Three

Dawn's light had not yet crept free of the horizon when Brian had what passed for breakfast. Orla had managed to make thin porridge with the last of her stock of dried oat flakes and the pan had been shared around the fireside. It was too thin to be like the porridge he loved, and was probably more like the gruel he'd read about in Victorian stories like *Oliver Twist*—but it was better than nothing. Pure water came fresh from the Clachie Burn so his thirst was quenched.

Mapon reappeared and sat down beside Tuadh.

"Are you aware that your daughter will already be claimed as a belonging of the Roman Empire?"

Tuadh's lips firmed. "Aye, druid, but I will still do everything I can to free her."

"What will that be?" Mapon was ever the peacemaker, his tone soft.

Tuadh remained silent.

Brian knew that the names of the new slaves would be written down on a wax tablet or on some parchment, or other. "When we rescue the girls, we need to snatch the scroll that contains their names. That way the slave-trader will have no evidence of who he has bought."

"Perhaps that will be sufficient." Mapon didn't sound completely convinced. He stared off into the distance for a while as though his thoughts were taking a long time to form. Eventually, Brian was aware of the druid looking at him. Before the old man spoke, he lifted his clarsach. Brian then watched the small harp coming towards him as if in slow motion because he could barely breathe. The act was somehow so significant.

"I wish to be reminded that you can make music from my Meriel."

It was such a strange request but Brian complied. After plucking the strings, to jog his memory of their sounds, he played a simple repeated refrain.

"Meriel does speak to you."

That was even more bizarre.

"Do you have news for us?" Orla looked to Mapon before she added more wood to the fire.

"Aye, indeed, I have. Scouts were sent to monitor activity at the Roman Durno camp last night. This morning they report that the Romans are dismantling their tents and packing up all of their tools."

Tuadh was energised by the information. "Severus and Caracalla's troops are leaving so soon?"

Unfortunately Mapon couldn't confirm that both father and son were about to exit the area. It obviously didn't matter too much, since Tuadh was bustling around and preparing to leave.

Brian tried again to persuade the druid to go with him to the coast but could see that the old man wasn't going to change his mind.

"Here is your mount," Thain said as he handed over the rein of the same filly that Brian had ridden before. It was impressive that Tuadh had managed to rustle up sufficient horses for his band of fifty warriors, having borrowed some from other local chiefs.

On the point of their setting off, one of Mapon's scouts arrived with a further update. "The warriors on The Mither Tap hillfort sent word that Roman troops are heading off in almost all directions."

"Which routes do they take?" Tyrnan stopped

attaching the bridle on his horse and came closer; not appearing bothered about the massive bruised lump at his temple.

Mapon studied Tyrnan before he asked his own question. "Have they followed Delnabo and his clan?"

The scout thought not since Delnabo had set off to the western high hills, to return home. He then answered Tyrnan. "A large force, maybe as many as a legion, has headed north-west towards Tap O'Noth."

"They are likely to be Caracalla's men. They will be going north again to ensure that the Vacomagi Celts are still behaving themselves and not attacking his Roman troops left at the temporary hillfort on the shores of the firth. He claimed as much during the final negotiations last evening. The High Chiefs agreed to this strategy of Caracalla's and will not interfere with his troops."

Tuadh snorted. "The Vacomagi answer to no invasive Celt so I do not believe they will rest long with Romans on their territory."

The scout continued, "Many of the troops from Durno are already on their Roman road heading south. A small force has also been noted heading due east, towards the coast."

"I told you!" Brian was now truly convinced that his sister would be among that small group.

"How small a group of Romans?" Tyrnan asked before gathering his rein and executing a perfect leaping mount, barely a wince on his features showing the pounding discomfort that must have given him.

"I only know that according to the warriors on The Mither Tap hillfort it was a much smaller force which was moving at a slower pace."

"We need to get going as well." Brian wasn't bothered about the Vacomagi tribe or the Romans going south—he was champing at the bit to get to the sea. The armband message had said to go after dawn and it now seemed an age since the first sliver of pink had lit the sky.

"I bid you farewell, Tuadh of Balbath, and wish you success in rescuing your daughter." Mapon's farewell was very solemn.

When the druid turned to him, Brian felt the man's old fingers curl around his shoulders in a reassuring grip. "Fear not, lad. I do not believe that your sister is destined to be a Roman slave. She may have many adventures in her life, but I do not believe that being a slave is one of them. I have not forgotten your friend, Aran, either. He has need of me. I can assure you that he will have my support till my dying breath. Yet, young tamhas, I have a dilemma. I must go now to a place where my Meriel may not. I wish to leave her in your capable hands."

Mapon lifted the clarsach from the ground and handed it to a stupefied Brian.

"But I'm riding off to rescue my sister. I may not be able to look after it properly," Brian stuttered. "My riding skills aren't actually all that good."

To Brian's surprise, there was a knowing smile on the old man's face. "Then I am certain Orla will care for her till you return?"

Orla, who had been hovering in the background, stepped forward to receive the instrument. "It will be my pleasure, Mapon."

Liam was at the head of the procession of Tuadh's warriors, Brian somewhere in the middle as they headed for the sea. The plan that Tuadh's warriors had made sounded like a good one but they first needed to skirt to the south to avoid the trail of Roman soldiers who had already begun to wend their way on their flattened Roman road.

Brian turned back to wave to Mapon but the druid wasn't looking as he trudged his way around towards where the High Chiefs had been camped. The old man had said some very strange things that needed more thought to work them out during the ride, and he needed to think about how to find Aran, as well.

When they crossed the River Don, not far from Balbath, Brian realised how long they'd been on the peculiar adventure that Callum had sent them on. Not many days but they'd been crammed full.

It was a crushing shame that he felt a catastrophic failure as he reminded himself of the terms of the quest.

Separated from the other two wasn't what Callum had intended. He couldn't think of any new information to share with the historians. He maybe had some evidence, though. He felt for the ocarina that was still under his tunic and he had a Roman gladius at his side. Had he helped the enemy?

He wasn't convinced he knew who the worst baddie of the story actually was. Delnabo and Carden had been pretty rotten; Blairdaff even worse, but he had no idea of just how rotten Severus, or Caracalla, might have been to his sister or Aran.

"We will stop here." Tuadh's command was whispered down the file as they approached the end of a small wood.

They'd been trekking in silence for most of their journey while Brian had fought with his thoughts and his conscience. Tuadh's band of warriors had been extremely cautious, advance scouts fanning around in all directions, since they had no idea of how many Roman patrols were in the area. The landscape seemed so different from his twenty-first century one but he had guessed where he might be from the occasional glimpse of the sea as they'd crested the tree-free hilltops

"Is this the place, Tyrnan?" Tuadh's low question was confirmed.

"Aye. Beyond is the flat plain of the machar. If the Romans are heading for their ships at Baile Mheadhain, having come from Durno, they will pass through the machar."

It didn't take long before Tuadh's best scouts returned.

"It will not be quick. There are three columns of chained prisoners, perhaps thirty in total. They are accompanied by auxiliary infantry, one soldier for perhaps three or four captives but there are also the same numbers of mounted legionary soldiers."

"Ha! We can easily deal with that." Tuadh grunted as though relishing the conflict to come.

***

The new morning had long dawned and Fianna was despairing. There had been nothing she could do to free her and Seonagh…or the handful of other higher ranking hostages that littered the space near the centurion's tent. Chained to each other they were powerless and she hadn't been too surprised to find that she was the one key person chained to a stake driven into the earth, trapping her even more. Her tendency to let her mouth run off had obviously not been appreciated by Caracalla or Severus…or the centurion.

The night had been long and colder than the one spent outside at the grove. She had huddled into her cloak but being chained meant it only covered parts of her leaving plenty of opportunity for cold draughts to creep around. Though curled up next to Seonagh they'd shared some body heat, propping each other up when one of them nodded off.

A while ago, like the rest of her fellow prisoners, a cup of water had been offered to her. She guessed it was breakfast though she'd refused it. It probably seemed like she was too proud to accept but it was the passing of germs on the rim of the one beaker used that she was concerned with. Which she afterwards regretted as completely stupid, because any moment now it might be Caracalla that killed her and not a few microbes.

Ages spent wondering where Aran and Brian were had brought no answers. She worried and worried next to the still occasionally sobbing Seonagh. Feeling such a failure was the pits. Callum would be so disappointed in her for not managing to stay with the other two though he'd be even more upset that she'd lost the precious computer!

Did that mean that she was forever stuck in AD 210? What an idiot she was!

Miserably staring down at the already well trodden grass, she was startled when a soldier came and yanked up the chain, almost breaking some wrists in the process. Leaving the chain to bind the group, he removed her extra tether from the stake.

The words he cackled were gibberish again as more of his fellow soldiers forced them along and out of the temporary camp.

"Where are you taking us?" Her cry was frantic.

He replied but it meant nothing.

Outside the turf walls of the camp there were lines and lines of prisoners.

"What is happening out here, Fianna?"

She gasped. How weird? She could still understand Seonagh's words. She didn't want to answer but she didn't want to distress Seonagh even more than the girl already was. "By the looks of it we're at the cattle market."

Seonagh's expression showed she hadn't a clue what she was talking about.

Pointing to a slightly raised platform where a young warrior was being poked, prodded and ogled she explained. "Those three men over there must be slave traders. They're buying slaves from the Emperor."

Seonagh looked around her. "I do not see Severus."

Fianna managed a poor laugh. "I don't mean literally buying from him. Those horrid men are paying the Roman Empire for the privilege of carting off the slaves."

"But the final treaty agreements only happened last evening. How can the slaves be sold so soon?"

Fianna recalled watching a film which had scenes showing slavery in the Roman Empire. Her stomach was telling her that she'd rather have not remembered. "The slave traders follow the Emperor when he goes on a campaign of terror. It means they can bargain for the captives when they are freshly gained."

"They follow till the Emperor has people like us to give away for gold?"

Again, Fianna's laugh was sarcastic. "Slave traders don't get so many to drool over every day, Seonagh. Exchanges of large numbers of prisoners during treaties only happens occasionally, but a few Celtic warriors are probably captured regularly enough after skirmishes to make it worth their while travelling the length of the empire."

"Bring that batch over here!" The order came from one of the muscled breastplates who bustled around the area with a toady at his heels taking notes on a wax tablet.

Thank goodness he was speaking the Celtic language because her ability to speak Latin had gone with her lovely bronze bangle.

Fianna had remembered that the officers of the legion were called tribunes. She guessed this one was in charge of getting the best price at the flesh stall.

Waiting for her turn was excruciating. Women and young girls wailed and sobbed all around the area, some male warriors joining in when they were whipped or set upon for not complying with orders. Latin words that were bandied back and forth around the Celts were pointless. The only good thing she could see was that the slaves weren't stripped bare before being set up on the rickety platform. The day was cool and misty, any early May warmth still in hiding, and she was glad to be able to keep her clothing – spared the horrors of being naked before all of these people.

"Seonagh of Balbath?" The tribune had stopped in front of her after his lackey had murmured something about there being high ranking prisoners.

When she didn't answer immediately, the chain that bound her wrists was yanked around. It took very little for the iron shackle to feel as though it would soon break her bones. Her temper rose as well as her fears. This disgusting man was going to sell her and she couldn't do a thing about anything. "I am not!"

"She must be Fianna of Durris." The lackey wasn't inclined to give more information than he needed to as he consulted a wax tablet. "Red like a fox."

The slave traders came closer to ogle her. They were all even worse than the tribune. One of them, a little guy who was as round as he was tall, piped up in a squeaky voice, his Celtic pretty basic. "High rank? Where is insignia to prove?"

"Remove your cloak!" the tribune demanded.

"What? Do you think I'm Houdini?" Fianna scoffed in his face and held up her shackled wrists.

In barely a whisker, she was free and set up on the mounting block, a legionary soldier pinning her squirming body in place.

The tribune walked all around her. "Has someone already removed jewellery from you?"

What was there to lose? Fianna was defiant. "Yes, you moron. My torque and my precious armband have been removed already." When the tribune looked at his scribe, she railed at him, "Not by an underling. You'd better go and see what your boss has done with my things and Seonagh's silver bangle and torque. Caracalla stole them from us!"

The slave traders started up a hullaballoo of noise that wasn't in Latin or Celtic. Whatever it was, she didn't have her armband to deal with it. The tears that fought to leak from her eyes she tightened back inside. She wouldn't lose her dignity in front of these disgusting men.

Seonagh caught her gaze when she avoided

looking at the traders. The plea in them was heartbreaking. Somehow, she had to persuade the tribune to keep her with Seonagh but her runaway tongue had already cheeked the man.

The scribe was wittering on as he read a different wax tablet.

"Release Seonagh of Balbath." The tribune pointed to her shackles and then turned to the little round trader. "These two are worth more than that whole line of men. Do you still want them?"

From the nodding of the trader's head he seemed to want them but the words he gibbered and angrily repeated, sounded like a complaint.

Chapter Twenty-Four

"Hello!" Aran cried but no-one was answering.

Being tethered up close to the post meant no chance of accessing his armband, and no chance of any other sort of escape. The occasional walk past of a solitary night guard changed to one of higher activity by many soldiers after the first hint of a pink dawn appeared.

As the sun gradually inched across the sky, he watched the contents of the officer tents being whisked out by the most menial un-armoured soldiers who packed the goods onto small carts that appeared from wherever they had been stored. Idly, Aran mentally noted their plain tunics, guessing that a whole bundle of them must be the 'immunes' he'd read about—the guys who were in the legion, who were soldier trained, but who were mostly non-combatant. They were the basic labourers and day-to-day organisers who kept the legion going in food and other services, though he knew that many other immunes were the highly trained land engineers, the medics and the more senior administrators.

All around him the guy rope stakes of the ordinary contubernium leather tents were whipped out of the ground and the tents rolled up in a blink. The speed and expertise of each team of soldiers was incredibly impressive—the men not looking particularly cheerful but they all worked hard. When the ground around him, apart from Severus' tent, became a vacant area and he was still manacled to his stake, he began to worry a lot. His concern for Fianna and Brian had escalated as the night had worn on but now it was at epidemic levels. What was going to happen to him was alarming, but not knowing what had happened to his friends was even worse.

"Get up!"

The order when it came was oddly relieving.

He was unhitched and bundled off by the same centurion he'd encountered the previous night, his legs not able to function at first because of the cramping in them.

"What's happening?"

"The luck of the gods seems to be with you!" the man sneered.

"Is Severus letting me go?"

The centurion guffawed. "The Emperor never gives anything for nothing. He has demanded a very high price for your liberty."

The town streets of tents were almost all collapsed by the time he was dragged out through the gate in the turf wall. Down below the encampment, he could see another show of strength of Romans and Celts. Hauled down the slope at a spanking pace towards the river he wondered what on earth was going on. Severus stood at the front, his aquilifer alongside him. Behind the Emperor, as before, were Caracalla, and the tribunes. This time, though, Aran could tell by the scutum colours that the soldiers flanking the Emperor were only those from his own special Danubian bodyguards. Not nearly all of his troop but a good fifty or so.

Unlike the day before, there was only a tiny band of Taexali Celts on the far side of the River Urie. Aran was too busy being forced down the slope to count but he reckoned they only numbered some twenty or thirty.

"Why are you having more negotiations with the

Taexali?" he asked when he was dumped to the side of the Emperor.

The centurion ignored his question. So did the Emperor. Severus didn't even look at him.

Aran was horrified when he looked closer at the men across the river. Mapon wore his druid robe, his staff held in one hand. What was the crazy old man doing?

The tribune who had interpreted the day before was first to speak when the Celts stopped around ten metres from the Emperor. After a blandly polite greeting the tribune continued. "The Emperor Severus believes the old will be a very good exchange for the young."

Aran didn't even get the chance to wonder what that meant. His elbows were locked into those of the centurion and a Danubian guard. He was shepherded across the temporary bridge towards Mapon but before he reached the druid, things got very hectic. As he was thrust into the hands of Mapon's followers, a rush of legionary soldiers came behind the centurion to tow the old druid back towards Severus.

"No, Mapon!" he cried. "Don't let them take you!"

He was being exchanged for the old druid.

That couldn't be right. He couldn't let such a thing happen. The Romans still hated the druids. They might kill Mapon.

Mapon wasn't able to turn around, the grip on him too tight, but the old man's shout was clear. "Do not fear, Aran of Durris. My time has come. Your Pin of Funach warned the tribes of the need to negotiate but your armband warned me of my fate. I go with the blessing of the gods and you must also go soon to that place from whence you came. Your journey here is now ending. Tell Brian the Bard to take good care of my Meriel."

Through his struggles to get back to Mapon, the voice of the druid interpreter was firm. "The deed is done, Aran. Mapon will tell them nothing new and his time on this earth is almost over. Fear not. He will not die being tortured by Severus. My druid master will leave this mortal life of his own accord."

Aran couldn't help it. As he watched the old druid being dragged to Severus' side, tears trekked a path down his cheeks and dripped off his chin.

Out of the blue, the focus shifted. Before Mapon even reached Severus, the old druid cried out, "Beware, Severus of Rome!"

There was a scuffle behind the Emperor. A pugio—a Roman dagger—flashed in the air as one of the officers rushed at Severus. In a whisker, the Danubian guard was upon the attacker, overpowering the figure to the ground.

Caracalla!

Aran gaped at the scene. Caracalla had indeed tried to murder his father.

He watched Severus turn and stare at the man pinned to the ground by four burly bodyguards. The Emperor's voice was clear, almost sounding unconcerned when he spoke.

"Leave now and follow your troops who headed north this morning, my son. Your place is no longer with me."

Curt flicks of his wrist had the guards silently, but efficiently, remove the protesting son of the Emperor.

Severus slowly circled and looked across the dividing space.

"Go in peace with your knowledge of the gods,

Aran of Durris. Rome has no further need of you but I do have need of your soothsayer druid, Mapon. I vow that he will be returned to his kin when he is no longer needed by me. Your friend, Fianna, will tell you when that will be."

"Where are Fianna and Brian?"

Aran's question wasn't answered. Severus hailed his litter and climbed in. The negotiations were done. Mapon was already being escorted up the hill and out of sight.

***

The walk was long and tiring. The sun had come out to play but it didn't cheer as much as it did in the idiotic song that kept running through Fianna's head.

She wondered if she had a fever. It wasn't a 'hip-hip-hooray' situation and she definitely wasn't at all merry. The view from the top of the rise they'd just been forced up, shackles and all, should have been stunning but it was scary. Way in the distance the sea spread before her in all its glory, twinkling and sparkling and gently rippling as the North Sea only did on glorious days. Looking down at the white sands visible beyond some of the dunes her heart hammered in her chest. Bobbing down there on the water were a few sails.

Roman ships.

She wasn't nearly as good as her brother at geography but from the view, she had an idea of how far away the water was. Along with Aran, they'd often been on the cycle path called The Buchan Way and she was sure she'd seen a similar outlook down to the sea. If she was correct, the water was no more than five miles away. They'd already been forced along at a spanking pace and had probably covered something like ten miles—another five was still possible before the sun set.

Once she and Seonagh were on one of those vessels, there was no hope of escape. They might be taken to Rome itself or anywhere in the empire. She'd begged the slave trader to release them. She'd asked where they were going to but answers hadn't come her way.

"Manaan looks happy." Seonagh whispered behind her.

"Well, your god Manaan isn't going to be happy soon because we are not going to get on those ships," Fianna vowed. "Do you hear me, Seonagh. We must not allow ourselves to be dragged onto one of those vessels."

"Do you fear being on the water as much as I do?"

Fianna felt a tiny smile break free. "I'm a good sailor. That's not what I'm worried about. I wouldn't give much for my chances of getting us our freedom if we're chained to one of the oars that power those ships."

"Halt the slaves!"

Relief. The words were the best that Fianna had heard for ages.

"We will rest here for a short while." The odious slave trader's voice was still whiny but he couldn't have given a better order.

Fianna could see the final trees of the dense wood that they'd just trekked through. Just below them, the last few saplings in the strong sunlight looked glorious, the sun's rays striking their way through the quivering branches. Seeing the open fields in the distance, and beyond that the blue of the sea, was amazingly appealing, the oppressive blanketing of the thicket having been quite claustrophobic. Normally being in a dark wood wouldn't have bothered Fianna one whit, but being robbed of the sunlight had seemed like just one more imprisonment, another thing that was sapping her strength, and by the looks of them that of her fellow slaves as well.

Her idea of not sharing a cup for water was being put to the test but it had been quite some time since they'd been allowed to drink from a stream as they'd passed across it. Being hot, thirsty and exhausted wasn't feeling so nice. From the tinkling and gurgling sounds she could tell there was another stream nearby, but if it was like the previous time, the slaves would be the last to get near the water.

On hearing the command to stop, the auxiliary foot soldiers guarding her and her fellow captives forced them into a tight circle and urged them to be seated.

Before hunkering down she did a quick head count. She'd thought there were about twelve in her first line of slaves but now she counted thirteen. Normally she wasn't in the least suspicious but she hoped it wasn't to be an unlucky number. Apart from two soldiers on horseback, one at the front and the other at the back of the three huddles of slaves, the only other mounted person at present was the revolting slave trader who looked like he was sweating buckets. The other equestrian soldiers had already moved away to water their horses.

When the slave trader dismounted upwind of her and Seonagh, Fianna could smell his stench. Yuck!

A flick of the man's hand and a few guttural noises sent a handful of the foot soldiers off to do a check of the area opposite the stream where the horses were happily slurping.

Fianna closed her eyes. Bliss. She'd thought herself reasonably fit but by the protest her calf muscles were making she guessed she wasn't. A noise at her ear roused her from a momentary sleep.

"What?"

Seonagh whispered. "Stay silent. I am not sure, but I believe there is someone else in this wood apart from Romans. I noted some movements before we were called to a halt but I do not know if our guards saw anything."

The next noises told their own story as, one by one, the soldiers who'd wandered off to check the area were picked off by well judged spear throws.

At the same time, on the far side of the stream, a wall of Celtic warriors sprang up from the undergrowth and hurled a volley of spears at the equestrian soldiers. Startled by the speed of the unexpected attack, the Romans could do little to defend themselves. Death screams mingled with Celtic warrior calls to defeat the enemy. What had been a silent wood was a horrendous and noisy battlefield.

While Roman bodies thudded to the ground, the slave trader's panicked shouts could barely be heard. "Attack! We are besieged!"

No more words came from the ghastly little man because he, too, met death at the tip of a whirling Celtic axe which was followed by Tuadh's long Celtic sword to the man's neck—just to be sure that the deed was done.

"Father!"

Seonagh's cry startled Fianna almost as much as

the gory sights around her.

Springing to her feet Fianna was never so glad to see the band of Celtic warriors who surrounded her slave group. She stared at the one who ran straight towards her.

"Fianna!"

It didn't matter that her twin couldn't hug her properly because the shackles got in the way; Brian had come to rescue her. Tears tripping her, she grinned at Brian. "I was scared that the Romans might have killed you and here you are with the Celtic rescue mob. I always knew you were a dark horse, my lovely brother!"

The last agonised cries of the besieged Romans died away and all of Tuadh's warriors gathered around the still bound but essentially freed slave groups.

"Hold still, Fianna." Tyrnan's order wasn't a nasty one at all. A huge grin was a sight to see below the multicoloured egg at his temple. "Please give me the pleasure of setting you free."

Happy thanks rang around as one by one the shackles were removed. Tuadh looked as though he was crushing Seonagh's bones; he was so pleased to have his rescued daughter back in his arms. After snatching a quick hug from his sister, Liam shouted over to Brian. "What exactly must we look for in this vile slave-trader's belongings?"

Reluctantly letting her go, Fianna watched Brian rifle through the leather bags that had been on the trader's horse. Having pulled out a wad of parchment scrolls Brian whooped. "Let's see if we can find your names."

Twisting her wrists, to sough off the feeling of

being trapped, she joined him on the ground. Knowing there was enough noise around for them not to be heard, she still whispered. "I can't understand the Latin, can you?"

Brian shook his head but kept his eyes on the scrolls, unrolling one after the other of what was a large pile of maybe twenty different ones. Chucking a few in her direction he eventually answered, "I don't have a single clue about reading what's on here. Can you read any of these?"

A quick scan had her shaking her head. "Will it matter?"

Brian held her gaze. He looked almost upset. "We're going to have to destroy all of these scrolls because we don't know which one has your name on it."

Fianna scrunched up her lips. "That's a pity. I quite fancy being known down through the ages as Fianna of Durris."

Her twin's nudge at her shoulder seemed almost back to normal. "It doesn't matter what you are called but Seonagh can't be known as the property of Rome. Someone in the months or years to come might try to snatch her again if these scrolls are found. They could really make her a slave of the empire."

"Oh, right! You're right." She looked across at Seonagh who was totally delighted to be back with her family.

Liam's shout interrupted everyone. From one of the saddlebags he had pulled out a silver object. "Is this your band Seonagh?"

When Seonagh looked her head shook, her disappointment clear.

"No matter. There are lots of treasures in these

bags. This was a very rich trader."

That was enough for Tuadh and his sons to delve into the leather bags.

Tyrnan called to the other warriors. "Strip the dead Romans of anything useful to us and bury the bodies as quickly as possible. Nothing must show that we have attacked this convoy."

Chapter Twenty-Five

Aran stood at the gates of Balbath alongside Mapon's acolyte who had now become the area's temporary druid leader in the old man's absence. Orla and Caitlinn were beside him, as well, and they were just as anxious as he was to greet the band of Balbath warriors who slowly padded their way down the hill, their horses in tow behind them.

"Look! My father returns."

Orla had declared there was no point in them waiting at the temporary camp at Tullos when Aran and the druids went there after the exchange of Mapon. The hillside was cleared of all visiting Celts, apart from Carden who had no settlement to return to. Scouts had broken the news that his roundhouse village was put to the torch by Caracalla in an act of petty vengeance as he and his personal guard passed by on their way north. It was as well that Blairdaff was long gone, as well, because Aran had no intention of even looking at the traitorous chief, far less talk to him.

On the way back to Balbath, Orla tried hard to convince him that Tuadh would rescue all of the slave prisoners and that those from their settlement would safely return, including Fianna. He believed her. He had to hold on to the belief that Fianna would be safe. He knew Tuadh's warriors would keep Brian safe as well.

Now, as he scanned up the hillside to see who was returning, he was sure she was right though they were still too far away. It was a large group making its way down so there couldn't have been many casualties.

Caitlin was beside herself. "Seonagh and Fianna

flank my father. I see them! My sister is safe and my new friend Fianna is also unhurt."

As the band drew closer Aran found he couldn't just wait at the gate. Grabbing Caitlinn's small hand his gaze pleaded with Orla. Her tiny nod and huge smile were all he needed to set off at a run with the little girl.

"Aran. You're safe!" Fianna's squeal was typical as she started off down the hill, Brian appearing at her heels.

The group hug and victory dance were absolutely perfect. These were his two best friends and everyone was fine.

"Ouch! You just got my best bruise," Fianna protested after he gave her another hug, just because he was so happy that she was okay.

Apart from some very obvious bruises to her cheeks and chin, she was fine. The signs of mistreatment under their cloaks didn't matter. They were all together again.

Orla had been busy since the return to Balbath. Although the Romans at Deer's Den had looted the Balbath roundhouses for anything left that was useful to them or portable, it was a great relief that they hadn't set the settlement on fire or destroyed the contents of the roundhouse interiors. The stalls and low cots were still there. Things like fire irons, cauldrons and larger tools removed by Roman scavengers would be replaced in time, but for now Orla had managed with what she had. Her hearth-fire blazed away in Tuadh's roundhouse, some pots above it already bubbling with enticing smells.

When their weapons—Aran's and Brian's Roman gladii and many Celtic long swords—were stacked at the entryway, as many of the important people of Balbath as possible crammed in around the blaze.

"Tell us your tale, Seonagh." Tuadh was almost back to his blustery self though maybe not quite so brusque.

The catch-up took quite a while. Everyone wanted to know about all the happenings to everyone else. The food that was passed around was only small game that had been swiftly roasted; the fare having been hunted by some of the warriors who had not been in Tuadh's rescue band. It wasn't a lot but was sufficient to stave off the hunger pangs of not eating all day.

Dusk was descending when the last of the tales had been told. Tuadh suddenly stood up and went to the back of his stall. On his return he called for attention. "I believe the time has come for me to give you this, Brian the Bard."

Brian's face was as red as the fire.

The chief handed him Meriel. "Orla has told me that Mapon has great faith that you will care for his instrument and I cannot think of anyone else who could use it better than you. This is Mapon's Meriel but henceforth she must be renamed by you. You may only speak of her being the Meriel once owned by Mapon, but you must never name her such yourself."

The whole room resounded to cheers and whistles.

Brian got in a thank you before the chief resumed his conversation though Aran realised that Tuadh's focus had turned to him.

"Aran and the tamhas of Durris. You have come to us at a time of much upheaval. You are all more than welcome to always remain at my hearth but

Mapon told me that you would need to leave soon, that your time here was coming to an end. Is this the moment for you to leave?"

Aran gulped. He hadn't even thought to check if the twins still had their armbands. How could he have forgotten such a crucial question?

Both twins came to stand beside him when he got to his feet. "Is the time and situation suitable for us to say…OOH, a quick goodbye?" He hoped his meaning was understood.

Two pairs of almost identical eyes sparkled back at him and both heads nodded, the grins also a mirror image. They both drew back their cloaks to reveal their armbands.

"Yep." Fianna whooped. "That slimy slave trader had bought it."

Aran's smile was huge as he bid the Balbath people farewell. "Many of you thought we came here with the blessing of the gods. Our leave of you is going to seem like that but fear not about what you might see, people of Balbath, because we will be safe going back to where we came from. We have loved being here with you all. We're sad that the Romans have caused you such hardship and regret that they may do so again if you do not honour their treaties."

Brian interrupted. "I've had a great time visiting you all, as well. Nobody is ever going to be better at using a sling as you are, Duhlain, but I'm going to be a close second." Aran watched his best mate lift up the pouch at his waist which must still have the sling and stones inside. After that Brian groped inside his tunic and pulled out the ocarina. "This belongs to you, Ailish."

Seonagh's grandmother's old voice drifted up.

"Aye. It did but it now goes to one who can play her."

Brian was quick to answer. "I'm sorry I haven't had time to teach anyone."

"No matter. Mapon will be pleased that the Pipe of Netherdaugh is also in your capable hands. Take it with my blessing."

Fianna had to get in the last word, as usual. "Seonagh. I'm sorry that I never had a sister but if I did I'd want her to be exactly like you." She smirked at Brian. "However, after my time here I realise I have got the absolute best brother in the whole world!"

She looked at him and Brian. "After saying goodbye, on the count of three we'll use the easy route?" Her head bobbed in time to her silently mouthing some more.

Aran was happy with that. Reaching for the knob on his armband, he pressed it. When all of the flaps popped open, they shouted in unison, "Goodbye."

As he counted to three, he watched Brian's frantic scrabbling to clutch the clarsach to his chest and also reach around to press the white cross.

"O.O.H." echoed around from three loud voices.

Aran felt that whooshing, front flip-flip-flipping sensation again. He wanted to grin but the blubbering was back at his cheeks so he just went with the flow. It was a mere blip before he felt his feet thud against hard floor tiles. Tipping over, he cannoned into Fianna and Brian, all of them falling down like tumbled skittles, Brian still clutching the clarsach.

"You okay?" He helped Fianna to her feet as he got up himself.

On the other side of the glass enclosed screen, the people at the desks all around the room clapped like mad.

"Oh, my Taranis! That was a fun ride," Brian hooted, still from the floor as he laid aside the instrument and collapsed onto his back, his chest heaving with massive chuckles.

Callum rushed over, opened the glass doors and grabbed Brian up. How he then managed to put his arms round the three of them after that was amazing—but he did.

"Well, you lot," Callum eventually croaked after he'd squeezed them all to death. "You've had quite an adventure, haven't you?"

"Adventure?" Brian stuttered, "You don't know the half of it!"

Fianna squeaked as she burrowed in for another cuddle from Callum. "It was totally amazing Callum…er…Dad…you have no idea."

"Dad?" Callum grinned as he gathered the twins in tight at his shoulders, once more.

"Gee, Dad!" Brian echoed his twin. "Yeah! Dad. You have no idea."

"Callum?" Aran said backing up his best friends, "You truly are the greatest Dad for sending us on that…interactive story!"

Aran could swear that Callum blushed, though Callum really did deserve to be called Dad for allowing his children, and him, to experience what they'd all just lived through.

Ronald bustled up to them. "It's great to see you back, guys. I'm guessing you liked our programme then? Did you have enough challenges and dangers?"

Aran and his two best friends looked at each other

and creased themselves, their laughter filling the room. He looked down to where Fianna pointed. His cloak was torn but a battered-looking Pin of Funach was still in place. His braccae were a disgusting mess. He only had one ripped leather shoe on but the knife sheath he'd been given still dangled from the strap at his belt. Fianna's dress was slashed in places, her potato sack of a cloak almost completely worn away.

"Hey! I've still got my torque but yours are gone" Her fingers smoothed the ring around her neck, her grin almost as wide as the bronze below.

Brian was in the sorriest state. The clarsach on the floor was almost decrepit, the beautiful wood scratched, chipped and mud encrusted. Some broken strings pinged and twanged, no longer singing as they did for Mapon. His cloak was non-existent apart from the cord around his neck and a frill of jagged-edged material that barely went half-way down his back. The legs of his braccae were split open to the elements.

Ronald chuckled along with them. "I'm thinking we maybe should see to fine-tuning the return clothing function a bit more?"

Aran felt the guy lift up a tangled bit of his long mess of hair as he was helped up to his feet. "And also hiring a hairdresser for this lot."

"Good thinking." Callum agreed with Ronald. "But first, let's hear what you three have learned."

Three voices deafened him.

Aran couldn't help himself. He was like a drip of oil on a searing hot pan. "The Emperor Severus. I met a real live Roman Emperor…"

Fianna burst in. "Yeah! He was really nice to you, wasn't he? And his stinkingly horrible son, Caracalla, was worse. I was sent to them as a slave, Dad, but my fabulous brother saved me. Can you believe that Brian came and rescued me?"

Callum looked at Brian who was smirking like mad. "You okay, son? Your sister just paid you a huge compliment and you've not even one single freckle of embarrassment."

Brian played it cool. "Couldn't let her sail away to who knows where. Nor Seonagh either. We had to rescue her, too."

Callum nodded, just once, whilst staring at Brian. "Guess I need to find out about your new love interest."

Aran guffawed. "If anyone was thunderstruck it was Fianna. She was all over those brawny Celtic warriors."

"I was not!" Fianna's protests were accompanied by a huge red grinning blush. "Well, only a little bit."

"Okay. Only a little bit." Callum pointed to the door. "We need to go to the debriefing room and get comfy. I've a feeling there's a lot I've got to learn about your incredible adventure."

"I'm pretty sure we covered all of our tasks." Fianna was jumping with glee as she towed after her dad.

"We know who we were with, where, when, what was happening—we got all of that stuff really easily." Brian's words were garbled by the smirk he couldn't control.

Smiling back, Callum acknowledged all his son had to add before Aran felt the focus was on him.

"Apart from that nitty-gritty, how did you get on with your other quests—like helping solve the nicknames for the hill and getting information for the archaeologists?"

"The Axeman!" Brian was so excited he was stumbling over his words. "Tell him about Tuadh."

Aran's beam nearly hurt his face he was smiling so hard. "I'll bet that nobody knows that Tuach Hill in Kintore was named after the fiercest Celtic leader who lived there nearly two thousand years ago. How that man could wield an axe was totally awesome."

"We can tell you loads about the old hillfort on The Mither Tap, as well, and about the roundhouse settlement at Balbath." Fianna was desperate to reveal everything she knew.

Callum held up one hand to stop her flow and stroked his chin with his other. "I'm thinking the adventure was a bit tame and wasn't as exciting as we had thought it would be?"

"Tame? We were nearly killed loads of times. We've got bruises and bumps all over. We've all been taken prisoner."

Callum's expression was doubtful, though behind his eyes was an unmistakeable twinkle. "I don't remember the eject icon being used because someone was facing imminent death."

Aran nudged Brian out of the doorway, wedged as he was with the remains of the clarsach. "Nah! But I think we might need to talk about that before our next adventure."

Callum stopped their progress along the corridor. "You're planning a next adventure?"

Fianna hugged Callum's arm. "'Course we are, aren't we boys?"

"We've still got loads of days off school during this holiday. What else would we do?" Brian's enthusiasm almost made him trip up when Callum's step forward wasn't quite long enough.

Aran managed to get in a word edgeways. "Bicker like mad and have Fraser Twins' fiascos. Save us from that fate, please, Callum. We really, really need your wicked interactive stories."

Entering a lounge area, Callum bid them sit down on the sofa before he picked up a tray loaded with chocolate cake and a jug of orange juice.

Three pairs of eyes drooled. Cake. They hadn't had anything sweet for an eternity.

"Where would you like to go next time?"

Somehow, the twinkle in Callum's eye told Aran that the man probably knew where that might be already.

To all of my readers,

Thank you for spending time reading ***The Taexali Game.*** If you liked what you read, would you please leave a short review on amazon.co.uk, or at the place where you purchased it? A few lines are all that's needed and are fantastic to let other readers know how much you enjoyed it. Reviews also help other readers to make up their minds about which books they might like to buy. Recommend it to your friends and family—adults love reading adventure stories, too. Thank you!

Keep up to date with **Rubidium Time Travel Series** news at the Rubidium Time Travel Series Facebook Page. https://www.facebook.com/pages/Rubidium-time-Travel-Series/916558555032004?sk=timeline#

Look out for **No Mean Demo** – Book 2 of the *Rubidium Time Travel Series* coming later in 2015.

Aran Bruce and the twins, Brian and Fianna Fraser, are itching to get going on their second adventure since Callum's been really nice to them. This time they've a little more knowledge of where they're about to pitch up. Victorian Glasgow is an incredible place for them to fulfil their task list—yet it's also hazardous to the naïve. Whilst coping with their own perilous situations, they must rescue their new friends from unthinkable events. The mystery item they have to find out about is only the tip of the iceberg.

About the Author

Nancy Jardine finds people of the past are fascinating, so it's absolutely brilliant that she lives in Aberdeenshire, Scotland, because there are so many ancient possibilities to explore right on the doorstep. The thought that some ten thousand Ancient Roman legionary and auxiliary soldiers possibly tramped over her garden, almost two thousand years ago, was sufficient inspiration for her to write more than one Celtic/Roman novel. If you don't find her at her desk writing, then she'll be blogging, trying to keep off Facebook, or playing Supergran with her grandkids.

For adult readers who have enjoyed ***The Taexali Game*** Nancy Jardine also writes novels for the general adult market—some are romantic mysteries and some are historical adventures. Discover more about her writing, or contact her at her:

Website www.nancyjardineauthor.com

Blog http://nancyjardine.blogspot.com

Amazon UK Author Page http://amzn.to/1ehiqSt.

21236231R00176

Made in the USA
Columbia, SC
19 July 2018